Life's a Beach
Then You Die

Falafel Jones

Life's a Beach Then You Die

Fourth Edition released November 2013

ISBN: 1484169778
ISBN-13: 978-1484169773

DISCLAIMER

This is a work of fiction. Names, characters, places, and incidents are the products of the author's imagination or are used fictitiously. Any resemblance to actual events, locales, or persons, living or dead, is entirely coincidental.

WHAT'S IT ALL ABOUT?

Max Fried is a former computer forensic examiner who devotes his time to swimming, drinking and bathing in the hot Florida sun, but today... it's a real killer. A murderer is coming his way.

When a smooth-talking lawyer persuades Max to find a deceased client's estate assets, Max takes the job, thinking it will be a snooze. Instead, an old killer with a new identity breaks into his home and steals the client's computer.

Max doesn't know the computer contains clues to a 20 year-old murder but then, the murdering thief doesn't know Max stored a copy of the stolen computer on his iPod. Too bad for the bad guy, the copy contains evidence that would get him the death penalty.

Now, Max is the last one alive who knows why people are dying. If he can outwit the killer, he can return to his bar stool on the beach. If not, he'll be victim number five.

LIFE'S A BEACH THEN YOU DIE is a murder mystery featuring a playboy lawyer, a billionaire heiress, our favorite forensic fellow, and oh yeah, a bunch of dead guys, some cops and a killer.

Max and I both worked in computer forensics, are licensed private investigators and live on a small island. Please don't tell him only one of us is real.

ABOUT THE AUTHOR

Falafel Jones was named for a Mediterranean sandwich Mom craved while pregnant. While this name may have been a burden growing up, it provided a distinction from all of the other Joneses in town. In fact, things could have been worse. Ask Falafel's brother, a construction worker named Sweet Pickles.

CONTENTS

CONTENTS

CHAPTER ONE

I noticed them the moment we arrived. She was a busty blonde bursting from a blue bikini and holding a lipstick stained cigarette. He looked like a handsome Irish football player grown older and puffy, a scotch glass a fixture in his hand. Besides Jack, the owner-bartender, they were the only ones there.

While we sat outside on bar stools admiring the ocean, Jack brought my AmberBock draught and Mariel's vodka tonic.

I said, "Thanks," and when I lifted my chilled mug, condensation dripped onto my crotch. I decided to sit until it dried.

Jack wiped the wet spot on the counter and leaned forward on his hands. "Max, we've been waiting for you."

"Who? Me?"

"Yeah, I know you come in about now, so I told them to wait."

Mariel and I turned to each other and then to Jack. Sometimes, you couldn't tell when he was kidding.

Jack AKA Jack Jr. worked at Bobbi and Jack's Beachside Patio since childhood. He claims to have been born behind the bar here when his dad ran it and where allegedly, his pregnant mother, Bobbi, served drinks until and immediately after she dropped him. He sometimes told gullible customers his real name is Jack Daniel's for the drink his Mom had on her tray at the time.

"Guys, I don't want to impose," Jack raised an eyebrow, "one of my lunch regulars needs a hand. Maybe you can help. Ed's a local lawyer. I think he's semi-retired," Jack pointed down the bar to the man and the woman.

She could be either a good-looking older woman who appeared

younger or a haggard younger woman who appeared older. It was hard to tell. Whatever her age, I'd say she was fond of the man she sat with. Her hands lingered on him whenever possible.

Despite her attention, when Jack pointed at him, Ed looked in our direction. I said, "Sure. I'll talk to him," and Jack waved him over.

After getting up from his stool, Ed bent down and whispered something to the woman. Then he straightened up and put some money on the bar. She smiled up at him and said something I couldn't hear. When he bent down again, they kissed. He picked up his drink and walked over to where Mariel and I sat. With a cigarette and his drink in his left hand, he reached out with his right. "Ed McCarthy," he shook my hand then Mariel's.

Mariel gave him her perfect smile.

Ed wore the New Smyrna Beach uniform of tan cargo shorts and sandals. He topped his version with a blue and white, short sleeved floral print shirt. I topped mine with a short sleeve golf shirt; black out of deference to the fact it was winter.

"Jack tells me you've moved down from New York to the corner of the bar," Ed chuckled at his own joke. "I'm from New York, too. In law school, I dated a girl from Daytona Beach so I got licensed in both states." He took a drag from his cigarette.

The way he rambled on told me he must have been waiting at the bar for quite a while. Well, that and the swizzle sticks all lined up where he had been sitting.

"Nice to meet you, Ed." I thought I saw him here before. The place is less crowded during the off-season and the regulars stand out over time. "I'm Max, my wife Mariel. Jack said you might need something."

Ed took a deep breath. "I'm handling an estate for a client. Ray was my first Florida account. I wrote his will and we had a lot in common. We'd fish together... Just this morning I attended his funeral. He took Friday afternoon off to do Christmas shopping and died instead. When you write those things, planning for someone's demise, you think days like today will never come."

Mariel took her eyes off him, stared at me for a long moment, and then back at Ed. "Oh, we're so sorry about your friend."

"Thank you. Kathleen and Ray didn't have anyone here so after the funeral she's going home to her mom and dad. She's busy packing so I'm drinking alone." He shook his head. I guessed that either the blonde wasn't drinking or for some reason, she didn't count.

Mariel appeared upset, "Kathleen's his wife?"

2

"Yes." His gaze turned up at the sky for a moment and then back down at me. "This one's for Ray." He raised his glass and took another sip.

Mariel and I raised our glasses and drank with him.

Ed said, "It's bad enough losing a friend, but when they die at someone else's hand, it's that much harder to accept."

I was about to tune Ed out, classifying him as a melancholy drunk but that statement caught my ear. "Your friend was murdered?"

"Police found his car overturned and crushed on the side of the road. A clear day, no traffic, no skid marks. It's an unattended death with suspicious circumstances so they're investigating it as a Homicide. I'm waiting to hear more from the M.E."

"If the police are involved, why do you need me?"

"Kathleen needs to locate their assets. The police found his notebook computer in the car wreckage. Kathleen wants it examined." He shrugged. "She says he used it for online banking." He took a long drink from his glass and placed it on the bar with a thump.

I didn't like the sound of this. I took early retirement because someone took a shot at me and I promised Mariel I'd stay out of harm's way. A case involving a homicide sounded risky.

Ed took another sip of his drink and went on to say. "I told Jack I didn't know anyone who could search the computer. I need to get past the passwords and preserve the information for court use. You know, in case someone contests the will or makes claims against the estate. Jack told me you used to do that kind of work."

"Used to, before retiring, I worked for the State as a computer forensics examiner."

"You mean you can search a computer, break the passwords, and find things?"

"Yeah, sure. That's what I did."

Ed put down his drink. He placed his hands flat on the bar and leaned toward me. "Max, that's what I need. Will you do it?"

"Sorry, no. I'm retired now. These days, we're working on our health. As part of our retirement exercise routine, Mariel and I walk two miles up the beach to get here. We have a drink. We walk back home."

Ed leaned his head back and squinted at me. "I never thought of bar hopping as exercise."

"Well," I said in my defense, "sometimes, if it's not too hot, we also walk the half a mile across the island on Flagler Avenue from the ocean side to the riverside. Mariel shops the boutiques and I

3

bench test the benches."

He shook his head. I don't think Ed thought I took exercise seriously enough. "Do you know anyone else who can do it?"

"In New York, yeah, but not here."

"If I had to hire a stranger, what would I look for?"

"I'm a stranger, but find someone with a certification in computer forensics. Get someone with a bunch of letters like ENCE, ACE or CCFE on their business card."

"Are you certified?"

I smiled up at him, "I'm an ACE."

"What's that?"

"AccessData Certified Examiner. AccessData makes computer forensic tools. But now, I'm a full time retiree and beach bum."

"Jack says you have a private investigator's license."

"Yeah, a lot of states require examiners be licensed."

"So you do P. I. work?"

I laughed. "No, I never used my license. I got it before I got shot. I figure that if I needed to work after I retired. I had to have a fall back plan and with my personality, I'd never make it as a Wal-Mart greeter. Turns out my experience qualified me for a Florida P. I. license. I applied for one and got it but that's it."

"Someone shot you? What happened?"

"I lived... I'd rather not discuss it."

Ed sat down on the bar stool next to me, waited a moment, and said, "Max, I need someone who can go over this notebook computer for bank accounts, investments and other financial information. I've been searching. Geez, I haven't been able to find anybody else. Would you please do this one job for me?"

"I'd love to help you out, but I retired a year ago, sold the house, and moved here to never work again. I still have some equipment and the license just in case I need work, but I don't need it. I don't want it and I don't want to give up beach time or Mariel time. Life is like a roll of toilet paper. It goes faster near the end." I raised my glass to drink.

Ed waved his hand. "Yeah, I can understand, but it shouldn't take long, should it? The results don't need to be back for a week or so and based on Ray's life style, there seems to be some money here. I'd be able to pay you a fee that would make it worth your effort."

"I'm not looking for trouble. I don't need any more danger in my life."

Ed made a dismissive wave with his hand. "Ah, it's a safe job. The Police are handling his murder. All you need to do is locate the family bank accounts... nothing more than that."

I felt Mariel touch my arm. "It's OK if you want to." She showed me her sad face. "I don't mind if you do this. I've some things to do which'll bore you. Besides, I feel bad for his wife and it's December. You're not going to spend a lot time in the water anyway."

After Mariel spoke, I felt bad too. It hurt to think of someone refusing her help after I'm gone. She was right. I did have free time lately. There was no good reason I couldn't spend a few days on this. There didn't seem to be any real risk, plus a few extra bucks could buy a roof rack to carry my kayak. I tilted my head at Mariel. "The boss has spoken. I'll take the case. How about an hourly rate plus expenses regardless of what I do or don't find."

Ed smiled for the first time since we met. "Very good. Thank you. I've got to get back to the office, finish some paperwork. How's this? I'll prepare a standard service agreement you can sign. Come by in about an hour. While you're reviewing it, I'll call the police and find out when they're releasing the notebook."

I nodded my approval and read the business card Ed handed me. His office was just a short walk down Flagler Ave.

When Ed got up to leave, the blonde blew him a kiss. He grinned and waved back. I was curious about their relationship, but thought it impolite to ask who she was.

Five minutes after he left, I forgot he had been there. In New Smyrna Beach, also known as "NSB", we were having a sunny, December afternoon. It was about 77 degrees and it was almost Christmas.

On Bobbi and Jack's patio, a two-piece band played "Rudolph the Red Nose Reindeer." A steel drum carried the melody and an acoustic guitar provided accompaniment. We liked to say NSB also stood for "Not So Bad." We had been down here about six months, six months in New Smyrna Beach, not six months at the bar. Well, that statement was mostly true.

Now that Ed had left, I felt pretty good and mellow. I had a steady pension income, a warm sunny day, a bar stool on the beach, live music and a beautiful woman. Who cared if I was a year older today?

"Happy Birthday, Max," Mariel said and handed me a small, wrapped box.

"Usually, I don't get my gift till dinner. Not that I'm complaining, but you got me curious. Why give it to me now?"

"You'll see when you open it. I thought you might want to use it later today. Besides, you'll get a nighttime gift of a different variety."

I opened the box and removed the iPod inside.

"I thought you'd like it for running on the beach," she said.

"Wow, great. Thanks. Now, I have no excuse for not staying in shape."

Mariel's looks provided enough incentive to keep anyone in shape. We're the same age, but people think she's ten years younger. She hasn't changed since we went to our High School Senior Prom together. Me? I look my age.

Her trademark high heels showed off her shapely legs. She wore a loose cut amber print sundress, the color complementing her butterscotch skin. The dress tied around her neck with a thin string and clung to her flat stomach and thin thighs. Despite her petite figure, Mariel filled out the top nicely. The dress fit her well. Everything did.

I wore shorts, a shirt, and sandals. My birthday was a "special event", so we "dressed up", meaning we both wore our wedding rings and underwear. Most of the time, we lived in our bathing suits and left our drawers in our drawers, along with the jewelry.

After a lifetime in the frigid northeast, living seven days a week in our bathing suits became a symbol of the casual island life we came here to live. Much like invitations that specified "Black Tie," we began categorizing a few of our own events as "Underwear required."

So far, aside from special occasions like this one, trips to the airport and infrequent cold days, there weren't many other items on the list. We even extended the rule so that wedding rings were only required when wearing underwear. When Mariel would ask me if I were wearing underpants, I would show her my ring finger and then she would know her answer.

Jack's meandering around the bar led him back to us, "Refills?"

Mariel and I shook our heads. "No thanks." I said.

He glanced down at the packaging on the bar. "What'd you get?"

I showed him the iPod. "Birthday gift from Mariel."

He raised one eyebrow at her and nodded. She beamed back at him, happy he approved of her gift selection.

"Hey, happy birthday. " He pushed the bills I had left on the bar back at me. "Then, this round's my treat."

"Thanks, I appreciate it." I raised my glass to him.

"Thank you very much, Jack." Mariel touched his wrist. "You're very kind." Then she turned to me, "Max, you promised that man. We have to go."

We said our goodbyes to Jack and headed out. When I agreed to help Ed, I thought the job would be a snooze. How could I know things would go so wrong? Who knew retirement could be dangerous?

* * *

We walked west on Flagler Avenue, stepping on the engraved bricks sold by the Flagler Merchants Association. For $50 a pop, tourists and locals had the chance to immortalize themselves with three lines of text for all to see. Mariel stopped to view the brick she bought to memorialize her dad.

After a few blocks, we turned left to Ed's office. The address he gave me led to a single story concrete-block house. A sign in the front window displayed a phone number and advertised the place was "For Rent 2Bd 1 Bth." We walked up to the door and I knocked anyway. Nobody answered. I verified the address against Ed's business card and decided we were at the correct place. While searching for a doorbell, I noticed a stone walkway leading to the left of the building.

We followed it and found a second entrance. I knocked again and this time, the door opened. The house included a small side bedroom converted into an office with its own entrance. Ed ushered us inside.

He grabbed my hand and shook it, "Max, Mariel. Thank you for coming."

"Please, have a seat." Ed directed us to two upright wooden client chairs with upholstered seats. The chairs didn't go with the rest of the room. I wondered if they might have come from a dining room set, maybe one broken up in a divorce settlement.

"What do you think?" He asked, gesturing around the room. The decor was half-beachy and half-lawyerly. Amid sailing icons and an Ivy League diploma, requisite bookshelves had the requisite books. He seemed to have everything he needed if not everything ever published.

"You appear to be well equipped," I told him.

"Thank you," Ed walked across the room to a stereo receiver next to a CD player and speakers. Classical music played.

He turned down the music and sat behind a huge old wooden desk. It was heavy and dark and could have come from some captain's quarters. I couldn't imagine how he ever got it in the door. I also couldn't imagine how he could ever find anything on the desktop.

So much paper covered the surface that if I hadn't noticed the wire leading up from the floor, I wouldn't have known there was a phone on the desk. Besides the shelves, chairs and desk, there wasn't any other furniture in the room. If there was more, I doubted there would have been room for Ed.

"It's ah, very cozy," offered Mariel.

Ed opened his mouth to reply a second before a muffled ringing sound come from under the papers on his desk. "Um, excuse me, please." He lifted a manila folder and then answered his phone.

"McCarthy Law, how may I help you...?"

"Oh, I'm sorry. I'm in a meeting now..."

"No, it was good seeing you again too..."

"No, I don't know if that's a good idea..."

"Well, it's a little bit too close..."

"No, no one else is interested in renting it..."

"Yes, I did have a good time, but..."

"Yes, I'm sorry. I really can't talk now..."

"I'll be back as soon as I can. We can talk about it then..."

"OK"

Ed hung up, and avoiding eye contact with us, pulled a folder from the pile on his desk. "Thank you and now to business." He continued our conversation as if the phone had never rung.

We agreed on an hourly rate and while Mariel and I read the service agreement, Ed called the police. He was right about the money. We just finished reading when he put down the phone and said, "The police will release the notebook to me tomorrow morning. Why don't you give me your address? I'll pick up the notebook and then come by." He rummaged through the piles on his desk, and pulled out a piece of paper.

"Sure," I said and told him the address. He wrote it down, and the paper disappeared back into the desktop.

"Just don't make it too early," Mariel added. "I think the birthday boy is going to be up tonight."

CHAPTER TWO

Asleep and dreaming I was in a concert hall, I heard the music start, but the orchestra played only two notes. A high note followed by a low note. The combination sounded familiar and the two notes played repeatedly, a high note and a low note. As I woke up, I realized the two-note song was the "Ding Dong" of my front doorbell.

My glasses stared at me from my night table. After putting them on, I jumped out of bed, pulled on running shorts left on the floor and ran for the door. An oblivious Mariel snored softly, her head buried under the cover. She was such a tiny lump under the blanket; I almost couldn't tell she was there.

I barely rounded the corner from the bedroom to the hall, then the one from the hall to the living room. Narrowly avoiding these collisions, heading for the foyer to answer the bell, I felt guilty being asleep when other people were out of bed. It was silly, but that's how I felt. My parents must have imprinted this on me as a kid. I was never a morning person. For a long time, I battled with my parents about getting up for school. The fights ended one morning when my father poured a pitcher of water on my head to wake me up.

Ed was at the door. His head went back and his eyes widened when he saw a shirtless, bleary-eyed old man with bed head hair. I knew I made an impact on him, but I couldn't tell if he was embarrassed about waking me up or disturbed by hiring someone who looked this way and was still in bed at 9:30 am.

"Here's Ray's computer. Kathleen signed the release. It's in the case. Um, I hope I'm not too early. I came straight from the police

9

station."

I assured him there wasn't a problem. Actually, any time before noon, visitors had a good chance of catching us asleep. We preferred later hours and if no one interrupted, we kept them.

"When I picked up the computer, the detective told me the M.E. confirmed it's a homicide. There weren't any skid marks because Ray died before the crash. He had a heart attack but no history of heart disease. They found nothing in his cardiac system to explain the attack. They're going to run some more tests... try to see if they can figure out what caused it. Then maybe, the cops'll figure out why... and maybe who..."

He had the notebook case in one hand and a paper coffee cup and a cigarette in the other. His face was red and blotchy and he wore what he had on yesterday. I looked past Ed and saw a silver Mercedes sedan in my driveway. My view wasn't clear, but I thought I saw a blonde in the passenger seat. I guessed Ed was hung over and upset, anxious to get rid of the notebook and intent on getting to the next thing on his agenda. It probably included more coffee and maybe Alka Seltzer. I took the notebook case. Ed took his leave.

Eyeglasses are fine if they don't slide down your nose, fog up when you enter a warm building, get speckled with rain or limit your peripheral vision. Unfortunately, mine did all of these things so I only used them to find my contact lenses. I went into the master bathroom, passed a still sleeping Mariel, placed the notebook on the counter and put in my lenses.

Once I could see well again, I took the notebook into the third bedroom, which we used as a combination office and secondary guest room. This room contains a TV and a desk for my computer equipment. Against the opposite wall is a sofa bed, which grants the room status as a secondary guest room. The main guest room is next door, furnished with a real bed, another TV, an empty closet and a view of the pool.

I placed the notebook on the desk and hunted for my gear. Since moving here, I had no need for my forensic tools, so they sat in a box -- somewhere. Inside my office closet, I rifled through the cardboard shipping containers until I found my tool kit. My desktop computer already had the forensic software installed.

About six months passed since I used these things. It felt odd working with them outside of the lab, but good to use them again. It was a comfortable feeling. I had to admit that I didn't miss the job but I did enjoy the work.

Despite what they do on TV, you can't just turn on a computer without altering important information. Date and time stamps change and the system overwrites space from which you might otherwise obtain evidence. So, my first step would be to create an exact copy of Ray's disk I could examine without compromising the original.

I removed the hard disk from Ray's notebook computer and placed it on my scanner. I needed to record the serial number from its label for my report and this method eliminated any transcription errors I might make reading and writing.

Then I connected the disk to my desktop computer. I had to place a device in between the two that would protect Ray's disk against any changes, so I used my write blocker. It's a connector that allowed my forensic software to read Ray's disk but which blocked any attempts to write to it.

Copying would take a while, so I got it started and went to the kitchen. Now I had a tough decision, eggs or cereal? I was awake now and there was time enough to cook, so I decided on a cheese, onion and pepper omelet.

If you like a challenge, try saying "Sharp Shredded Cheddar" three times fast while drunk. I used the Latin coffee, Bustelo, advertised as muy sobroso y mas fuerte, (very tasty yet strong) made café con leche (coffee with heated milk) and poured some orange juice.

The aroma of onions, peppers and strong coffee filled the kitchen. Just as my omelet finished cooking, Mariel staggered out to the kitchen drawn by the smell of the coffee. She wore high-heeled slippers and a baby blue nightgown with white dots that could pass for a sundress. Even without makeup, she looked great.

With half closed eyes, she gave me that great smile of hers. Without a word, I handed her a cup full of coffee and a glass full of orange juice. She smiled again with half closed eyes and silently staggered back to the bedroom. We had a good night. Content, I peeled a Clementine orange, put it on my plate alongside my omelet and sat down to eat.

After breakfast, I checked on Ray's disk. It was still copying so I showered, shaved and dressed while Mariel did her morning exercises. From the bathroom, I could hear the thumps of her jumping jacks and then the squeaks from the exercise bike. She spent a lot of time on that bike and had the legs to show for it. By now, she should be able to talk. I finished dressing about the time the disk finished copying. Now, I could get to work. I had what examiners called an image, a copy of the notebook disk, on my desktop computer.

I loaded Ray's disk image into a forensic program, which would catalog every single one of his files, bypassing any logins or passwords he might have used to secure his computer. Since this process also takes a while, I got a second cup of coffee, went to the living room and watched a movie on the big 58" plasma screen TV.

Mariel, awake, fed, dressed and made up, came into the living room. She looked good enough to take my eyes off the TV. When I did, I saw she was waving one of my T-shirts at me. "Clean or dirty? I found it on the floor next to the bed."

"Oh, that's from last night. I like to have clothes handy in case I need to get the door in the middle of the night."

"Clean or dirty? I'm doing the laundry."

"Dirty. I guess laundry waits for no man."

"That's because no man will do it." She left the room with my shirt.

I turned up the volume. After a bit of big screen, surround sound bliss, I went back to the office. The disk image completed processing and was ready for examination.

It took me a few hours, but as requested, I found Ray's banking and investment accounts. His online passwords were in one of the computer registry files. I also found a number of spreadsheets, emails and other financial documents. The emails showed Ray Kenwood worked in sales for a local division of a worldwide corporation, A. V. Designs. The banking records indicated Ray had a lot more money than you'd think a sales guy would earn but nothing else stood out as unusual.

One of Ray's documents was password protected and encrypted. When I made it readable, I saw it contained three columns. The first one was a list of dates, the second consisted of six digit numbers and the third contained six-character combinations of letters and numbers. People don't encrypt documents unless they hold something important, but even after decrypting this one, I had no idea what it meant.

Ray's files also included emails, sales brochures, slide show presentations and other documents which appeared work related and had nothing to do with his finances.

Mariel came into the office. "I'm going to the library to work on my paper." A former Spanish teacher, she enrolled in a college class on *Don Quixote* for "fun."

"I'm going to go to the library and then I'm going to go the Starbucks on campus or maybe I'll go to the Starbucks and then to the library. I'll decide when I get there. Te amo." She leaned over and kissed me goodbye.

She had read that book at least three times, once in English, once in Spanish and once in Old Spanish. I guessed she couldn't get her fill of it. I told her I loved her too and she left.

I went back to work and wrote a report detailing Ray's finances. It included the bank names, account numbers and passwords for five different money market accounts, two checking accounts and an online investment account. The money market account records listed Ray's deposits.

I found one recurring amount, direct deposit of his paycheck. For a short period, starting recently, another recurring amount was a series of cash deposits. I couldn't find the source, but it was the same amount each week, indicating the possibility of an additional source of income. Other sporadic deposits were wire transfers of varying amounts.

Ed would need a copy of the disk as well as the report, but there were too many files to fit on a DVD. If I were working on a regular basis, I would have had a spare hard drive to hold everything. Since I wasn't, I didn't.

However, I did have an almost empty 120 GB iPod. I decided to copy Ray's image and my report to my iPod. Later, when Ed paid me, I could copy the iPod contents to Ed's office computer. I started copying, but like every other part of the examination process, it would take a while. It was a good time to have lunch so I headed for the kitchen.

Again, I sautéed some onions and peppers but this time covered them with Tofurkey Brand Philly Cheese Steak, a steakless steak, and American cheese. Once the cheese melted, I put the pile on a roll and headed out to the pool to eat my lunch.

When I lay down on the chaise with my sandwich, I could smell the hibiscus and citrus trees in the yard. So many trees and bushes grew in the yard, you couldn't see much of the fence surrounding the property. Birds chirped and sang and the water in the pool rippled from the pump action of the pool filter. Boy, what a treat. I retired here just so I could do stuff like this.

Done with lunch, I checked on my disk copying and found it completed. At this point, back in my old lab, I would have locked up the notebook and disk drive in a safe, but again since I wasn't working, I didn't have a safe. When I thought about it, I didn't think it would be a problem. I keep my house locked and I was only trying to locate assets.

The job finished, it was time to notify Ed and collect my fee. I called his office and got no answer. I called his cell phone. Again, no reply. A few minutes later, I tried both again. When I got no answers this time, I left messages at each number telling him I finished examining the notebook.

I had time to kill. It was 76 degrees out and I had a new iPod to take for a run. I put on my trunks, a T-shirt and sandals, grabbed a towel and a water bottle, and left for the beach. When I got to the end of the block, I crossed route A1A, and then the dune crossover to the sand. It was low tide, so the beach was wide enough I could run in the surf without dodging the vehicles driving on the sand.

I dropped my sandals and T-shirt in a heap with my towel and water bottle. George Thorogood and the Delaware Destroyers roared to life on my new iPod. They played great running music with a good solid beat. When George started singing advice to "Get a haircut and get a real job", I took off and ran south. I started where they allow vehicles on the sand. Then I passed Chases on the Beach, a bar-restaurant, where they'll serve you drinks in their in ground pool. By the time George sang the chorus, I arrived at the 27th Avenue beach ramp. This is the southernmost point on the beach where you can drive on the sand and the absence of cars makes it easier to run. I wouldn't have to pay attention to avoid being an accident victim.

I ran barefoot, dashing into the surf whenever I got too hot. My mind wandered as I ran and I realized it was a lot more fun examining Ray's notebook than I thought it would be.

Since I had only one case to do without the pressure of a full-time workload, I was able to enjoy the hunt for answers. I liked figuring things out. I'm hopeless in that I always want to know the answer to the question why.

Others have noticed this tendency. One year at an office holiday party, Santa Claus read out a list of holiday wishes for all the staff. He granted me, "Complete understanding." My first reaction at the time was, "What does he mean by that?"

I completed the first two miles in 17 minutes and then ran a little longer to make it an even 20 before turning back. I finished the total run in about 40 minutes. I said I ran. I never said I was fast. After a dip in the ocean to cool off, I sat on the sand for a few minutes to rest while I finished off the pint of water.

CHAPTER THREE

When I got home, I saw it right away, but it didn't register. I knew something was odd about the front door, but I didn't know what. Then shock gave way to recognition. Someone moved the welcome mat and next to the lock, there was splintered wood where the doorframe had been. I didn't need to be a detective to realize someone had broken in.

I also didn't need to walk in on someone who might still be there. Since I don't carry my phone when I run, I went across the street to use my neighbor Karl's. I could watch my house from there while I waited for the police.

I rang his bell and stared at his lime green door while I waited. Folks on the island seemed to have a thing for tropical colors. After what felt like a long time but was probably less than a minute, Karl came to the door. He opened it just enough to see who was there, then opened it fully. "Hey Max, you're pretty sweaty, huh? What's going on?"

Karl's a lean but muscular retiree with a shaved head and an unshaved goatee. He's about six feet, three inches, 170 pounds and in his early sixties, but he looks a lot younger. Karl lives alone and seems to spend all of his time on the beach. I see him more on the sand than I do on the street. When I thought about it, I was surprised he was home.

"I just got back from running and it looks like somebody broke into my house. Can I use your phone to call the police?"

"Sure. You're not kidding, are you? Wow, c'mon in man." I followed him into his kitchen where he pointed to the phone. Then he went to the window to look across the street. I had never been inside his house before and was surprised. For a bachelor, his kitchen was surprisingly clean. Actually, it was clean for anyone. Either he was fastidious or he never used it.

I picked up the phone and dialed 911. A woman answered. She sounded calm and professional. Her voice was reassuring and I answered her questions.

"OK sir, I'm sending officers over to investigate. In the meantime, stay where you are and don't go back into the house. Now, give me the address where the break-in occurred."

I gave her the address, hung up and joined Karl at the window facing the street. We could see the entire front of my house and I watched intently. I wanted to make sure Mariel didn't come home and walk in on anything. Karl and I stared out the window together in silence.

While we waited, I worried. I worried Mariel had come home and was there when the break-in occurred. When I realized our driveway was empty, I worried she had put her car in the garage. Then I remembered she never put her car inside until the evening. She liked me to guide her in so she wouldn't hit the lawnmower or my bike.

I was also bothered by the possibility the people who broke in had vandalized our home. We had just spent six months and thousands of dollars remodeling the house when we bought it in July. We painted the interior, installed new floors, and purchased new furniture including the big TV and the audio system. These were luxuries, but we saved for years when we both worked so we could buy them when we retired. We didn't expect to have that kind of income again. I was only gone an hour. It didn't seem long enough for something so significant to have taken place.

Two city police units, one marked and one unmarked, silently pulled up in front of the house. Each vehicle contained one man.

The taller of the two men was in uniform and he drove a white sedan lettered "New Smyrna Beach Police." About six and a half feet tall, slim, and gangly like a basketball player, he appeared to be in his early 30s and had longish blonde hair.

The other officer was in plain clothes and drove an unmarked, black SUV. He was a slightly older, shorter, darker man with short, thick, curly, black hair. Just less than six feet tall, he had chest and stomach muscles that pushed against the front of his tight short-sleeved white golf shirt. His muscular upper arms filled the shirtsleeves. He wore khaki slacks, thick-soled black shoes and a matching black belt that carried his gun and badge. I wondered if he had his clothes tailored to show off the time he spent in the gym.

Karl and I went outside to meet them. "Hi, I'm Max Fried. I live across the street. When I came home, it looked like someone broke in. I figured it would be better to call you than to go in and surprise anyone who might still be there."

The taller of the two officers gestured for us to get out of the street and onto the curb behind a parked car. He looked at me, then Karl and asked him, "Who are you?"

"I'm a neighbor. I live across the street," said Karl as he pointed back at his house.

The cop looked from Karl to me and pointed to the ground at our feet behind the parked car, "Get down and wait here." Then both officers headed up my driveway to my house. They had their hands on the grips of their holstered guns and moved in a slight crouch.

One went around to the back of the house while the other headed for the front door. After a few minutes, they both came out of the house alone. The uniformed cop got into his car and drove off. The other stopped at his SUV, removed a clipboard and walked over to me.

"I'm Detective Leon Torres," He nodded up at the house. "There's nobody there. Let's go inside," he said. Karl and I started towards my house and Torres put his hand up, stopping him. "You see anything?"

"No, I didn't know anything till Max came over to use my phone."

"OK, you stay outside," Detective Torres looked at me, "Just you."

Karl looked disappointed but stepped back. Torres started towards my house. "You're going to look around and see what, if anything is missing. I'm going to complete an official report. You notice anything after I leave, you come down to the station. We'll file a supplemental. You'll need copies of the report for your insurance company. If you see anything that was touched. Anything. Don't touch it. Call me. I'll dust it for prints. Do you understand?"

I said, "Yes," followed Torres in and started to look around. When we entered the foyer, I noticed the splintered wood near the door lock and I had to step over a long piece of broken molding. I looked to the left, into the kitchen. The cabinet doors and drawers were all open, but the dishes and kitchenware items were pretty much in place. I guessed whoever intruded was too smart to throw glassware and knives around. Someone could cut themselves.

Falafel Jones

From the kitchen, I stepped gingerly into the great room, our combination dining room-living room. The cabinets in the dining area buffet and the entertainment console were open, their contents scattered on the floor. Mariel's Spanish books formed lopsided piles in front of the buffet cabinet in which she stored them. My Blues CDs carpeted the tile floor. I had to step carefully not to destroy them.

However, items of value such as the TV and stereo equipment were all in their places, apparently untouched. Detective Torres stopped in the great room to dust some CD cases. Using my foot, I cleared a path through the debris. I didn't want to lose any more of my music collection than I may already have. He finished checking for fingerprints, took a few steps and stopped to write something on his clipboard. I moved on to check the rest of the house.

In the guest room, the closet door was open. Aside from that, there was no sign of any break-in. I wasn't too surprised, since our guest room is empty except for the furniture.

I walked into the master bedroom. The intruders emptied the bureau and nightstand drawers onto the floor. Clothing and other personal items were scattered and the drawers lay upside down on top of their contents. My wallet and wedding ring lay on the floor near the bed. I picked them up, put on my ring and looked in my wallet. My cash and credit cards were intact and my ring is solid gold so it seemed odd that the thief left them behind. The door to the walk-in closet was open and items from the shelf covered the floor, but the clothes hanging on the rods were still in place.

When I got to my office, it was also a mess. Once again, if it could open, the intruders opened it. If anything was inside, it was now outside, on the floor. They even cut apart the cardboard moving boxes in the closet. Carefully packed contents fell in piles preventing the door from closing. I guessed now, I'd finally have to finish unpacking.

I found the disarray upsetting, but what I didn't see was more disturbing. My desktop computer, Ray's computer and his computer disk were gone and with them, the case on which I was working.

I was a fool. I took a case and didn't secure the evidence. It was a rookie mistake and I made it. Actually, it was worse than a rookie mistake. I knew better than to leave evidence unsecured. I could have taken the disk to my bank and put it in my safe deposit box, but I had convinced myself I didn't need to do it. I wasn't guilty of naivete. I was guilty of arrogance, thinking I could be exempt from the rules. I was pissed and I had only myself to blame.

Since nothing else of value was missing, the computers must have been what they had come to steal. What I didn't understand was why they opened and searched my cabinets, closets and drawers if the computers were in plain sight? I could imagine only one reason. They must have also wanted something else they thought I might have.

I was just leaving my office to tell Detective Torres what was missing when I heard the clicking of high heels on tile and voices came from the foyer. Apparently, Mariel had come home and was talking to him in a high-pitched voice. I couldn't hear what he was saying but I heard him speaking in a calm, quiet voice. When I got to them, she ran over and hugged me tightly. "Are you all right?"

"Sure. I was out for a run when this happened." I turned to Torres who had turned his attention back to his clipboard. "Apparently, the only things missing are my desktop computer and my client's notebook computer."

Torres stopped writing and looked at me. "Client's computer?"

Mariel stepped back to observe our discussion, but kept hold of my left arm. With my right hand, I opened my wallet and showed Torres my P. I. license. It was still new and I still got a kick out of flashing it. "I was examining the stolen computer for a client."

"What were you looking for?"

"I've been hired to locate assets from Ray Kenwood's estate."

"The same Ray Kenwood who we found dead in his car?"

"Yeah."

"And now, somebody broke in and stole his computer?"

"Yeah."

"Why? What was on it?"

"I don't know. I mean just some bank account and investment information. I was looking for estate assets. I didn't see anything that would explain why someone would steal it."

He stared at me in silence for a moment or two. He shifted his weight back onto his heels. I didn't think he liked what I said. Without taking his eyes off me, he clicked his ballpoint pen and put it in his shirt pocket. I admired the move. If I had tried it, I probably would have missed my pocket and stabbed myself with the pen. If not that, at best, I would have written on my shirt.

"I'm finished here," he said. "You can pick up a copy of the report sometime tomorrow morning."

"What are the chances of finding the stolen computers?" I asked even though I knew I'd never see them again.

"Not likely," he said. "Probably, some kids've already hacked your online bank accounts, wiped your drives and loaded computer games. On the other hand, if you found anything on the victim's computer, we could possibly have a clue -- Detective." He handed me his business card and left.

I watched him leave and then I looked at Mariel. Her eyes were wide and her mouth was open. She looked up at me and gently touched my arm. "You realize, don't you, whoever took these things knows you've already seen whatever it is they don't want anyone to see."

She changed her touch on my arm to a grip. "If it was important enough for someone to steal, it may be important enough for someone to kill. The poor man who owned that notebook is already dead."

"Yeah, well, just because they wanted the information; it doesn't mean they care if someone else has seen it. Without the actual disk, someone just knowing what was on it may not be a threat. It all depends on what was on it. They just took the computer. If they wanted me dead, they could have just waited for me to come home." I countered, not convinced I was right.

She leaned towards me, "So, what's on the disk?" She leaned back, threw her hands up and started to walk away from me. "No, wait, don't tell me. I don't want to know. It's safer that way."

I followed her. "Aside from routine banking and family finances, I don't know what's on the disk... It looks like I better find out."

She stopped walking and turned to face me. She jerked her head back and tilted it to the side. "They took both computers. Isn't it kind of late for that?"

"No, I've got a copy of Ray's entire disk on my new iPod, and if my notebook computer is still in the closet, I can use it to read the iPod until I get a new desktop."

She started to walk away again and then turned and walked back to me. Her hands hung down by her side. "Max, this isn't what we planned. We were going to spend our time here relaxing and playing together. Now, this. Now, we can't even be safe in our own home. I can't live like this." She turned away from me and brought her hands up to her face.

I was afraid she was going to cry. I hated to see her cry. I can't stand to see her cry. I walked over and put my arms around her. I was sympathetic to her being upset, but the break-in wasn't my fault. She wasn't happy but I was a victim of the break-in too; plus it was my stuff they took.

I thought about pointing out she said it would be ok to take the job, but thirty seven years of marriage taught me it wouldn't be a smart move. Instead, I said one of the only two things husbands could say at times like this. "I'm sorry."

She didn't reply. She just stood there with her back to me. I put my hands on her shoulders and then said the only other thing husbands could say at times like this. "I love you."

"I love you too, but I'm leaving," she pulled away, turned and looked up at me. "I'm too upset to stay here. I'm going to my sister's. You should come with me. It's not safe for us here. I don't want anything to happen to you again."

"I can't go. I have to stay here and work this thing out. It doesn't seem likely the police will resolve this. To them, it's just another burglary. Neither you nor I are going to feel safe here, until someone catches the thieves. Sometimes, in order to be safe, you have to do the thing that scares you the most. "

She looked at me in silence for a moment, turned away and left the room. Her packing was loud enough to be a clear signal. I knew better than to try to stop her.

CHAPTER FOUR

I phoned my handyman, Steve, to come and fix my door. While I was good with computers and electronic devices, I'm far from handy. In metal shop, my 3 ½ by 5 inch file card box ended up as 2 ½ by 5 inches. I couldn't measure worth a damn. Worse than that, I was clumsy and dangerous. While building a C-clamp, my metal stock slipped out of the bending jig and flew across the room. I finally transferred out of the class after setting my lab coat on fire while forging a chisel. You never saw a happier shop teacher.

Despite this experience, I would sometimes underestimate the challenge of a particular task and attempt a home repair. Whenever I did so, swearing ensued. Next, there would be blood and a call to a professional to fix the original problem plus whatever else I broke trying to fix it myself. Mariel had long ago learned to disappear whenever she saw me reaching for my toolbox.

Since we bought this house, Steve quickly became one of Mariel's favorite people, second only to our exterminator. Florida has some big bugs. Luckily, Steve promised to come by later in the day. I was oddly amused by the realization that at least this time he wouldn't need someone home to let him in.

I phoned Ed McCarthy again. I needed to tell him about the theft and to see what he thought about sharing the disk data with Torres. It was doubtful kids stole the computers. More likely, the theft was related to Ed's client and I needed to find out what I could tell the police without violating confidentiality rules. Ed still didn't answer either of his phones. I left another message. "It's

Max. You need to call me right away. There's been a theft." It seemed odd he was still unavailable at both numbers.

After hanging up, I remembered what Detective Torres had said about making an insurance claim, so I phoned my agent. Vicki had just sold us new policies when we moved in a few months ago and I still had her direct line in my speed dial. She answered right away, told me how to file my claim and went on to ask. "When did the break-in take place?"

"About an hour or so ago."

"In broad daylight? Did any of the neighbors see anything?"

"You know, Vicki. I feel stupid I didn't think of that myself. I must be more upset than I realize. Checking with the neighbors is a good idea. Thanks."

"You're welcome, Mr. Fried. If you need anything else, just give me a call."

"Thanks."

We hung up and I sat, staring a while at the empty spot under my desk where I kept my computer. The office looked odd with only a monitor and no computer, so I went to my bedroom closet to see if my backpack was still there. Luckily, I found it on the closet floor under some golf shirts I wore in cooler weather and some sweaters I was saving in case I had to travel north. The backpack compartments were unzipped, but nothing was missing. My notebook computer was still inside. I got it out, set it up on the desk and turned it on.

While waiting for it to start up, I realized just how much business I conducted on line and then how much of it was stored on my desktop computer. Since I just harvested all of Ray's personal information from his notebook, I was reminded how vulnerable I now was. Whoever had access to my stolen desktop computer would also have access to any emails, letters or any other documents I had containing my account numbers. They could obtain from my computer registry files, any passwords I used for online banking or investing. All they needed was some free software from the Internet.

So, the first thing I did with my notebook was to access my bank account on line to change my password. Then I changed the passwords for my 457K retirement plan and for Mariel's two 401K retirement plans. I also checked all of the balances and looked for recent withdrawals. Everything looked OK I guess I got there in time.

Next, I went to my paper files and pulled out a list of my credit card numbers. When we moved, I had photocopied all of my credit cards onto a sheet of paper I filed away in case I lost my wallet. I spent the next two hours on the telephone arranging for new cards. Since I didn't like the idea of merchants having direct access to my checking account, I still had an unused debit card that came with my new Florida checking account.

Lastly, I ordered a new computer online, paying extra for express shipping. I congratulated myself for having the sense to use my debit card instead of a credit card. The break-in shook me up enough that I could have easily charged the cost of a new computer on a cancelled credit card. Clueless, I would have spent weeks wondering why my purchase didn't arrive. On a positive note, every time I bought a new computer, I was amazed how much more I got for the same money I paid for my old one.

Finally done with all of the requisite notifications, I had time to take a shower. Even if it didn't make me feel better, at least I'd smell better. By the time I came out of the steamy bathroom, I was surprised to find my mood somewhat improved.

Standing there clean, wet and wearing a towel, I was also thinking a bit more clearly now and Vicki's comment came back to me. One of my neighbors might have seen something. I got dressed so I'd be more presentable. Since my wedding ring was still on my finger anyway, I put on underwear, cargo shorts, sandals and a golf shirt. With a pen and a pad from my desk, I went out to the front porch. When I reached for my key to lock the door, I realized it was unnecessary.

I stood on the porch and surveyed my prospects. Across the street was Karl. He already told the police he didn't see anything. To my right was Clara. She didn't work and spent a lot of time at home. To my left was Diane. She worked days, but her pickup truck was in her driveway. Maybe she had been home today. I walked over, rang her bell and started to admire the Christmas lights on her palm tree.

Diane opened the door wide, jingling the keys in her hand. She must have just arrived home. "Hi, Max. How are you?"

"I'm fine, but someone broke into my house and I was wondering if you might have seen anything unusual."

Her mouth opened when she heard the news and then she said, "No, Max, I'm so sorry. No, I just got home. I just walked in the door."

"Oh, I didn't realize you got off so early."

"I don't. I left early today to pick up my mother at the airport." She ran her fingers through her short hair. How's Mariel taking this? The poor thing."

Life's a Beach Then You Die

About a week after we bought our house, Mariel encountered a land crab in our garage and started screaming. Ever since Diane heard that noise, she has acted as if Mariel were a delicate flower. While it's true Mariel claimed she saw an octopus in the garage, I like to think that her reaction was simply due to her unfamiliarity with Floridian fauna and flora.

I chased the crab out with the pool net, but to be fair, the crab wasn't the only incident. For example, since we arrived six months ago, there was also:

1.   The lizard that scooted in under the dishwasher when Mariel opened the front door. Later found dead in a cabinet (The lizard, not Mariel)

2.   The lizard Mariel found in the garage sink. I washed it down the sink drain.

3.   The lizard that Mariel found on the garage floor. I blew it out with the leaf blower.

4.   The GIANT grasshoppers (bigger than the lizards, even bigger than her fist) that hung on the outside of the pool screen. I blasted them with the water hose.

5.   The black snake that found its way into the pool cage. Pool net to the rescue again.

6.   The orange peel on the kitchen floor that someone (Mariel) thought was a lobster.

7.   The piece of lint on the garage floor in front of the clothes dryer that someone (Mariel) thought I should kill.

Hence Mariel's "Door Rules." Rule number one stated that the garage, front and patio doors must remain closed at all times except for the time actually required to move something in or out. Rule number two applies only to the front door and the foyer door to the garage and it states one must open the door only a crack before opening fully. The intent of rule two is to startle the geckos so they run from the door instead of through it.

After thanking Diane for her concern about Mariel and our misfortune, I walked down her driveway toward Clara's.

When I got to the curb, I saw the garage door opening on the house next to Karl's. As it opened, a blue car pulled onto the driveway and into the garage. I didn't know the folks who owned that house. Karl told me they lived about an hour and ½ away near Orlando and used an agency to rent their place to vacationers. A man got out of the car carrying a hardcover book and a shopping bag from the Publix Grocery store. I called out to him.

"Hi."

He turned to look at me. He was tall and slim, slimmer than I was but not quite as tall. Probably in his late forties, he had medium length blond hair and a neatly trimmed moustache. As I approached his car, he walked out of the garage towards me and said, "Hello?"

"Hi, I'm Max Fried. I live across the street." I pointed over my shoulder.

The man shifted his shopping bag and his book to his left hand and offered me his right. As he extended his hand, I noticed an anchor tattoo on his forearm. "Nice to meet you, I'm Ralph. We're renting the place for the week." He gestured with his head towards the house behind him.

For some reason he felt the need to explain using the word "We" because he went on to add, "My wife and kids are down the block at the beach. I got stuck with lunch duty." He held up his grocery bag and smiled.

"Nice to meet you, Ralph. I don't want to put a damper on your vacation, but earlier today, someone kicked in my door and stole some computer equipment. I was wondering if you saw anything."

His smile disappeared. I was developing a real knack for spreading holiday cheer. "Really? Here? Geez, I asked about this kind of thing. The realtor told me this was a safe neighborhood."

"Did you see anything suspicious?"

"Nah." He shook his head. "I was here most of the morning on the phone with clients back home until I had to go out and run some errands. I'm really sorry to hear about this. I saw a patrol car on the street when I went out, but I thought he was just driving through. I really didn't stop to think there was a crime."

I thanked him. He told me some more how he couldn't believe things like break-ins could happen here, closed the garage door and went inside the house. I was willing to bet his vacation plans for next year would be different.

I walked back across the street to Clara's, rang her bell and waited. It took a few minutes but then I heard a cane on tile and movement behind the door. The door opened just a crack so she could see out. When she saw me, she opened it all the way and looked up.

"Oh, Max. How are you and Mariel doing? The police were here earlier asking me if I saw anything. Unfortunately, I didn't. The only time I went out today was to get my mail and I'm not one to sit by the window staring out. How can I help you?"

"Thanks, Clara. You just did. I appreciate it. Bye."

She gave me a puzzled look, not the first I earned from her, and closed the door. I walked down her driveway, went home and into my office. Questioning more neighbors wasn't going to help. I had already spoken to the closest ones. Besides, the police seemed to be canvassing the neighborhood. On the other hand, Clara gave me an idea.

Perhaps, Eileen, the mail carrier saw something. I met her several times when she hand delivered packages too big to fit in my mailbox. I also spoke with her a few times when she delivered while I was doing yard work. She seemed to be a bright woman who didn't let much get past her. Hopefully, she was driving up and down the block about the time of the break-in. Since she didn't live on the street, I didn't think it likely the police would speak with her. I looked up the phone number for the local post office and called.

"New Smyrna Beach Post Office," a man answered.

"Hi, I'd like to speak with Eileen, the mail carrier please." The phone was silent for a minute. Then he said, "I'm not sure if she's back yet. Hang on. I'll check."

After waiting a minute or two, I decided they forgot me. I was about to hang up when I heard a woman's voice. "Hello?"

"Hello, Eileen?"

"Yes. Who is this please?"

I told her who I was and my address.

"Oh, yes. How can I help you?"

I told her about the break-in and asked if she had seen anything unusual.

"Well, there was this one blue car parked for a long time. It was there long enough for me to visit all the houses on the block. It seemed odd because the driver sat slouched down in the driver's seat with the engine off. I had to maneuver my truck around it to get to a mailbox. For a while, I thought the driver may have been hurt or asleep, but as I passed the car on my way back up the block, the driver sat up."

"Thank you, that's very helpful. Do you know the plate number or what type of car it was?"

"No, I'm sorry. Just that it was blue. I think it may have had four-doors. I'm not sure. I'm sorry I don't recall. Next time I see something off, I'll write down the plate number."

"Oh, it's OK. Thank you very much. You've been a big help."

"OK, thanks. Bye."

"Bye."

I didn't get much for my efforts, but you never know. I didn't think this information would help much, but I decided to keep it in mind.

Now that I exhausted my canvass, I was finally ready to take a closer look at the data on my iPod, a much closer look. Now, I had a reason to think there was more there than I had originally found.

CHAPTER FIVE

Ray Kenwood, the dead owner of the now stolen notebook, seemed to do quite well financially. He also traveled a lot and his notebook computer contained documents and presentations regarding specifications for some of his employer's products. I guessed he must have made the rounds of trade shows, sales meetings and such, but I still didn't see anything that would explain the theft – or his murder.

While I was searching Ray's disk copy, my phone rang.

"Hello?"

I could hear female voices laughing in the background and then, "Max? Ed."

"Ed, I'm glad it's you. I've been trying to reach you."

"We were out on the boat. When I'm on the water, all business stops. I just got back, turned on my cell and got your voicemails. It's not that easy to sail a boat while you're talking on the phone. Hard to believe pal, I'm just not all that coordinated. Now what's this about a theft?"

"Someone broke into my house and stole Ray Kenwood's notebook computer. They also took the desktop computer I was using to examine it." When I finished speaking, I heard more feminine giggling over the phone.

"Shush, you two. Max, your first message said you finished with it. So you finished the examination before it was stolen?"

"Yes, and I think that's why my desktop was also taken. It contained my report." I told him about the financial information I found on the disk and about the break-in. "Ed, all of the personal information I found on Ray's notebook will also be available to whoever stole it. Ray's wife is going to need to contact some banks and credit card companies, take steps to protect their accounts."

"But she doesn't know about any of that stuff. That's why we hired you."

"I know, but it's OK. I still have a copy of my report here. It details all of the account information I found. I'll email it to you and you can forward it to her."

"No, print it out and we'll bring it over to her this evening. I'll pick you up around five. This way, you can explain everything. Thank goodness, you still have that report."

"Yeah, and it's probably a good idea to meet Kathleen. Maybe she'll know something that might explain the break-in."

"Maybe. You can ask her when you see her. How's Mariel? Is she OK? Are you OK?"

"Mariel's worried for my safety because I've seen the disk contents."

"Why would that put you in danger?"

"Well, according to her, someone stole the disk to keep anyone from seeing what's on it and whoever took it knows I've already seen it. She thinks if it was important enough for someone to steal, it may be important enough for someone to kill. She thinks it may have something to do with Ray's death."

"Well, geez, I don't have any clue why anyone would want to steal Ray's notebook or even why somebody would want to kill him."

"Me neither, but I'm taking a closer look."

"A closer look at what? If they stole the notebook, the disk and your computer, how're you going to do that? You've got nothing to look at."

"Actually, I've got everything to look at. You know when you make a forensic image of a computer; you've got the entire disk contents in a file, right?"

"Well, yeah, but..."

"I've got a copy of that file on my iPod along with my report. I'm going to use it and try to find out why the notebook was stolen."

"Wow."

"Ed... the cops weren't pleased with me. They seemed to think there might have been something on the disk relating to Ray's murder. I got the impression they thought I screwed up by not finding it."

"Did you?"

"Well, no. I don't think so. I didn't see anything unusual, but then I was only looking for assets."

"Are you going to look again?"

"Yeah, and this time, I'm going to look for anything that might explain the theft or the murder. Any reason I can't share my findings with them?"

"No, no reason In fact, I think you should, but let me know what you find before you give them anything. I've still got to protect my client's estate."

"OK, but in the meantime, what can you tell me about Ray's death? Do you have any details as to what happened?"

"Well, Ray died from a heart attack while driving, went off the road into a fence. Poor guy was only about 45. Even though he didn't do much to take much care of himself, he was healthy. He just passed an insurance physical. This is despite the fact he was overweight, smoked like a chimney and ate like sugar, salt and grease were three of the food groups. The only things unusual about his death were he had no history of heart disease and no one seems to know why his car was found where it was."

"Where did he have the accident?"

"State Route 44, they call that stretch, East New York Road. It happened on 44 right by Damascus Road. They found his car up against the fence by the electrical towers."

"Who knew I had Ray's notebook computer?"

"No one else knew. I didn't tell his widow. I figured I'd wait and see if anything turned up. I didn't want her disappointed if we didn't find anything. The only ones I discussed this thing with were Jack at the bar, you, and Mariel."

"Then, the only ones who could even know there was a computer are Jack, someone who could have overheard about it at the bar, you, Mariel and me."

"You don't think that Jack..."

"No, but that doesn't mean anything. Let's keep looking at the facts. What about the woman you were with at the bar?"

"Nope. I didn't mention anything about it to her and she wasn't around when I talked to Jack."

I thought it was odd Ed glossed over the woman's presence at the bar. I thought at least he would have mentioned her name, but he didn't. I tried to dismiss this, thinking maybe she was a client and Ed was just being discreet. Then I remembered the kiss she gave him when he left her at the bar. Maybe, I'm too suspicious, but I mentally filed this information for later. "I'm going to exclude you, Mariel, and myself because we already had access to the notebook. We didn't need to steal it."

"Right, and except for Jack, there wasn't anyone else at the bar close enough to hear."

"Was the bar the only place you discussed this?"

"Yeah, except for when we talked in my office."

"Ed, whoever took the notebook needed more information than just the fact there was a notebook. They would have also needed to know where it was and when it was there."

"Let's see. The police took the notebook from the accident scene. I only had it long enough to bring it to you. The first opportunity to steal it didn't come until I left it with you. Someone would have to know you had it, when you had it and where you're located."

"Even we didn't know when I'd have it until you phoned the police from your office. It was only after you hung up that we knew you'd be picking it up in the morning."

"Yeah, and we were also in my office when you gave me your address."

"Add to that me leaving a message on your office machine saying I was finished with the notebook. Someone hearing me would know I still had the notebook but not for much longer. Your office must be bugged."

"Jesus! I have confidential client consultations there!" Ed exploded.

"Yeah, OK. Look, until I get a chance to get over there and sweep for bugs, let's assume there is one. Until we clear this, don't say anything in your office you don't want overheard. If we need to, we can try to use this to our advantage. In the meantime, talk to me only on your cell and only talk when you're out of the office. OK?"

"Yeah, I guess so. Sure. OK."

"Good. First thing tomorrow morning, I'll drive to Orlando, pick up something to find hidden transmitters. It'll probably take about three hours there and back. I'll call you when I'm done and we can meet at Bobbi and Jack's, go to your place, and see what we can find. OK?"

"Yeah, sure. Fine."

We hung up and I turned to my notebook computer. I launched Google Earth and looked at the corner of SR 44 and Damascus Road, where the Police found Ray's car. One of the nice things about Google Earth is it not only shows you pictures of a location complete with roads and buildings, but you also get to see the names of businesses located in those buildings.

One of the local business names on the Google map, PC

Gadgets, looked familiar. Ray had sent emails to someone at PC Gadgets. I remembered the name because they're a small, local outfit. They make and sell computer peripherals like mice, keyboards and so on. Their products were standard. They didn't make anything someone else didn't already make, but their products were decent quality and inexpensive to buy. I actually owned a few. Ray worked for a much larger company in the same field, A. V. Designs. They not only made and sold similar products, but they also designed and developed new technology.

I looked again at the emails Ray had sent to PC Gadgets. Each one contained a photo of men on a sailboat, more like a yacht. I don't know how many feet it was but I never saw one this big before. Maybe Ray and the email recipient were sailing buddies who worked for different companies in the same field.

A couple of things seemed odd, though. The photos looked like someone took them all on the same day yet Ray mailed them one by one over several weeks. In addition, the hairstyles and clothing looked dated. I hadn't seen hair like that since the mid 80s.

I wanted to know more about these old pictures, but I didn't have much hope of learning more from the photos themselves. These styles predated consumer market digital cameras. If they were shot with a modern digital camera, I would have been able to determine not only the date and time, but also the camera model, shutter speed and aperture settings.

I searched Ray's data for graphics and I found the scans of the original film photos. Possibly, because there was handwriting on the backs of the original prints, whoever scanned them scanned both sides. Someone marked each photo backside with a date in 1984. Each date was the same and unfortunately, the only thing written on the back.

These emailed photos probably meant nothing, but they were all I had. I created a time line of emails from Ray to the competing company and then searched Ray's drive for activities that took place between the day before and the day after each of the emails.

The search was worth the effort. Ray's banking records showed large deposits each day after his emails to PC Gadgets. Also, one of those encrypted spreadsheets came up again. This one contained three columns. The first column listed dates, the second column, six-digit numbers and the third a combination of letters and numbers. This time I noticed the dates in the date column were in the date ranges I had searched. I imagined the six digit numbers could be dollar amounts but didn't know for sure. I still had no idea what the letters and numbers in the last column were.

I compared a few of the date entries to Ray's deposit records and got matches not only on the dates, but also on the six digit numbers that followed. They equaled the deposit amounts. For the last few months, Ray was depositing thousands of dollars. He was also recording the deposits in a spreadsheet next to some kind of letter and number entry that I didn't recognize. This was looking very interesting, but I still didn't see anything to explain what was really going on.

When I first started working for the State, they sent me to training. One of the trainers told my class, "When you don't know what decision to make, get more facts." In the past, I found it was good advice, so I thought it might help if I knew who the men in the photo were. There was a good chance one of the men might be Ray so I used Google to search for images of Ray Kenwood. I found two. One of him in an article about the fatal accident and one from an A. V. Designs sales presentation at a trade show. Both photos displayed a much heavier man than the one in the 1984 photo, but he was clearly the same man.

I had no way of identifying the other two men yet so I made a mental note of their appearances. One was taller and had long, blondish, and wavy, hair. He wore a Fu Manchu moustache. The other man was clean-shaven, shorter and had a flat nose. He also had a crooked smile with the left side of his mouth looking higher than the right.

I puzzled over these photos a bit more. Nothing came to me, so I looked more closely at them. The pictures didn't appear to show anything significant. Each one was one or two of the same three guys on a boat. No big fish on a line or any other significant moments captured. Just some guys sitting or standing on a boat. Based on the number of photos, all looking alike, it seemed odd Ray would send one old picture at a time over several weeks. How many photos does one need of what appeared to be repetitions of the same boring thing?

Back around 440 BC in Greece, a man named Histiaeus shaved a slave's head. He tattooed a message on it and when the slave's hair grew back, he sent him to the message recipient. Such was the birth of Steganography or concealed writing. A distinguishing advantage of this method is that the existence of a hidden message is not readily apparent.

On one hand, a coded message is usually very clearly a coded message. It tends to be combinations of random numbers or letters. The coding advertises that a secret exists and all one needs to do is crack the code.

On the other hand, if steganography is used, the existence of a hidden message isn't apparent. You first have to find the message before you can try to crack the code. People use a similar technique today, to hide text and images inside of photos. To the naked eye, the photo looks normal, but someone with the correct software, found free on the Internet, could encode and decode hidden messages in photos.

I saved the photos from the emails to a folder and ran them through a Steganography program. Sure enough, I found something. Each photo contained hidden text and images regarding some kind of A. V. Designs product. The amount of specificity and detail exceeded sales and promotional information normally provided to potential customers. Each of the decoded files contained a file number consisting of letters and numbers in the top left corner. I compared them to the entries in the last column of the spreadsheet. They matched.

Ray's spreadsheet contained file numbers of A. V. Designs technical documents next to dollar amounts and dates. In turn, the dollar amounts and dates matched wire transfers into Ray's personal bank account. Ray Kenwood had been emailing trade secrets to the competition for profit. So, Ray was a crook, but is that what got him killed?

CHAPTER SIX

I thought, "Isn't this case going well? I've lost evidence that may benefit my client's killer and I've found Ray's guilty of a crime. Ed's going to love this." I looked at the email address where Ray sent the photos, Ben.Horton@PCGadgets.com. At least, I had a handle on the man who appeared to be Ray's buyer. I ran a Google search on Ben Horton and PC Gadgets and discovered he was a high profile executive there. One online newspaper displayed a picture of him coaching a company sponsored soccer team. The article described him as a Research and Design Executive and business owner.

I also found a company newsletter containing his name and photo. His picture appeared over an article he wrote on the company's history. I saved a copy for later perusal. He looked like he could be one of the men in the emailed photos. Probably, Ray stole the secrets and Horton bought them. There was no apparent reason why a third person would be involved. On the other hand, the third man's lack of identity nagged at me. Ray emailed Horton several photos of just himself and Horton. Why did he also email photos that included one of them with the third man? I like complete understanding so I wanted to know, "Who was the third man?"

If the police had Ray's computer, Ray's files would incriminate Horton in the thefts. This gave Horton a motive for breaking into my home and possibly for killing Ray. I'd need more information. Maybe murdering Ray would have been, if you pardon the expression, overkill.

The industrial theft was another thing, even if Horton didn't kill

Ray, following the trail of Ray's crime might lead me to his killer or at least the reason for his murder. It seemed the best way to learn more of Ray's crime would be to investigate Horton but I couldn't exactly approach him directly. What would I say, "Hi, I understand you've been buying trade secrets. Did you break into my home and steal the evidence? Oh, and who's the third guy in the photos containing the stolen information you bought?"

Since Horton and Ray communicated by email and trusted hiding their secrets in plain sight, I decided to watch Horton's emails to see if they lead to anyone else. In addition, prior correspondence might be helpful. If I had access to the PC Gadgets email system, I could monitor Horton's emails. Unfortunately, I didn't have access, but I knew someone who could get it for me.

Angie D. was a colleague from back in New York. We met in the hospitality bar at a white hat hacker's conference when his smiling picture suddenly appeared on my computer screen. Since the white hat hackers are supposed to be the good guys, I took his prank in the spirit of the moment and we became friends. He makes his living as a consultant, but he's a programmer, a surfer (the kind who uses a wooden board), a digital forensic examiner and oh yeah, a lock picker. Angie D. is the type of guy who doesn't really care what's behind the locked door. He just wants to see if he can get in.

I called him on his cell. "Hey, Angie, it's Max."

"Hey, Bub. How're you doing, man?"

"I'm good. What's up?"

"Up is a directional indicator. How's Florida?"

"Nice and warm. You should come down and visit. I've got wireless Internet access throughout the house. You can surf the net from my pool. Tell you what, to make your visit more entertaining, I won't give you the password and you can hack in instead."

"Tempting as that may be, I'm kind of booked these days. You got something on your mind, don' t you?"

"Yeah, I need to monitor emails coming from and to a corporate email address."

"I take it this address is not your own, you don't have a court order, you don't have a subpoena and we never discussed this. Gimme the email address and watch your own account for something from Bill Gates."

"Thanks, Angie. It's Ben.Horton@PCGadgets.com"

"Later, man."

While I was waiting, I decided to see what, if anything, I could find out on my own about Horton and PC Gadgets. The first thing I did was visit Sunbiz.org. This is the web site of the Florida Department of State, Division of Corporations. Every corporation in the state needs to file with them and luckily Florida makes this information available on line.

I searched for the corporate name PC Gadgets. In return, I was able to view their Articles of Incorporation, which showed me the name and address of the registered agent, the address of the principle place of business and the names of the corporate officers. The original filing showed Ben Horton was both the registered agent and the president of the corporation. No other officers were listed. The address for the business was the same as the registered agent, the PC Gadgets office on Damascus Road.

While at the Sunbiz.org website, I also searched for Judgment Liens, and found the IRS had filed a lien against PC Gadgets for $10,347. I could also see the lien had been satisfied about a week before Ray made his first deposit. It was beginning to look like Horton and PC Gadgets were in financial trouble, had found some kind of benefactor and somehow this tied in with Ray getting pay offs.

Since the Horton's business was located in Volusia County, I looked at the County website at Volusia.org where I was able to access the Property Assessor records. I typed in Horton's address and found his property information. I could see the details of his house such as how many bedrooms, baths and so on, as well as when he bought it and for how much. He paid a lot, but considering the riverfront neighborhood and his own private dock, that was to be expected. None of this information was especially useful.

Next, I did a search on the Revenue Division's Tax files for Ben Horton's name. I found the records for his home again, but a second property he owned also came up. I checked the address and saw Horton's name listed as the sole owner of the property on which his business was located. He paid all of the taxes in full on both properties. Again, I found nothing useful except to find he had many expenses maintaining both properties and trying to keep his business going. It looked like he was stretched thin, got in trouble with the IRS and some how got some money to dig his way out. My question now was "Where did he get the money?"

I went back to the Sunbiz.org website and looked again at the corporate records. I noticed he filed the most recent annual report about two weeks before the IRS Lien was satisfied so I took a closer look and found a change. Below Ben Horton's entry as

President, a new entry added Corky Eastwood as Vice President.

Who was Corky Eastwood? I couldn't even tell if Corky was a man or a woman. I wondered, "Did Corky bail out Ben?" And if he or she did, was he or she in on stealing secrets from A. V. Designs? Every time I got something that led somewhere, it just seemed to raise more questions. The closer I got, the further I got. Well, if Corky had the kind of money Ben needed, then there was a good chance there would be something on Corky in the newspaper or the web; maybe a business or society page thing.

The Daytona Beach News Journal, the local print paper, has a web site, so I searched their papers archives for Corky Eastwood. I got lucky and found one article. It was an obituary, not for Corky, but for her father, Grant Courtland Eastwood III. He died from a heart attack on his boat. Apparently, the vessel was too big to dock so he anchored in the river and was unable to take his dinghy to shore in time to get help. He was a widower affectionately known to his friends as Zorky. God knows why they called him that. Geez, Zorky and Corky, I guess the rich really are different.

I followed up that lead by Googling Zorky. He was a local attorney who had managed a large family fortune into an even larger family fortune. He was a back stage kind of guy in local politics and had once run unsuccessfully for senator. It appeared Corky, his only heir, inherited everything. I didn't have any proof yet, but it looked like I found the source of the money Ben used to pay the IRS and Ray.

I also had a name now for someone other than Ben who could have broken in, but the image of a society woman rolling in wealth breaking in to steal a computer just didn't make any sense. What did make sense was that if she were daddy's heiress, she would probably be on the Board of Directors of more than just Ben Horton's company. So, I went back to Sunbiz.org, to check the corporate filings again, but this time, I did a name search on Corky Eastwood.

Aside from getting a hit on PC Gadgets, Corky Eastwood's name appeared as President of Eastwood Family Holdings, Inc. Ben Horton's name didn't appear in any of the Eastwood corporate papers. In an attempt to learn more, I Googled "Eastwood Family Holdings." A few articles from trade papers and web sites came up. I read them and learned "EFH" as their logo showed, was a serious top shelf company invested in many high tech development projects here and overseas.

A business magazine ran a story of how successful the company became since Corky took over after Dad's demise. From all accounts, they were blue chip. They looked legit and I was beginning to suspect Corky was unsuspecting when it came to PC Gadgets.

I played this all out in my head, and came up with the following explanation. Ben Horton overextended his finances to the point he couldn't make his tax payments. In danger of losing his business and house, he steals designs from an outfit known for innovative products and bleeding edge development. Somehow, he hooks up with Ray who sells him design documents. Horton then uses these stolen designs to entice EFH into investing in his company. So she can keep an eye on him and more importantly her money, Corky Eastwood becomes vice president at Ben's company. I thought this made sense, but it still didn't prove Horton broke into my home.

About two hours after I talked to Angie D., a new email arrived. It supposedly came from Bill.Gates@microsoft.com and contained the user ID and a password for an account on Yahoo. I signed on and sure enough, I saw copies of Ben Horton's incoming and sent emails. I looked through them. The most recent one was a daily statement from a hotel in California listing his current room charges as of noon that day.

The statement showed Horton was out of state and charging brunch when someone broke into my office. He also had an email from TransCon Airlines confirming his scheduled flight home tomorrow morning. I had to revise my theory. Horton may have a motive to steal Ray's computer, but at the time of the break-in, he was three thousand miles away. Except for that and the emails, I had already seen from Ray, there was nothing else unusual.

CHAPTER SEVEN

I was pondering my discoveries about Ray when the doorbell rang. It was Ed, standing there with a cigarette in his hand. I thought about telling him what I found, but it didn't seem like the right time. We were on the way to visit Ray's widow and telling Ed his dead buddy was a crook now didn't seem seemly. I'd tell him later.

"Hey, Max. You ready?"

"Sure, let me get my report." I went back to the office, got my briefcase and joined Ed in the car. As he backed out of my driveway, he said, "We're getting to her just in time. She's leaving early tomorrow to visit her folks."

Ray had lived on the mainland in Venezia, an upper class riverfront neighborhood in Quay Assisi. The Kenwood home wasn't far from mine, maybe a ten minute drive. It was a big house, L-shaped with a three-car garage forming the small side of the L. Even in a depressed real estate market, it was probably worth a couple of million.

Ed pulled into the Kenwood driveway next to a silver Mercedes SUV bearing the Florida license plate "ONE BBW." I could see luggage piled high in the back of the vehicle.

We walked up to the house and Ed rang the bell. After a few moments of silence, the door swung open and a very large, very pretty woman in a sleeveless red dress filled the doorway. She was as tall as I was and as wide as Ed. She looked sad at first, but brightened when she saw Ed.

"Ed!" She cried and hugged him. She wrapped both arms around him and squeezed. For a moment, I thought his feet might

41

have left the floor.

Ed grunted out, "Kathleen, this is Max Fried."

She released Ed, turned and hugged me tightly, too. If I were a foot shorter, her expansive breasts would have had me struggling for air.

"Boy, you're a puny one, aren't you?"

I just smiled. At six foot three, 180 pounds, I had never thought of myself as puny, but I guess when you're as large as Kathleen is, size is relative. I wondered how to extricate myself when Ed said, "Max has some papers for you. Shall we go inside and sit?"

She released me. "Of course, where are my manners? C'mon in." I thought I heard a touch of the Carolinas in her voice.

We followed her through the house into the living room. Soft jazz playing on the sound system gave way to Nat "King" Cole singing "The Christmas Song." Kathleen sat on a sofa facing an unlit fireplace where two empty red stockings hung from the mantle. She tossed her head, flicked her hand to throw her long black hair over her right shoulder, and patted the seat next to her. Ed sat down and I took a white leather chair across the coffee table from them. There was an empty glass sitting next to a book on the table. I strained to read the book title but could only see the cover photo. It looked like a romance novel. She pushed the closed book away and said, "I just finished."

"Kathleen," Ed began, "we found what you wanted on Ray's computer, but first, Max has a few questions, OK?"

She nodded her approval. I removed a photograph and my report from my briefcase. Ed took them from me and placed them on the coffee table in front of Kathleen. The photo was on top.

"I found this image in one of your husband's emails. Do you recognize anyone?"

She picked it up and Ed leaned over to take a closer look at it. "Just Ray," she said. "Boy, does he look young there, probably taken before we met." She smiled, "Mmm, Ray was a good looking kid." She handed the photo to Ed. He looked at it, grunted, and handed it back to me.

I put it back in my case and asked, "Do you know Ben Horton?"

"No, who's Ben Norton?"

"No, not Norton, Horton, apparently someone Ray did business with. They exchanged emails. I thought you might know him."

"What if I did?"

Her question made me uncomfortable. I realized I should have thought this through more before I started asking her questions. "I uh, thought he might know more about some of Ray's business dealings... that he might have additional information."

She sat up straighter and stuck out her chest. "Then ask him. Why are you asking me these things?"

Ed pointed to my report on the table, "Max found the bank accounts, credit card and investment information you wanted." Kathleen softened a bit and looked down at the papers while she lit a cigarette. Then she reached out and thumbed through the pages. "Ray was a lot of fun and he always provided for me, but he never let me in on his business. Thanks, I really needed this."

Ed put his hand on hers. "There's a small... complication."

She sat back and looked at him. Ed looked at me, paused and then continued. "After Max obtained the information, someone broke into his home and stole Ray's computer."

Kathleen looked genuinely surprised. "What? Why would someone do that?" She looked at me as if she expected an answer. I didn't have one so I said nothing. Saying nothing when I knew nothing was a recently acquired skill I wished I had learned earlier in life. It seemed to work now because Kathleen turned back to Ed and said, "None of this makes any sense."

Ed asked, "What do you mean?"

She shook her head from side to side. "First, the police tell me that Ray had a heart attack. Now, you tell me that someone stole Ray's computer. Ray was a fit as a fiddle and he was a simple sales rep."

I didn't realize it but I must have reacted when she said Ray was fit because she glared at me and said, "People just assume that if you're big, you're not healthy. Ray had good numbers. Low cholesterol, low blood pressure and good sugar levels. The guy just had good genes. His Daddy was over 100 when he died. I don't believe Ray had a heart attack. No, not Ray."

I asked her, "So you think he had an accident and that's it?"

"I don't know. I wasn't there, but if he did, I can collect money from his accident policy too."

I asked, "Did you tell this to the police?"

"You kidding? The first sign of any foul play and the cops come after the spouse." She looked me up and down. "Don't you watch TV?"

CHAPTER EIGHT

We sat in Ed's car, headed to my place when he asked me, "OK. Who's this guy, Horton and what do you think he knows?"

I didn't have all of the information I needed yet, so I limited my response, "Like I said, he did business with Ray. Sometimes people discuss investments with business associates. I thought he might know something more about Ray's finances."

Ed appeared satisfied with my explanation. If he wasn't, he didn't let on but he still seemed upset from our visit with Kathleen. I was going to see Ed again tomorrow morning. I decided I'd give him the bad news about Ray's criminal activities then.

He dropped me off and as I entered my house, my stomach growled. I looked down at the culprit and realized I hadn't eaten since lunch. Now was about the time Mariel and I would plan dinner. Maybe "plan" isn't the correct word. Maybe I should say, "negotiate." Due to my size, I have what I like to think is a healthy appetite. On the other hand, Mariel is five feet two inches and slim with a limited capacity for food. One reason Mariel stays so slim is she hardly eats. The other reason is she is obsessed about exercising.

When we lived on Long Island, I once showed her a Newsday cartoon of two ragged, emaciated men stranded in the desert. One was crawling on his hands and knees. The other was doing sit ups. The caption read "I just don't feel right when I don't exercise." She didn't get it. When we went out to eat, I'd have dinner while she'd have a dinner salad. I don't like to think I wolf down my food, but while I'd be sitting there groaning, wishing I could loosen my pants in public, she'd still be working on her dinner salad, dressing

44

on the side.

Due to her minor and my major interest in food, I did the cooking and she did the cleaning. I cared a lot more than her about what I ate and how it was prepared. She cared a lot more than I did about what kind of mess I left after I made our meals. It was a match made in heaven.

All of this thinking about food made me hungry and made me miss her. I decided to call her at her sister's. Her sister and their mother moved down from New York a few months after Mariel and I did. They each owned units in a condo about a mile south of us. It's close enough we can see each other when we want to and it's far enough we don't have to when we don't.

Not wanting to get the whole family involved, I decided against calling my sister-in-law's home phone. Instead, I would dial Mariel's cell. I knew I was kidding myself about them not being involved. I was sure the three of them and possibly my niece, if she were home from college, had already rehashed things a couple of times. I tried to admit to myself my real reason for calling the cell instead of the house phone was that I didn't want to talk to any of them except Mariel. I felt bad enough about her being upset. I'd feel worse if I had to talk with one of the other people who loved her.

"Hello?" she asked.

"Hi, it's me," I said. I knew she knew it was me. Mariel never answered her cell without first looking at the caller ID to see who was calling. This was my pitiful way of buying some time so I could assess her mood before we spoke.

"I know."

On the Mariel Scale, a count of three words in two exchanges usually means she's still upset but willing to talk. So far, so good. Maybe I could build on that if I were careful. "I was thinking this is when we usually talk about dinner."

"I'm going to have dinner here. We're going to have some cottage cheese and fruit."

Cottage cheese and fruit for dinner sounded revolting, but the fact she told me what she was having was a good sign. If she were mad at me, she'd have only told me she was eating there. On the other hand, maybe she told me the menu to revolt me.

"OK. I just wanted to check in and see how you're doing. I'll make something here."

"I'm doing fine, but how are you? Are you still at the house? I'm worried about you."

"Yeah, I'm still here." My doorbell rang and I got up to answer it. "Wait a minute. Someone's at the door."

"Don't answer it," Mariel said. "You don't know who it is. It could be dangerous."

"I'm sure it's OK. Crooks don't generally ring the bell and announce themselves."

"They might if they want to know if someone is home before they break in. They might just ring the bell and hide."

"I'm sure it's ok. Besides, the door is broken. I can't lock it anyway." I opened the door.

"Max, please be careful. I'll stay on the line. If there's a problem, hang up and I'll dial 911."

"Hi, Steve, Mariel, it's Steve. He's come to fix the door."

"Oh, Max. I'm so worried about you. Please come and stay here with us."

"No thanks, I need to see this through or you'll never come home. We didn't work this hard to get to the point where you're afraid to be here."

She said nothing and then. "OK. I love you."

"I love you too."

Steve had been standing there patiently looking over the broken doorframe while we talked. When I hung up, he said, "Hiya, Mr. Max. This doesn't look too bad. I don't have any new molding in the truck, but this piece broke off pretty clean. I think I can put it back with wood screws, slap some mud and paint on it and it'll be just fine for now. If you want to beef it up, give me a call next week. I can come back with materials, strengthen the frame and install a stronger lock."

"OK Steve. Thanks."

We exchanged small talk while Steve repaired the door frame. As usual, he was quick, cheap and did good work.

After he left, I realized this would be my first night alone in this house. Since we bought this place, six months ago, Mariel and I had spent each night here together. Our first night after taking ownership, we went out and bought an inflatable bed. We slept on it for a few days until our furniture arrived from New York. Now, it felt odd to be here alone.

The house was strangely quiet. Neither CNN nor MSNBC blared from the bedroom. Mariel's a TV news junkie. When she's home, she always has a TV on one of the cable news channels. The only exception is baseball season. Then she bounces back and forth between METS games and the news.

On the bright side, I had a chance to make whatever I wanted for dinner. I decided to make an old favorite, pasta pesto primavera. Mariel used to love it, but recently decided the carbohydrates in the pasta were evil. I got out the old stew pot my father used to use when I was a kid. In my parent's home, my Dad used to do all of the cooking. He did it until the day he died. He liked to say he had to teach my mother how to boil water. Since I ate my mother's cooking from time to time, I don't think he was joking. I liked using that pot. It was of my few links to my old man.

Early in our marriage, I burned some food onto a small pot and Mariel threw it out as she thought it would be too hard to clean. After that, we had a long talk and she assured me she would never do that with the old man's stew pot.

I filled the pot half way with cold water. While the water heated, I boiled a can of cannellini beans, blanched a bunch of broccoli, cooked some cauliflower and nuked a pack of frozen chopped spinach. After the water boiled, I poured in a box of rotelli and watched it dance in the hot water. When the pasta was al dente, I strained it and tossed it in a huge bowl along with pesto sauce, the beans and the vegetables.

I filled a bowl with some pasta, found a fork, a glass, a bottle of red wine and brought my dinner out back to the pool. It was nice, cool, and quiet. The covered patio extended about 20 feet to the concrete pool deck, which was as wide as the house and covered half the backyard. A screened enclosure around everything kept the bugs out, but there was still a nice breeze. Patio lights glistened on the shimmering water as I sat at the table and ate.

"How'd I get into this?" I asked myself. I should have asked a smarter person, because I didn't know the answer. I knew I needed more information but had no ideas on how to get it. The only lead was the bug in Ed's office... if there really was a bug in Ed's office. I'd have to get equipment and look for one.

I finished dinner, and went back into the house. By now, the path through the CDs on the floor was so well defined I almost didn't notice the mess anymore. I realized I had better clean up before Mariel came back. If she saw all of this again, it might just remind her of how scared she was. Maybe, if things looked normal when she came home, she might feel more comfortable here. I spent less time than I thought getting the CDs and books picked up. Of course, now the previously alphabetized books and CDs were all stored in random order, but at least they were off the floor and out of sight.

I picked up the things on the bedroom floor and stuffed them back into drawers and onto shelves. I shoved some of the stuff on my office floor into the closet and then piled the rest on top until I could get the door shut. Neatness would have to wait until I got some new boxes.

Back in the kitchen, I got out the yellow pages, looked up a few likely places where I could buy what I needed and picked one. Tomorrow, I'd get up early and sweep Ed's office. After loading the dishes into the dishwasher and tossing the empty wine bottle, I staggered off to bed.

CHAPTER NINE

At 7:30 am, a beeping noise startled me even though I knew I had set my alarm for that time. I wouldn't say I woke up, but I did manage to open my eyes. I had to so I could find my watch and press the button that would stop the damn beeping. I couldn't believe that before I retired I had been getting up earlier than this for over 30 years. I don't know now how I had managed to do it.

I pulled down the covers, figuring I could build some inertia now my eyes were open. I thought I could do this if I did it one step at a time. Rather than being the next step towards momentum after opening my eyes, pulling down the covers slowed me down again as it revealed another reminder Mariel wasn't there. I stopped a moment to think about that. Then when I realized getting out of bed was the first step to getting her back into bed, I sat up and swung my legs over the side. Did I mention I wasn't a morning person?

I took my glasses from the nightstand and staggered into the bathroom. Some days, it takes a blast of steamy, hot water in the face to get me going so I took off my glasses and walked into the shower.

After a few minutes of scrubbing, I felt revived and clean enough for public contact. I put on my boxer-briefs, cargo shorts, sandals and an emblem marked golf shirt I got free at a forensic tools training class. If I was going out to buy P. I. gear, I should look the part and it was too hot for a trench coat and fedora. I dragged myself into the kitchen. I had to get on the road quickly so I settled for a glass of orange juice, a bowl of Kashi cereal with skim milk and cup of café con leche.

I got my camera bag from my office, my car keys from the kitchen drawer and went out the foyer door into the attached garage. Mariel's car was gone and my Monte Carlo looked lonely in the two-car garage all by itself.

I left the house, crossed the southern bridge to the mainland and after 15 minutes, turned onto Interstate 95. I still couldn't believe that this was the same road, which stretched north far enough to be the Cross-Bronx Expressway in New York. I traveled about 30 miles south to exit 50. Then west another 15 until I came to the Spy Shack of Orlando. The name was so cheesy I was embarrassed to go in. The Spy Shack wasn't so much of a shack as it was a former gas station. It looked like the building owner wanted to save money while keeping his future rental options open. Removable wood fill-ins covered the repair bay doors.

I slinked from my car to the shop and opened the door. A small bell jingled. An Italian opera played softly in the background. A golden retriever on the floor to my right lifted his head up from resting on his front paws. He looked at me and then put his head back down.

To my left, a man sat on a stool behind what looked to be the counter for the old gas station. It ran along the entire left wall. In front of the man, small tools and a soldering iron covered the countertop.

He held something in both his hands close to his face and squinted at it through thick glasses. He wore a short sleeve shirt with a pair of thin blue stripes running both vertically and horizontally across a white background so the lines formed a pattern of blue double-lined boxes. Over that, he wore a pair of thin grey suspenders stretched over his potbelly to snap onto his baggy blue jeans. He looked like he might be in his fifties with a full head of unruly black and white hair and a thick, wide, moustache to match. He ignored me as he attempted to focus on what he held.

Welcoming his lack of solicitation, I turned to my right and passed the still disinterested dog. I wandered through the shop looking at the devices used to both pierce and protect privacy. I thought it was odd to see a Christmas wreath for sale until I realized it contained a hidden camera. Despite myself, I become fascinated with all of the ways people pried into each other's lives and with all of the ways to prevent and to catch them.

I made a full circuit of the shop and came to rest in front of the man on the stool. Without moving his hands or his head, he raised his eyes over his glasses and looked at me. He said nothing but that which he said with his raised eyebrows.

"Hi," I said. "I'm looking for something I can use to detect a hidden transmitter."

He looked at me a moment as if deciding whether my need was worth him pausing his efforts to help me. When he sat up straight, I guessed he decided to help me. "Sure, fella. Lemme put this down gently first so this wire don't come loose."

As much as I didn't want to succumb, I couldn't help myself. I leaned forward. "What do you have there?"

"Oh, it's a new design I'm working on. I make some custom devices. From time to time. For special customers. Sometimes, a fella needs something that isn't a standard product." He gently placed his work on the counter and looked up at me. You trying to find a bug?"

"Yes. My client and I discussed something in his office and it appears a third party also heard it."

"And you're sure your client didn't tell anyone else?"

"So far. That's why I want to look for a bug."

"OK, so this wasn't discussed on the phone. It was said in person?"

"Yes."

"OK, so you're probably not dealing with a tapped telephone line here. If you were, the conversation would have had to take place while talking on the phone. Was it said near a telephone?"

"The closest phone was a few feet away."

"If you were near a phone but not on the phone, someone could be using an Infinity Device."

I must have been giving him a blank stare because he paused a moment and then said, "It lets someone dial a phone without ringing it so the caller can listen in on whatever is in range of the telephone microphone."

"I guess that could be. The phone was close enough on the desk, but a huge pile of papers covered it. Would it still work when buried like that?"

"Possibly, but if there's no Infinity Device, then if anything, you probably have a separate listening device hidden somewhere. Now, if that listening device is a microphone connected to a recorder, you won't detect anything when you sweep for radio signals. On the other hand, if there's a microphone there connected to a transmitter, you stand a chance of finding the transmitter when you sweep for bugs. Luckily for you, stashing a mic and a recorder means the stasher has to return and retrieve the recorder before they can hear anything."

"Why is that lucky for me?"

"Well, since you gotta go back for the recorder without knowing if what you want is on it, most folks wouldn't choose that approach. Plus if you don't know where it is and it looks like you don't know, finding the thing can be tough. If you got a transmitter hidden there, then it's transmitting on a radio frequency. If something's transmitting on a radio frequency, I gotta couple devices here that can hear 'em."

He got down off the stool and walked behind the counter to a wall mounted cabinet where he took a key from his pocket and opened the glass sliding door. "This here's what I'd recommend. If there's something transmitting, you should be able to find it with this frequency finder. You put on these headphones, plug them into the finder and then turn on this switch."

He held the device so I could see where he was pointing. "Then you move the finder around until you've covered the entire room. It's got a range of about 25 feet so you don't have to move too much. If the finder finds something, one of these lights here on the top start flashing. This'll scan as high as 8 GHz so you'll be able to find the latest breed of bugs. It's $279.95. It's no spectrum analyzer but then this gadget's about eight thousand dollars cheaper. Oh, and it will also detect an Infinity Device."

I looked at the device. I looked at the man. I looked at the device.

"You're skeptical," he said.

"How does it distinguish from equipment that's supposed to be there?"

"Depends. Some household appliances like microwaves and telephones will transmit frequencies this finder can detect. That's where you come in. You've got to use common sense, move things around, turn things off and on. In-vest-igate. You know, sometimes folks will intentionally use a bug that transmits on a common frequency to try to hide the signal. Of course, they run a risk of the signal being drowned out by someone making popcorn, but life is full of choices."

I looked at the man. I looked at the device. I looked at the man. I nodded.

"You'll take it?"

"Yes." I handed over my VISA debit card. He put the device back in its box and put the box in a yellow plastic bag. The bag bore a smiley face and the advice to "Have a nice day!"

He rang up the sale and gave me a receipt to sign. I signed it and we swapped my signed receipt for my customer copy. I put my card away and he handed me the bag with his left hand while he reached up with his right to shake my hand.

"Mr. Steed, it's been a pleasure doing business with you. My name

is Sid Speichek. Please come by again."
I started to correct him about my name when I realized why he called his business the Spy Shack. Mentally shaking my head, I smiled and left. Maybe he'll debit Mr. Steeds' account instead.

CHAPTER TEN

I got into my car and drove back to New Smyrna Beach. The ride went quickly. Trips home always seem to be faster than trips to new places. I parked in the lot at Bobbi and Jack's and went inside.

I didn't see Ed so I called him on his cell, said I was back and climbed onto a bar stool. The band wasn't there today but great blues recordings came over the sound system. The current song sounded like an old recording of a young B. B. King.

Jack walked over with a chilled mug in his hand. It's never too early for a cool beer on a sunny day. He looks like he's really casual and laid back, but don't be a rude drunk in his bar or you'll see a very different man. He put it down in front of me, showed me that pleasant expression he wears and said, "AmberBock draught. How are you doing today?"

"You ask everybody that."

He laughed. "It's an old customer service trick. When you say that to someone who's been here before, they think you remember them and you're asking how they're doing compared to last time they were here. If they've never been here before, they think you're just being friendly. It beats trying to remember everyone you serve."

He raised his eyebrow at me, wiped the counter where the chilled mug made it wet, and went to serve another customer. I sat there for a while watching the action in the bar and on the beach. The weather was beautiful. Again. The air temperature was about 79 degrees. The sky was blue, clear and cloudless. The ocean looked inviting but I knew this time of year, it was a too cool to most locals for swimming and guessed the few folks playing in the surf were tourists. It looked like another day in Paradise. I had difficulty reconciling this idyllic scene with the reality of Ray's murder, the break-in and Mariel's self-exile.

I was finishing my drink when I saw Ed through the glass door. He was getting out of a small white convertible in the parking lot. The driver was a slim, pretty brunette. Young, she wore a tan baseball cap with her hair in a ponytail pulled through the opening in the back. Ed walked around to the driver's side and the brunette reached up, hugged him around the neck, pulled him down and kissed him. Ed straightened up and the brunette drove out of the lot.

Ed entered the bar and stopped in the doorway when he saw me. I placed a few bills on the counter, motioned to him and went out to the patio. I walked through the patio and down the beach near the surf. The sound of the waves would make it tough for anyone who might try to listen in. Ed followed.

He caught up and we walked south on the beach. I watched the waves while Ed watched the bikinis. "Ed, before we get to the main event, I need to talk to you about something."

"Yes?"

I got as far as "I found some..." before Ed's cell phone rang.

He held up one hand palm first towards me "Er, excuse me, please," looked at his phone, opened it and said, "Hi..."

"Uh, huh..."

"Yeah, it was fun. Yup, just like old times." Ed smiled. "Look, I'm with a client now. How bout I call you when I'm done...?"

"Let's think about it for a while first..."

"I may have another idea. We can talk later..."

"OK. I'll call in a bit, bye."

Ed closed his phone and put it back in his pocket, "I'm sorry. My ex is in town from New York. We spent the morning on the boat with our daughter. Just like old times."

"Sounds nice, she staying long?"

"Well, that's the question. Sheila left her job at the firm in New York. Now, she's staying with our daughter Brenda who only has a one bedroom. Sheila's stuck on the couch and she wants to use the apartment next to my office. She doesn't want to stay at Brenda's, says it's not right to cramp her style."

"Sure, what mother would want to get in the way of her daughter's social life?"

"No. Brenda is getting in Sheila's way. That's why she wants the empty apartment."

"Oh, and you think it may be too close?"

"Maybe...I thought so at first, but the other day on the boat...it was so nice being a family again, the three of us. I was actually thinking of maybe inviting her to stay at my place..."

"You mean she's thinking of staying down here?"

"Yeah, she's left the job for good this time, due to the sexual harassment."

"That's not right. Can't you represent her and get them to stop."

Ed stared at me for a moment. "No, you've got it wrong. First, she's an attorney. A good one. She can represent herself. Second, she's the one who's been charged with harassment, again. This time, some guy in the mailroom."

Things began to become clear, even to me, "Was she the one at the bar when we met?"

"Yeah. How did you know that? Never mind. I'm sorry, Max, you were trying to tell me something..."

"I found some things on Ray's disk... he may have been involved in some things that weren't kosher."

"What do you mean?" Ed's eyes started following the path of a young woman in a neon pink bikini.

"I found some emails on Ray's disk he sent to a competitor, Ben Horton at PC Gadgets. They contained photos embedded with trade secrets from Ray's employer A. V. Designs. Each day after sending the emails, there were large sums of money deposited into one of Ray's accounts."

"Jesus!" Ed stopped walking. I could tell how upset he was because he also stopped looking at the woman in the bikini.

"Somebody must have stolen Ray's computer because they knew information on it could hurt them. So, the Police know a murder and a theft took place, but don't know the motivation may have been to cover up a crime in which your client was involved." I started walking again.

Ed nodded his understanding and began to trail me. "Oh, so that's why you asked Kathleen about Horton. Look. We've got a bit of a problem here. We've got to cooperate with the police... especially on Ray's murder, but I certainly can't turn in a client, even a dead one or work against the interests of his estate."

We walked a bit in silence and I watched Ed chew his bottom lip. Finally, he said, "I think we're done, Max. I don't want to muddy Ray's memory any more than you have, and I expect you to keep quiet about this. We both have to respect confidentiality rules." Ed paused for a moment and then said, "I'm also not keen on you having questioned Kathleen like you did. Give me a bill for replacement of the stolen equipment you lost. Add up your billable hours and we'll call it a day." He stopped walking and turned to face me.

"What about the police?"

"They're going to want a killer more than a thief and they cut deals for live crooks all of the time. I should be able to cut one for a dead man's estate. I'll give them what you've found so far in exchange to leaving Kathleen's money alone."

"I'd like to be able to just walk away too. Some of my information was obtained in a way that isn't exactly admissible. I'd like to just ignore this and hope it goes away but I'm not so sure we can."

"What do you mean, 'isn't exactly admissible?'"

I ignored the question. I wasn't about to reveal I illegally read Ben Horton's emails. "Well, let's think this through. First, someone may have bugged your office. Second, not only did the thieves take the computers from my office where they were in plain sight, but they also tossed the place. Why would they do that if what they wanted was in plain sight?"

Either there were no more bikinis in sight or my question just captured Ed's attention. I hoped for the latter and pressed on.

"They must have been looking for something else. Something they think you might know about or something I might have. It would have had to be something in Ray's possession. If there's something out there they still want and they think we can lead them to it, they're not going to just leave us alone. If someone already killed Ray for it, we could be at risk and the police aren't going to guard us twenty-four seven."

Ed nodded and I thought I was starting to get through to him, "Hmmm."

"There's also the proximity of Ray's accident to PC Gadgets. The crash took place right near Horton's office but all of his payoffs were wire transfers. Up to this point, Ray and Horton did all of their business without meeting. Why go there now? The only thing that makes sense is Ray going there to drop this thing off. We need to figure out if he did and we need to figure out what it is."

I knew Ed was starting to catch on when he said, "So, it would help to know if he died on his way to PC Gadgets or on his way back. If he died on his way there and he was dropping something off, he should have still had it. Likewise, if he died on his way back, he wouldn't still have it. We need some more information."

"Exactly, do you have a copy of the police report from the accident?"

"No, but I can get one." Ed waved his hand dismissively.

"Good, can you scan it and email it to me?"

He shrugged. "FAX is about as high tech as I get."

"OK, FAX will be fine. Brenda dropped you off?"

"How did you know?"

"Detective school 101, the brunette in the car was young enough to be your daughter."

"So what? A lot of younger woman enjoy my company."

"I'm sure they do, and while this one may have grabbed you around the neck to kiss, you got it on the cheek."

"Hmmph."

"I've got my car. Let's drive over to your place, go bug hunting and see what we find. We can talk afterwards about how to proceed. If we don't see a bug, we can reevaluate, but if we find one..."

Ed thought about it for a moment or two. "OK, fair enough."

On our way out, Ed stopped to chat with Jack and to bum a cigarette. I took the time to stop in the Men's room. While I washed up, a tipsy, muscular guy with a shaved head and a USMC tattoo stood at a urinal and said to no one in particular, "There are no rules."

I was the only there and I can't keep my mouth shut so I said, "Mmm, sounds like a rule to me."

The guy looks at me and said, "I never thought of that. You're right. I've had this motto my entire life and you screwed it up in one second. Now, what do I do?"

That's me spreading cheer wherever I go.

CHAPTER ELEVEN

I joined Ed and Jack at the bar, and then Ed and I left for the parking lot. When Jack said goodbye, he smiled and I had a fleeting thought. I wondered if he really brought Ed and me together just to boost his bar business.

I used my remote to unlock my car. I knew it was a safe area, but I'm one of those folks who lock their cars. Even when it's inside of my locked garage, I lock my car. Years of going to school and working in New York City caused me to develop some particular habits. If I had to work hard to buy that car, so should someone who steals it.

Ed got into the passenger seat and asked, "So, how are we going to do this?"

"Well, I'm going to park in front of your place and we're going in your side door, the one that leads directly into your office. We're not going to talk. You unlock the door, go straight to the stereo, and put on a CD. After you've done that, I'm going to do a bug sweep."

He looked at me sideways, "Why am I putting on the CD?"

"Two reasons, one is we want it loud enough to mask any noise we might make looking for the bug. The other is the bug may be voice activated."

"Why does it matter if it's voice activated?"

"The detector works by sensing radio transmissions. If the bug is voice activated and the room is quiet, the bug won't be transmitting and we won't be able to find it. Playing music should activate it so it transmits."

"I see. So by using a voice activated bug, listeners can minimize detection."

"To some extent, but voice activation also extends battery life and makes it easier to review surveillance recordings."

We pulled up in front of Ed's office. I stopped the car, pocketed my car keys and reached into my camera bag. "Here, take this. If we find a bug, shoot it."

Out of the corner of my vision, I saw Ed tense when I said that. I glanced up at his face and he looked shocked. I pulled my hand out of my bag holding my digital camera and he relaxed. "Uh, I thought you had er, I thought you meant...never mind."

I laughed. "No. Ed. I don't even own a gun."

He took the camera, stared at it and then looked at me with a blank expression.

"Do you know how to use it?"

"Umm, yeah, turn it on, where? Here?" He pressed a button and the telescoping camera lens whirred to life. "Point and then press this button on the top. Right?"

Ed's head shot back as the camera went off and the flash filled the car. "Oops."

"Exactly."

I reached around to the back seat and got out the bug detector. I checked the battery, put on the headphones, and switched on the detector. If it detected a radio signal within 25 feet, a light would flash and a beep would sound in the headphones. The closer I got to the source of the signal, the faster the light would flash and the faster the sound would beep. The beep would also get louder as I got closer.

If there were more than one radio signal, the detector would respond to the strongest one. I would have to sweep the entire area carefully or a more powerful signal could drown a weaker one. This could be a problem, as a typical house would have all sorts of normal radio signals. Microwaves, cordless telephones, wireless computer equipment, remote control lights and fans all transmitted on frequencies a bug could use.

Plus, there were the inadvertent radio transmissions that came from malfunctioning or poorly designed household equipment like cable TV boxes, VCRs and appliance motors. Hell, even the mini-fridge behind Ed's desk could produce a radio signal when it kicks on. I wasn't optimistic. I turned to Ed, smiled with false confidence and said, "OK, let's go."

We walked up the path to the house. Ed opened the side door with his key and went directly to the stereo on the bookcase. He pressed some buttons and the CD left in the player started to play.

It was a bright sounding classical piece featuring violins. I wasn't a whiz on classical music, but I thought it might have been Vivaldi. It played at a good volume and filled the room so I expected it would easily trigger any voice-activated equipment. The problem was some of the high notes the violins played sounded a lot like the high-pitched beep of the detector. More than once, when I thought I heard a beep, I looked down but saw no flashing light to indicate the device had detected a signal.

I was in front of Ed's desk, by the client chairs when I thought I heard another beep. This time, when I looked down, I saw a flashing light. I stopped and slowly rotated my hips from left to right. When I went to the left, towards the client chairs and the bookcase behind them, the light and the beep stopped. When I rotated to my right, towards Ed's desk, the light flashed faster and the device beeped louder. As I turned to face Ed's desk, it became obvious there was a radio signal coming from under the pile of paper.

I looked up at Ed and saw he was watching the flashing light on the bug detector. I could see he got it. He could tell we found a bug hidden under the papers. He also seemed to realize one other important thing. He was going to have to do one of the things I guessed he probably dreaded most. He was going to have to clear off his desk and worse, he was going to have to do it quietly without complaining.

As Ed moved papers from the desk to the floor, I used the time to sweep the rest of the office. Just because I found one device, it didn't mean there weren't others. During the few minutes it took to check the rest of the room, Ed cleared the desk of everything except for the telephone and the answering machine. After carefully moving the phone to one side of the desk and the answering machine to the other, I waved the detector over each one, monitoring the beeps and flashes. They were stronger over the answering machine.

I turned off the detector, put it down on the desk and leaned over the answering machine for a closer look. It looked normal. No odd attachments or wires protruded. I picked it up for a closer look. On the top was a lid. I opened it and saw nothing inside but a small recording tape. I hadn't seen one of these in ages. I thought by now, everybody had changed to digital machines. I closed the lid and turned the machine over. On the bottom was a small hatch, like the kind that covers a battery compartment. I had seen machines like this before. They had a back up battery so the machine could still function if the electricity went off. Since telephone lines carry their own power and could function during a power outage, these backup batteries made sense.

I opened the battery cover and saw the bug. It was easy to identify since I knew what a battery looked like and the device in the battery compartment was clearly not a battery. I looked over at Ed and saw him leaning over the desk chair watching me as if the bug were a bomb. I pointed to the bug, and touched my thumb and forefinger together twice in front of my right eye.

He nodded, lifted the camera to his face and took two shots. After each, he showed me the image on the camera screen. They looked good. You could clearly see the bug. When he was finished, I carefully replaced the battery cover and put the answering machine down. I pointed to the stereo and then to the door. Ed turned off the music and we walked briskly out of his office.

I could see it took a great effort for Ed to contain himself inside his office. He was silently moving his lips and shaking his head from side to side. Once outside, Ed looked like he was ready to burst. He was shaking. He was sputtering. His lips were moving but he wasn't saying anything, at least nothing intelligible. I hurried to the car so he could unburden himself in a private spot. He followed. We got inside. Ed slammed the door shut and then he exploded. I even learned a few new curse words. I was impressed. I guessed that was just one more advantage of an Ivy League education.

Interspersed between the expletives, I thought I heard something about "client privilege", "not since 1577" and then "Berd v Lovelace." Then he mumbled something like "not even" and then "1988" and "Swidler & Berlin v. United States." After a while, his muttering began to slow down and he gradually became more coherent.

"Max. I can't believe what I saw. I can't believe what they did to me, did to my clients. I have to stop these people. We've got to stop these people." He made a fist and pounded the air.

"Then, you want me to continue pursuing this?"

"Well, yes, dammit." He slapped his right hand on his thigh and looked at me as if I were an idiot. I know because I've gotten that look before.

"What about Ray and his widow?"

"I'll call the D. A. I'll work something out. I'll call in favors if I need to. Get those bastards. They compromised me." He pointed his finger at me and shook it. His whole body shook. "They compromised my clients. Get 'em. The bastards." He clenched both fists and shook them once at chest level. "The bastards."

"OK, Ed. I'm going to head out now. In the meantime, we'll leave the bug where it is. It's better they don't know we found it. Just don't say anything in that room that can't be public. Now, how about you get the police report and I'll drive out to the accident site to look around."

"Yeah," he said, shaking his head. We split up. Ed got out of the car and I started the engine. With any luck, the police report would tell me which way Ray was driving when he crashed. In any event, I wanted to see the site for myself. I was sure the officers at Ray's murder scene weren't looking at it in connection with a break-in that hadn't yet occurred.

CHAPTER TWELVE

I left Ed's, headed south and made a right turn onto Third Ave which crossed over onto the mainland and became state route 44. It was a straight 20-mile ride to Damascus Road. It took me around 35 minutes.

When I got there, I noticed a few things of interest. First, there was a wreath on a cross, driven into the shoulder on the right side of the westbound road. Unless some other poor soul was lost here too, that marker indicated Ray was heading west when he died.

In addition, route 44, at this point, was a divided highway with the eastbound and westbound lanes divided by a grassy median. While eastbound traffic could turn right onto Damascus from SR 44, westbound traffic on 44 couldn't turn left onto Damascus. The median blocked access.

Of course, Ray could have been going east and could have crossed the median when he had the heart attack, but there were no marks on the median grass and there were no skid marks on the pavement in either direction.

I took this to mean Ray died with something in his possession; something someone wanted enough to bug a lawyer's office and to break into my home. Something to kill for.

I parked my car near the cross in the ground and got out. I took some pictures of the pavement, the road, and the shoulder. Then I pulled out my cell and called Ed. "It's me. Can you talk?"

"Yeah, I've got that police report and faxed you a copy." He sounded like he had finally calmed down.

"I'll bet it says Ray was traveling west when it happened."

Ed was silent for a moment. "Yeah, it does. How'd you know

that?"

"I got lucky, I guess. Someone placed a marker, a cross on the side of the road."

"OK, so he died while driving west." I could hear the shrug in his voice.

"West is the way to PC Gadgets. You told me that Ray took Friday afternoon off after lunch to shop. What time does the report show for the accident?"

"Hmmm. One forty five."

"That's just enough time for Ray to leave A. V. Designs and drive to the accident site. Since he died on the way here, instead of coming from here, he may have been coming this way to drop something off but never arrived. If that's true, it may still be among his effects. We need to find out what that thing is. Look, someone bugged your office, stole the computers and killed Ray. If this person already committed a capital crime and thinks we're a risk, we know how far he'll go to protect his interests. We need to know what he's after."

"Yes, we do. You know, I only picked up the notebook so you could start work in it. I planned to get the rest of his stuff later when I hoped Kathleen would be better able to deal with it, but I should be able to get a complete inventory list from the Police. I can check it and see what else was there. You think it's one person acting alone?"

"Could be. I don't know, but it appears somebody knew the computer and maybe something else was in Ray's car. They probably thought you could lead them to whatever it is they wanted. The next question is how they knew you were handling the estate."

"They must have gotten that from Kathleen but I can't imagine her telling anybody. I mean, who would care? Besides, she had nobody close here."

"Maybe they bugged her place too."

"We should check it for microphones?"

"Yeah, we better. Can you set it up?"

"Kathleen's still out of town, but I think so. I'll call you after I make arrangements. So do you think this other guy, what's his name? Horton? He stole the computers?"

"No, he was in California, meeting with clients. He was eating brunch with them at the time of the break-in. He wasn't scheduled to get back until this morning."

"How do you know that?"

"Don't ask. That's the inadmissible part. You don't want to

know."

"So, there may be someone else involved besides Horton?"

"I think so. I think there has to be."

"And this person killed Ray to get something he had in the car?"

"Well, I'm not sure. I think if someone were going to kill Ray for something he had, you'd think they'd make sure they got it. Also, didn't you say he had a heart attack and died before the accident?"

"Yeah, according to the Medical Examiner's report."

"Did they figure out how the killer induced the heart attack?"

"Not yet."

"Let's be careful. OK?"

"OK. What's next?"

"You check on the inventory list and call me at home. I'm going to look into a few things... should be there in half an hour. If I'm not there, leave a message on my machine."

I hung up with Ed and pulled off the shoulder onto S.R. 44 heading west. At the first break in the median, I stopped, made a U-turn and drove back east again, toward home.

The next right turn was Damascus Road, where Ben Horton's PC Gadgets was located. It was close to one in the afternoon on Tuesday so he could be back to work by now. Now that I had seen the accident site, I wanted a closer look at Horton. I turned right and then left into the P.C. Gadgets parking lot.

It was a small lot for maybe 50 cars without any security booth or marked spaces. It was almost half-full with most of the cars parked in front of the building. In the middle of the lot was a rectangular, one story building. It looked like a long, white shoebox. I parked in a spot that allowed a view of the front door and a portion of the back yard. I watched for a while. Behind the building, on the grass behind the back parking lot, people ate lunch at two wooden picnic tables. Except for the lunch crowd and the brief appearance at the front of the building by a U.S. Post Office carrier, there was no activity.

Since I didn't see anything threatening, I was tempted to go in and try to talk to Horton. I could show him a photo of the men on the boat and ask him who they were, but I didn't have the pictures with me. I thought of going back home to get one and then thought better of it. It wouldn't be smart to wave a document in his face that he knew contained stolen designs; especially stolen designs he had paid for.

Also, since the computers had been stolen from my home, I shouldn't know about the photos. I realized it was better for me if he thought I hadn't seen them.

If Horton was involved in the break-in, he would know who I was and that I was associated with Ray. Even so, there was no reason I couldn't also be investigating related matters that presented him with no threat. If I played dumb, an easy trick for me, he might even slip up and reveal something. Since the police were keeping the murder quiet, the papers only reported Ray's death as an accident. I could be a PI gathering information for a lawsuit.

I got out of my car just as the lunch crowd returned to the building. They went in the back while I went in the front. When I opened the door, a pleasantly plump, grandmotherly woman sat at a reception desk. She looked to be in her mid-60s and had a kind face. It was not hard to imagine her at home wearing an apron and baking a hot apple pie or maybe teaching in a one-room schoolhouse out on the prairie. "And how may I help you today sir?" she smiled at me. Her whole demeanor inspired good manners. Her desk was tidy and well organized her posture perfect.

"Good afternoon, ma'am. My name is Max Fried. I'm looking into an automobile accident that occurred just across the street. A man died in it and his family has asked me to look into whether road conditions may have contributed to the crash. Since you work across the street, I wondered if you knew anything that might be useful."

"Oh, my, yes, I read about that in the paper and I saw the wreath someone placed across the street, but no," she shook her head from side to side as her hand went to her throat, "I know nothing of the accident or anything regarding the road that may have caused it. I drive on that street and see the memorial marker every day." She dropped her hand to her lap. "It's so sad."

"Thank you, ma'am. Would it be all right if I spoke with some of the other employees? Perhaps someone else saw or heard something?"

"Well, I don't know. You'd have to check with Mr. Horton, the owner." She clasped her hands together on the desk in front of her and nodded her head as if she were agreeing with herself.

"May I please?"

"Just a moment and I'll see if he's free. He just got in a little while ago." She leaned forward, dropped her voice to a whisper and as if to excuse his tardiness said, "He's been traveling today." Then she picked up the telephone on her desk and pressed a button.

"Hello, Mr. Horton, sir. I have a gentleman here. He's looking into that horrible accident across the street." A slight pause ensued. "Yes sir. He was wondering if he could ask some questions." She paused and nodded as if Horton could see her. "Yes, sir. I'll send him right in."

She replaced the phone, smiled up at me, and said, "Mr. Horton, himself, will see you." She turned and pointed down the hall. "Fourth door on the right."

"Thank you, very much, ma'am," I said in my best Gary Cooper voice wishing I had a hat to tip. I headed down the hall.

When I got to the fourth door on the right, it was open and a man sitting behind a desk gestured for me to come in. The nameplate on the door read, "Benjamin Horton". As I entered the room, he stood up at his desk and reached out with his right hand to shake mine while his left hand gestured to the two chairs facing him. A garment bag covered one chair. The other was clear except for a small, black, leather case.

"Good morning, I guess, good afternoon. Please forgive me. I'm still on California time. I just got back. I'm Benjamin Horton. I'm sorry. I didn't get your name."

"Max Fried." I shook his hand with my right and gave him the black case off the chair with my left.

He shrugged. "I'm sorry. Like I said, I just got back." Horton's office was nicer than I would have expected given the building in which it was located. He sat at a large, brown, wood desk. On the desktop was an old-fashioned green felt ink blotter, a desk lamp with a green glass shade and of course a computer monitor. I saw no keyboard or mouse so I guessed his desk also had a keyboard drawer.

Behind the desk was a wall full of matching floor to ceiling bookcases. Some shelves were open, some glass covered and some had matching wood doors. To Horton's right and on the wall behind me were large tasteful paintings of a variety of classic styles. To his left was a large window that looked over the parking lot. I guessed he could have seen me sitting in his lot.

At first glance, Ben Horton didn't look much like any of the men in the photo, but that photo was 24 years old. As we sat there, I began to see a similarity. If you took off 40 pounds of 1980s big hair and added 40 pounds of 2008 fat, you'd get a match. Horton was balding and wore his remaining hair in a crew cut. He was about five feet eight inches, 200 pounds, and dressed in a blue suit with a pale blue shirt opened at the collar. His suit jacket and blue and white striped tie hung from a wood hanger on a wood coat rack in a corner behind the door to his office.

He sat down, leaned forward on his forearms and clasped his hands on the desk in front of him. "Marge tells me you're looking into that accident across the street?"

"Yes sir. The family is looking into whether there was any liability in the part of the State. You know, improperly maintained road. Long lasting hazards, that kind of thing." I sat back, crossed my legs and tried to look nonchalant. If Horton didn't know the Police were treating Ray's death as a homicide, I wasn't going to tip him off.

"You're an insurance investigator, then?"

"I'm a private investigator."

"May I see some ID please?"

"Sure." I got up and handed him my Florida P. I. license. He looked at the photo on the ID and then looked at me.

"Losing the beard was a good idea." He grinned and handed me back my license.

"Thanks." I put it back in my wallet and sat down again.

"So, you're working for Ray Kenwood's family."

He surprised me by mentioning Ray's name. "I'm working for the attorney handling the estate. Did you know Ray Kenwood?"

He sat back with his elbows on the arms of his chair and lifted his hands up. "I could tell you I know the name because I read it in the paper. I could say I remember it because the accident took place across the street, but you're a detective and it's a matter of public record so you'll probably find out anyway."

"Find out what?"

He put his hands down in his lap and leaned forward. "That I knew Ray back in the 70s and 80s. That we got in trouble together." He leaned back and waved his hand in the air as if to indicate how old and far away his story was. "You see, when we were young and stupid, about 25 years old; we got caught smuggling Cuban cigars. We got lucky, very lucky. I got a fine and three years of probation. Ray just got probation." He leaned forward again. "I'm telling you this because I want you to believe me when I tell you I haven't seen or had any contact with Ray in over 20 years."

"Why would I care if you've seen Ray in the last 20 years?"

"Because he's dead and I threatened to kill him." He sat back and smiled as if he had just delivered the punch line to a joke.

I like to think I'm unflappable, but this was the second time Horton surprised me in just a few minutes. My expression must have given me away because the next thing Horton did was laugh.

"That threat was also a matter of public record. It's in the transcript from the trial. During the trial, Ray testified against me to sweeten his deal with the prosecutors. I was young. I thought I was a tough guy. Turned out probation was a piece of cake. It was foolish to make the threat, especially like that in open court. Look, if I really wanted to kill him, I wouldn't have threatened him like that and I would have killed him years ago. I mean years ago." He looked in my eyes and slowly nodded his head as if to emphasize his certainty.

His stare convinced me and I sat there not knowing what to say next.

After a moment, Horton quickly leaned back in his chair and smiled a familiar twisted grin. Now, I was sure he was in the 1984 photo. "OK, I probably would have made the threat anyway. I was a hothead back then, but I really wouldn't have waited 20 some odd years. Hotheads don't wait. I would have done him back then." He paused and looked at me as if he were evaluating my reaction. After he seemed satisfied, I believed him, he continued. "Besides, I was in California when Ray died."

I was beginning to believe that if Horton really wanted to kill Ray years ago, he would have. On the other hand, I also believed there was something else going on here. I had no other directions to go in my questions so I just pressed on.

"Don't you think it's odd that of all the places to have an accident, Ray crashed and died across the street from your office?"

"Frankly, no." Horton clasped his hands over his belly. "He didn't die across the street from my office. He died on State Route 44. My office may be on the corner of 44 and Damascus, but my address is on Damascus Road. You need to make a turn to get there from here. Plus that road goes on for miles from the ocean to halfway across the state." Horton paused for emphasis and with his elbows on his chair arms, held up his hands again. "He could have been going anywhere."

"You seem pretty determined to distance your office from the accident site. If you haven't seen him in over 20 years, why should you be so concerned?"

"Look, Mr. Fried. I know how these things go." He waved one hand dismissively. "Once you've been convicted of something, everyone thinks you're guilty of everything, no matter what. I've done my penance. I don't want any more trouble. I want to be honest with everyone, just live my life and do my business." He tilted his head to one side. "Is that too much to ask?"

"OK, then." I nodded. "I guess you don't have anything to add that might help the family in handling the accident?"

"No. I'm sorry. I don't."

"Well," I said, rising from the chair, "thank you for your time, Mr. Horton." I left his office knowing he was lying about having no contact with Ray. I had seen the emails, so I was wondering what else might be false. As I walked out down the hall, I saw several other names on other doors, but I noticed not one of the other doors were marked "Corky Eastwood."

CHAPTER THIRTEEN

I left Ben Horton and drove home to an empty house, Mariel was still at her sister's. I wanted to see her but if she was scared enough to stay there, my visit would only add to her worries. She'd wonder if anyone followed me.

When I went inside, the quiet and stillness surprised me. It's amazing how much a small woman can fill up a big house. The place felt different without Mariel there, like I was in someone else's home.

It was after lunchtime, so I decided I'd better eat while I could. Once I started thinking about food I remembered how good the onions and peppers smelled at breakfast and again at lunch yesterday. Then I was surprised to realize only one day had passed since Ed dropped off the notebook and Mariel left. I usually looked forward to making a nice lunch but I wasn't much in the mood for that now. I wanted something easy so I nuked a veggie burger, poured some diet tonic into a glass, and squeezed an orange wedge into the soda. The fruit came from one of the trees in the backyard and its juice tasted better than any I ever had. Having grown up in New York, I got a big kick out of having our own orange tree.

On the way home from talking to Ben Horton, I had been thinking. We should probably turn him over to the Police. When Ed called me back, I was going to suggest it. I knew from his emails Horton was out of town during the break-in at my house, but he was the only person I knew of who had a connection to Ray and Ray was the only connection I had to the break-in. Maybe the Police could sweat him to reveal more information.

I was also thinking it might be helpful if I could talk to Corky

Eastwood. While I watched my burger going round and round in the microwave, I figured she probably wouldn't talk to me, but hey, what did I have to loose?

The microwave dinged. I ate my lunch and tried to plan my approach to calling her. Nothing came to mind. I was just going to have to dial and see what came out of my mouth.

After cleaning up the kitchen, I went into my office and looked up the number for EFH. I dialed and a woman with a professional sounding voice answered. She had perfect enunciation with no hint of any regional accent.

"Good afternoon. EFH, how may I direct your call?"

"Hi, I'd like to speak with Corky Eastwood, please."

"I'm sorry, sir. Ms. Eastwood is unavailable." She responded so quickly and so automatically that I got the feeling Ms. Eastwood was never available. Big surprise.

"When might she be available?"

"I'm sorry sir, but that's hard to say."

"Well, then how does one get in touch with her?"

"Well, sir. You can leave a message, if you like."

"Sure. Why not? Please tell her Max Fried would like to speak with her. I have information for her regarding a risk to one of her investments."

"Is that Jack Snead?"

"No, Max Fried. M-a-x F-r-i-e-d"

"Yes, sir. How can she reach you?"

I gave the receptionist my phone number, hung up and looked out the window. Since I didn't see any pigs flying, I figured it might be a long time before Corky returned my call.

I sat there staring at the phone, trying to decide what to do next, when it rang, startling the hell out of me. Was Corky Eastwood so impressed she was returning my call immediately? I fantasized as I picked up the phone.

"Hello?" I said, deepening my voice and trying to speak without my New York accent in order to sound my most professional.

"Max?" a man's voice inquired. "Is that you? It's Ed."

"Oh, hi, Ed. What's up?"

"I spoke with the Police and I'll have that inventory list tomorrow. I also have access to Ray and Kathleen's for the bug check. We can do it at any time."

"Great."

"You sound disappointed."

"Yeah, well, I was trying to reach someone on the phone and got blown off by her secretary."

"Yeah? Who were you trying to reach?"

"Corky Eastwood."

"Corky Eastwood? You mean Zorky's daughter?"

I was beginning to wonder if I was the only one who didn't know about Zorky and Corky. "Yeah."

"Hell! I can help you there. You know, I wasn't always a beach bum lawyer. At one point when I practiced in New York, I was Zorky's real estate attorney. He had a bazillion lawyers. He had a team for each area of law. He only used specialists. For a while, I was his real estate guy. I headed up a team of attorneys and paralegals. I also handled Corky's New York townhouse and her place in Key West. I can get you through. What do you want to talk to her about?"

"She's listed as Vice President of Ben Horton's business, PC Gadgets. I want to know the connection between her and Ben."

"Hmm. Yeah. I see." Ed paused. "Tell you what. I have an attorney-client relationship with her. You're working for me. I can get you access provided you respect the attorney-client privilege. You can't use anything she tells you against her. OK?"

"Ed. I'm not a cop. I can't use anything against anyone."

"You know what I mean Max. Don't get her into any awkward position like the one Ray Kenwood and his wife are in."

I think what Ed really wanted to say was "Don't screw things up for her like you did for the Kenwoods."

I wanted to point out that not only was Ray killed before I got involved but that the reason he was dead and his estate was in trouble was because he was a crook. It probably would have done me no good so instead, I just said. "OK."

"I mean this, Max."

"OK, me too, Ed. Thanks."

"Sure, give me a couple hours, maybe a day, I'll have her call. Any idea when you want to check the Kenwood place for bugs?"

"How about tomorrow morning?"

"Did you say 'morning'? You must really want to get this thing settled. How's tomorrow at 9:00? I'll meet you at Ray and Kathleen's. That way, I'll be done in time to help Sheila move her stuff."

"So you decided. She's agreed to move into your place."

"Yup, going to give it a try, see what happens."

"Good for you. Uh, Ed?"

"Yes?"

"One other thing I want to discuss. I think we need to turn Horton over to the Police."

"For what?"

"Theft of trade secrets."

"Why's that?"

"Ray's our only connection to the break-in and Horton's our only connection to Ray. Besides, this might all be connected to Ray's murder."

"How can the police hold him?"

"Well, we have the emails from Ray to Horton selling him secrets and corresponding wire transfers to Ray's accounts. But we don't have any way to get proof Horton wired Ray the money. The police can obtain subpoenas. Maybe more importantly, Horton not only admitted he knew Ray over 20 years ago; he admitted he had threatened to kill him. Maybe the Police should take a closer look at Ray's death."

"Horton threatened Ray? He admitted that? When? Why?"

"When I stopped by to see him this afternoon. He said it was a matter of record in a court case against him and Ray when they were younger. Personally, I think he told me so I'd find him more believable when he denied seeing Ray in the last 20 years."

"Max! Talking to you is like pulling teeth. You keep giving me little pieces of information that beg more detail. You visited Horton? What's this about a court case?" Ed let out a long breath over the phone.

"After we talked, I drove past Horton's office on the way home. I decided to stop in and chat about the crash. I figured it would be ok to ask questions an accident investigator might ask. When we started talking, Horton volunteered a whole lot more. He told me he and Ray were arrested for smuggling Cuban cigars. When Ray turned on Horton for a lighter sentence, Horton threatened to kill him."

"But, he claims he didn't?"

"Yeah. He claims."

"Max. You just dumped a load on me. Let me see if I have this. You think there's a case to be made against Horton for killing Ray and breaking into your place, even though you say he was out of town at the time. You want the police to arrest him for his part in the trade secret theft and then sweat him for murder, breaking and entering, etc. at your place, bugging my office even though he was away during the break-in and when Ray died."

"Sure."

"And this makes sense to you because, even though we don't think Horton burgled your place, he may have killed Ray and whoever did burgle your place and bugged mine has to have some connection to the trade secret thefts and the only 'whoever' we can identify with a connection is Ben Horton."

"Yes."

"What about Corky? Was she involved in this theft from A. V. Designs? Will arresting Horton incriminate her?"

"Not if she's innocent."

"No, Max. Fifth amendment, even if she's guilty, it's my job to protect her interests."

"She didn't seem to have an office in Horton's building and I didn't find anything to indicate she knew what Ray and Horton were up to. It looks like she's just an investor."

Ed let out another long breath. "OK. I'll call the D. A. again. Last time I spoke with him, he agreed to leave Ray's estate alone, if I gave him somebody else who happened to be guilty and alive. I'll have to do this sooner or later. Look, email me a copy of that report you made but revise it to address only the theft. Leave out Corky's being a V.P. in Horton's company and the irrelevant personal stuff I originally asked for. Include copies of the incriminating documents and explanations of what they mean. I'll send it on to the D. A."

"Sure, Ed. I'll do it right now."

It didn't take me too long. I had already stored all of the evidence in a folder on my iPod. All I had to do was document the documents and explain the explanations. I did that and emailed the files to Ed.

CHAPTER FOURTEEN

Now that I had free time, I wanted to go for a run. If I didn't run on a regular basis, I found it hard to get started again. It wasn't mentally difficult. The problem wasn't motivation. It was physically difficult to run because my body had to get used to the heat and exertion all over again. I found it was easier to keep running than to stop and start.

I changed into swim trunks and a T-shirt, grabbed my iPod and headed down the block, past tropical trees bearing Christmas lights, to the beach. There weren't many people around and the beach was quiet except for the crashing of the waves. Running here always helped to clear my head and often, after running, I'd have a new perspective on things. I was hoping this would be true today, but so far, I was coming to the end of my first mile and nothing was gelling.

I did see something though. Each block that runs west to east terminates in a wooden platform that crosses over the dunes to provide access to the beach. I was approaching the dune crossover near my sister in law's condo and I saw a woman walking. She was leaving the beach headed for the crossover stairs that led to the street. She was slim, about five feet tall with long dark hair and wore a black two-piece bathing suit, like Mariel's. I thought it might be her. I ran faster so I might catch her before she left the beach. It was close. She was over the crossover and almost out of sight when I caught up. When I got close enough for her to hear me, I started to call her name, but by then, I could see it wasn't Mariel.

I was disappointed. I slowed down and finished the rest of my run thinking about how much I missed her. I guess I must have been thinking about her without realizing it when I mistook that other woman for Mariel. After completing my four-mile roundtrip, I was back near the beachside of the dune crossover at the end of my street. I was ready to walk home, so I headed for the stairs.

When I climbed up the weathered wooden steps, I saw my neighbor, Karl coming towards me. Many of the houses on the block are second homes to snowbirds who only occupy them a few months a year, but Karl lives here full-time. A fellow New Yorker, he understands my accent. He was carrying his fishing gear to the beach, but stopped and waited for me.

I got to the top of the stairs and he pulled a small scrap of paper from the pocket in his sweatshirt. "Max, I saw this car parked on our street with a guy in it. He was just sitting there, not really doing anything, except maybe watching your place. At first, I thought he might have been, you know, waiting for you, but he parked too far from your house. I didn't know what to make of it so I copied down his plate number -- in case you knew him. He was driving a blue Ford Taurus, a four-door." Karl handed me the paper. I remembered the mail carrier commented about seeing a blue car the day of the break-in.

"Thanks. Hey, our neighbor Ralph has a blue car. Look anything like his?"

"Nah, Ralph's got a two-door Chevy with Jersey plates. This was a four-door Ford with a Florida plate."

I read the number Karl wrote on the paper. "I don't know what to make of this, don't recognize the plate or the car, but thanks."

"Yeah, well, after the break-in, I thought it would be a good idea to keep an eye out for anything unusual. See you later. I've got to catch my dinner."

"Thanks. Later." I folded the paper and stuck it inside my iPod case.

Karl nodded and walked down towards the surf. He looked determined to get some fish. I went in the opposite direction and walked home vigilant for any blue cars on the street. I saw none.

It's easy for me to lose things in my pockets when I run, so I tie my house key to the drawstring on my bathing suit. After I turned into my driveway, I looked down to untie my key. I felt the first impact immediately. It threw my body and my head back so that my eyes moved up and then I saw him. I also caught a fast but close up glimpse of his face as he ran from hitting me hard with his shoulder. I felt myself fall and I saw my feet in the air in front of me. My arms waved with no control over my ability to stop. Then I

78

felt the second impact as my head and shoulder hit the concrete driveway.

It seemed that only a second later I was lying on my back and I couldn't see. My vision was black. I wasn't sure my eyes were open or that I was even awake. After a moment or two, the center of my vision started to glow white. The glow expanded to the edges of my field of view and gradually revealed the white ceiling of an ambulance. I had no idea how long ago the man ran into me and no clue about what happened since he did. I was stiff, sore, groggy and disoriented.

A slim, young man in a blue uniform, wearing a stethoscope and white gloves sat next me. "Mr. Fried.... Mr. Fried.... Can you hear me?"

I turned my head in the direction of his voice and opened my eyes

"Good. That's good Mr. Fried. Do you know where you are?"

I nodded.

"Very good. Tell me where you are."

"Ambulance?"

"Know how you got here?"

"Knocked down."

"How many fingers am I holding up?"

"Two."

"Very good. We're taking you to Bert Fish. The doctor's going to check you out."

I nodded and fell asleep only to feel the EMT gently tapping my cheek. "You have to stay awake."

I fought sleep and drifted in and out as people lifted me from a gurney onto a bed in the Emergency Room. All I could think about was how clean, fresh and stiff the sheets felt. I was in baggage mode as they handled me.

I went back to sleep.

I woke to a man shining a flashlight in my eyes. First one eye, then the other. He saw I was awake and pocketed his flashlight.

"Mr. Fried, I'm Dr. Bashouri. I understand you've had a fall. It appears that you've hit your head. Are you nauseous?"

"No."

"Headache?

"No, well slightly and... the bump hurts."

He nodded. "Can you sit up?

Slowly and with effort, I swung my feet over the edge of the bed and sat up. I felt woozy. I must have looked wobbly because the doctor held out his hands as if preparing to catch me should I fall.

After I steadied myself, he said, "Remove your shirt please."

I lifted my shirt chest high and then the pain prevented me from lift my arms any higher. The doctor helped me with it and started fingering and probing my cuts and bruises. When he got to my left shoulder, he asked, "This gunshot wound. About hmm... one year old?"

"Nine months."

"It seems to be healing well. You can put your shirt on, now." He helped me get it back on and then used his flashlight to examine my eyes. "OK. Can you stand now?"

He helped me stand up and then said, "Now, close your eyes and touch your finger to the tip of your nose."

I did so.

"Yes. I see no signs of serious damage. I'd like you to rest here a little while, see if you have any new symptoms. Then you can go home, but for the next 24 hours, I don't want you to sleep more than two hours at a time. You may have a concussion. We want to be careful."

He smiled, patted my right shoulder and left. I lay down, closed my eyes and slept.

"Fried."

My rest was too brief. "Detective Torres. What are you doing here?"

"Heard it on the radio and recognized the address. Neighbor says he found you on the driveway. What happened?"

"Someone came running out of my side yard. Knocked me down."

"Know who?"

"Never saw him before, but he looked familiar. Maybe like some actor or someone I might have seen in a TV commercial. He was wearing a hard-hat and wraparound sunglasses."

"Sounds like one of the Village People. Maybe you saw him at the Y." He smiled. I didn't join him. "Too bad you didn't have a hard-hat too. This connected to the Kenwood case? To your break-in? To anything?"

As he talked, I heard the rapid clicking of high heels on tile. "I don't know." I said.

Torres turned to his left. I couldn't see who was approaching from behind the curtain, but I had a good guess.

Torres looked at Mariel's disapproving expression then said, "OK. Call me if there's a crime," and quickly left. I guess he's not as tough as I thought.

Mariel came over to the bed and took my hand. "Max, what

happened?"

"I got knocked down. How did you know I was here?"

"Karl called my cell right after he called the ambulance."

"Karl found me?"

She nodded. "I spoke to the doctor. You can go home but you have to take it easy. You also need to wake up every two hours. You'll come with me to my sister's."

"No, I'll go home."

"No, it's not safe there."

"If someone is after me, it's not safe anywhere. Besides, if someone wanted me dead, I wouldn't be here now. I mean I'd be here now, but in the basement, not in the ER."

"You can't go home alone. Someone has to be there in case you can't wake up. I'm not going home. I don't feel safe there." She let go of my hand and stepped back. "Why won't you come with me?"

I said nothing.

She stared at me for a few moments. In the past, she said she could tell how I felt or what was on my mind just by looking at me. Good or bad, history has supported her claim.

"I know why you won't come. You're in danger. You don't want anyone to follow you to my sister's. You're worried about me."

Silence wasn't helping my cause, but I didn't think speaking at this point would help me either.

"Max, it wasn't supposed to be like this. We're supposed to be having fun. You never should have taken this job."

There it was. I was waiting for that. I didn't remind her that it was a joint decision. It would have been pointless. Instead, I offered a compromise.

"You can phone me every two hours. If I don't answer, you can call 911. That way, you can stay at your sister's. I can stay home and no one will follow me where they can hurt somebody else."

Mariel nodded her agreement, leaned over the bed and hugged me. I hugged her back. It felt good to hold her again.

CHAPTER FIFTEEN

We checked out of the hospital. A nurse wheeled me to Mariel's car, gave me my iPod, a printed sheet of care instructions and a dose of Tylenol for the road. With one arm around Mariel, I climbed into her passenger seat. It was worth the pain and losing consciousness just to be able to hold her again but I discovered new pains when I bent and twisted to get in. Mariel drove me home in silence. I think there were things she wanted to say but she said nothing.

On the way, I thought about the man who knocked me down. From the way he hit me, he must have come from my side yard. He wore a white hard hat, work boots and some type of line worker uniform with a tool belt. The hat and large wraparound sunglasses covered most of his face. I couldn't see enough of it or see it long enough to identify him. He didn't hurt me after knocking me down, so I surmised he only hit me so he could get away and I wouldn't have time to recognize him.

I'd only been living here a few months and this was my first case. I only knew a handful of people, yet since Ray's murder, someone robbed me and now someone sent me to the hospital. There had to be some connection, but it didn't make sense. If Ray's killer attacked me, why did he let me live? Then I remembered the break-in. Someone searched my home even though the stolen items were in plain sight. The burglar must have wanted something he didn't get. Something he thought I had. Something that's kept me alive. I had to find it before he did.

It took me a while to get out of the car. Mariel stayed inside so I walked around to the driver's side to say goodbye. Through the open window, she gave me a perfunctory kiss as if to indicate that she still loved me but wasn't happy with me right now. I thanked her, turned and slowly walked inside the house.

This time, there were no signs of entry or attempted entry. In the kitchen, I bent to take a bottle of water from the pantry and my back started to stiffen. My left elbow began to feel sore, the old gunshot wound in my left shoulder throbbed and I wondered if there was any other damage. When I got into the bedroom, I looked in the mirror to find out. A pattern of scratches decorated my left side where I fell and the face of an achy old man with a bald spot in his short, silver and black hair stared back. That seemed to be the extent of it.

When I took a closer look, all I saw was a lined face with my grandfather's high forehead and his crooked tooth. He didn't give me the lines. They came from experience. Maybe that's why my mouth turned down at the sides. I don't know why Mariel thinks I'm good looking. I'm just glad she does.

I lied down on my bed and took inventory. Nothing felt broken. I had scratches, bruises, and a bump on my head but I wasn't bleeding and the headache was starting to become dull. I wasn't dizzy. Well, I wasn't dizzy as long as I didn't make any sudden movements. I guess I was lucky, I didn't hit my head too hard on the concrete driveway or lose consciousness for too long. I was just sore and I probably would be for a while. After resting a bit, I got up and left the bedroom.

I put the paper Karl gave me with the plate number down on the nightstand and headed for the shower. The hot water felt good and soothed my sore spots, but I was starting to get annoyed. It was getting to the point where something happened every time I left the house to run.

I toweled dry, put on clean swim trunks, and went out the back sliding door. I knew I was going to run the plate number Karl gave me, but after that, I had no idea what to do next. Maybe a little aimless floating in the pool would help my mind. If nothing else, the warm water should ease my body. I swam a few laps to work out the muscle kinks from the fall. Then I dripped dry on one of the patio chaises. I rested from my ordeal and thought about what just happened.

The man who knocked me down came to my house for a reason. His attire indicated he wanted people to think he belonged where he was. A hardhat, boots and tool belt are things you might wear if you worked in construction or as a lineman of some type. My assailant didn't have a ladder, but some utility poles have rungs and trees can be climbed. I looked around my yard. Not a single utility pole, but I had plenty of trees.

When I looked up into one of them, I saw something shiny. It reflected the fading sunlight, but I couldn't tell what it was. Whatever it was, I was sure it didn't grow there. I dried off a bit, went into the house, and got my binoculars. You can't live near the beach and not have binoculars. Between the boats, the birds and the porpoises, there's just too much to see.

The bright spot on the tree was a glass lens inside of a small black tube about three inches long. I recognized it immediately. It was a weatherproof bullet camera. I had seen one like it at the Spy Shack. Someone was interested enough in my activities to spend a couple of hundred bucks, but the location of the camera violated privacy restrictions. Without a warrant authorizing the camera, I doubted the video would be admissible in court. I started to wonder who would want to watch my house and why.

They positioned their camera so it had a view of the front yard. What were they hoping to see? The police had no reason to watch me. Did they? Who would install a camera without caring if they could use the video in court? The only purpose this camera could serve was recording who came to the house and who left the house. I began to think Mariel's concerns might be well grounded and I had better do something. This latest incident renewed my motivation. I started to develop a plan. First, I'd check for listening devices and then try to find who was watching me.

I ran around the house turning off any thing that could transmit a radio signal that might confuse my bug sweeper. This included the cable box, my computer, my wireless network router, and my cordless telephone. I put a Bruce Springsteen CD in the stereo and turned it up enough that I could hear the lyrics throughout the house. If I could hear the music, it would be loud enough to activate any voice activated listening devices.

Starting in the foyer, I swept from the kitchen to the great room, covering the dining and living room areas. No signals. I moved to the hall and then to each of the three bedrooms. Still no signals. I even ran the bug detector in the bathrooms and on the pool deck. Except for the proximity of the tree, there were no other signals anywhere. All the camera could do is watch who came and who left my house. I began to realize that watching me was all they wanted.

It seemed each of the bugs we encountered were very specific in their purpose. They must have planted Ed's to learn what he knew.

They must have planted mine to learn when my house is empty. All I could surmise was someone expected Ed to learn something he might eventually bring to me. Perhaps they'd also want to know when they could come and get it. Maybe that's why I was still alive. Now, if I could get a handle on whom they were and what they wanted. I didn't know what they expected to see, but I did have a license plate number that might tell who was watching.

One nice thing about having a private investigator license is the legitimate access you get to things most people can't legally acquire. For instance, The Driver Privacy Protection Act protects against most people obtaining your name and address from your license plate. However, the act states there are exceptions. For example, "For use by any licensed private investigative agency or licensed security service for any purpose permitted under this paragraph."

Luckily, one of the purposes listed under this paragraph is "Investigation in anticipation of litigation by an attorney licensed to practice law in this state or the agent of the attorney;" I anticipated I would sue this guy for something eventually, so I figured I was on safe enough ground. Since I didn't have time to wait days for a response to a DMV form, I sprang for $25 and used one of the online services, which promised same day service.

As I was finishing the online transaction, my phone rang. I picked it up.

"Hello?"

"Is this Max Fine?"

Close enough. "Yes."

"This is Amanda Finch, Ms. Eastwood's Personal Assistant. Ms. Eastwood will be available to meet with you tomorrow at the EFH office at 2:00 pm."

"That's great. Thank you very much."

"Do you need directions?"

"No, thank you."

"Very well, sir. We will see you then." She hung up.

Hmm, I guess old Ed must still have it, whatever it was he had. I sat there planning my discussion with Corky in my head when I noticed that while I was on the phone an email arrived. It was a DMV report and contained the registrant's name and address, the vehicle VIN, and type. The owner of the Taurus was A. V. Designs, the company that employed Ray.

I couldn't imagine a big outfit like A. V. Designs watching me with any criminal intent, at least not when they were so easy to trace. Considering the use of a company car, the surveillance Karl detected seemed more like corporate security at work than criminal enterprise, so I decided to approach this head on. I called A. V. Designs to make an appointment. If I had to get dressed for Corky tomorrow, I might as well go see A.V. Designs too.

"Good afternoon, A. V. Designs. How may I direct your call?"

"Hi, I'd like to speak with your Security Director."

"Regarding what, sir?"

Hmm, what I can say to get him or her to see me? "It's confidential. I'm a private investigator and can only discuss this matter with the appropriate corporate security folks."

"Yes, sir. Please hold while I connect you."

"A. V. Designs, Corporate Security Office. How may I direct your call?" Deja Vue all over again.

"My name is Max Fried. I'm a private investigator and I have a confidential matter to discuss with your Security Chief."

"I'm sorry, sir. The Chief is in a meeting now. I can't connect you. Would you like to leave a message?"

"Actually, I'd like to make an appointment. It's better we discuss this matter in person. Is the Chief free tomorrow morning?"

"Very good sir, let me check..., his only available time tomorrow would be 4:00."

I thought that might be cutting it close as I was seeing Corky at two, but I really didn't expect her to give me much of her time. "OK, Fine," I agreed.

"Is that Mack Reed?"

"No, Max Fried. M-a-x F-r-i-e-d"

"I'm sorry sir."

"No problem, I'll be there then. Bye."

When it rained, it poured. Tomorrow, I would be a busy boy.

CHAPTER SIXTEEN

I woke in a stupor to the sounds of pounding and ringing. I sat up in bed and assessed what I heard. Was it was real or was it from a dream? I decided it was a real person who was determined to get my attention no matter what the damage to my bell, the banger's fist or my door. Based on their persistence and the volume of noise, my first thought was fire.

I grabbed my glasses, put on my running shorts and bolted for the front door. When I opened it, I almost ran into a uniformed police officer.

"Where's the fire?" I asked. "I don't smell any smoke."

The officer was one I hadn't seen before. He looked like a High School senior. "Mr. Fried?"

"Yeah?"

"Detective Torres wants to see you. You're to come with me, sir." He pointed inside my house, "but first, let's go in and get you dressed."

I turned and went back into the house. The officer followed me.

"What time is it?" I asked.

"Just after midnight, sir."

"Where're we going?"

"The hospital, sir."

When he said "hospital," I must have turned white. I turned on him and grabbed his shoulder. "Mariel? My wife?"

"Oh, no sir. The Detective wants to see you about a case. Sorry if I shook you up. Let's get you dressed now. The Detective doesn't like to wait."

I went to my bedroom to dress but the sudden awakening and

the possibility of Mariel being hurt left me shaky. I had to sit a moment. The soreness in my arm and side from being knocked to the ground didn't help any. Somehow, I managed to put in my contact lenses and get dressed. I stepped back into my living room where the officer had been waiting on my couch.

"OK. I'm ready." By now, I was alert enough to ask, "What case?"

"Sorry, I can't say. sir."

"You don't know or you can't tell me?"

"Yes, sir."

He was young, but I could see I wasn't going to get any more information until I got to Torres. The officer got up and we walked to his cruiser in my driveway. He had to wait a moment to back out while a blue car drove down the street. I watched it pull into Ralph's garage and then we were on our way. Except for periodic squawks from the police radio, we rode in silence up Saxon Drive to Third Avenue.

A left turn over the South Causeway and we were on the mainland. At the foot of the bridge, he pulled into the lot at the Bert Fish Medical Center. I always thought Bert Fish was an odd thing for a hospital on the water. I eventually got curious enough to learn they named the place for a philanthropic Judge.

The officer pulled up in front of the main door and parked at the curb. He locked the car and we entered the building, navigating the maze of halls and the islands of nurse's stations. I followed him for about five minutes until we came to a waiting area. He pointed to the assembled chairs and sofas. "Have a seat. I'll tell the Detective you're here."

It was a typical waiting room complete with places to sit, magazine covered coffee tables, and coffee covered magazines, so I sat down and waited. Across the room, alcove really, a thirty something woman sat on one of the couches. She read a paperback while a young girl faced her and danced from side to side with her hands on the woman's crossed knee.

I examined the magazines but none appealed to me. CNN ran silently on a TV hanging from the ceiling, while the closed captioning fought the screen-bottom news scroll for clarity. If she were awake, Mariel was probably watching now, flipping back and forth to MSNBC or maybe to the local channel 13 news.

I waited some more and then after that, I waited again until Torres appeared. When he did, I stood up. By now, the girl had the woman reaching into her purse for something.

"Sit down, Mr. Fried."

I sat down. The High Schooler cop came in and stood silently by the waiting room entrance.

Torres asked me. "Do you know why you're here?"

I looked up at him. "The last time a cop asked me if I knew why he did something, I got a speeding ticket. I don't like to guess."

"I just left Ben Horton's room. Someone tried to kill him and you were the last person to see him."

I didn't expect that. I decided to sit down and then realized I already had. "What happened? You don't really expect that I... me..."

"Please, just answer the question. In any event, I need to know what you discussed with Horton. If you're cooperative, I'd be more inclined to think you didn't do it."

I thought about that while I watched the girl standing on her toes feeding money into a vending machine. "OK. We talked about Ray Kenwood."

"Anything else?"

"No. Ed passed everything we discussed onto the D. A. I thought that information was the basis for you guys picking him up for questioning. What happened?"

"We sent a car to get him at home. When the officers got there, no one answered so they looked in a window. Horton was down on the floor. They broke in and found him in anaphylactic shock. He gasped something about a black leather case in the kitchen. One of the men found the case with a hypo in it and shot Horton with epinephrine. When the paramedics arrived, they said that shot saved his life. He's been recovering here for a few hours. I just talked with him."

The girl left the vending machine with a bag of nuts and sat down beside the woman. "Sounds like a peanut allergy." I said.

"You knew that. Very good, now, you can see why you make such a good prospect."

"Lots of people know about anaphylactic shock, peanuts and epinephrine. Why do you think peanut warnings are on so many food labels? More importantly, why did Horton eat peanuts? If he had the syringe, he must have known he had the allergy."

"We're checking that now. The crew at the scene thinks someone may have crushed peanuts into Horton's Cheese Doodles."

"Cheese Doodles? Death by Doodles? Why do they think that?"

"The TV was on. There was an open bag of Cheese Doodles on the floor by his lounge chair and his fingers were orange. It's possible someone snuck in while Horton was away and sprinkled crushed peanuts or put some peanut oil in his Cheese Doodles bag. We found one of those bag clips by the lounge chair. It looks like he was eating from a previously opened bag."

"His attacker would have had to know Horton has this allergy and that it was severe enough to kill him. Any signs of entry?"

"It looks like one of the windows was recently replaced. The putty is still fresh. We think someone broke a window to get in and then replaced it to avoid detection."

"How come Horton didn't inject himself?"

"His syringe was in the kitchen, he was in the TV room. Too far to go with such a severe reaction. I'm guessing since he was in his own home, eating his own bag of previously consumed food he just got careless. Either that or somebody moved it where he couldn't get to it."

"Wow. Someone went to a lot of trouble to get Horton out of the way. I'd like to know why."

"Yeah? Me too. Well, I guess I've got all I'm going to get out of you. Go back to bed. You look like hell." As Torres walked away, he waved to the officer who brought me here. "Take him home."

CHAPTER SEVENTEEN

After the officer dropped me off at home, I staggered back to bed and had a fitful sleep. I switched from my right side to my left, back again and then again. I still ached from my fall and had too much on my mind to sleep. I knew once I drifted off that I'd be so tired I wouldn't want to get up.

I woke up alone during what I thought was the middle of the night to see light illuminating the blinds on my bedroom window. My first thought was that it must really be morning after all. My second thought was Mariel must be in the kitchen making coffee. My third thought was the recollection Mariel wasn't home with me.

Lying there on my back, I looked at the clock radio, 6:58 am. Two minutes before my alarm would sound. I stared at the ceiling and squeezed out my last two minutes of bedtime. I couldn't remember a single day since I stopped working that I had so many things to do. When I worked full time, I couldn't imagine ever being retired. Now that I supposedly was, I couldn't understand how I ever had a job.

The alarm began to chirp. I sat up, threw my legs over the edge of the bed, and silenced it. One step at a time. I picked my running shorts up off the floor, put them on, and dragged my tired body into the kitchen. I made coffee. Usually, Mariel made our coffee. Making my own was just another reminder she was gone. Too tired to cook, I poured some orange juice and then some cereal with milk. I took my coffee to my office and checked my email. There was nothing. Nothing from Mariel, nothing from the Yahoo account that was watching Ben Horton's emails, nothing from nobody. On the other hand, at least my SPAM filter was working.

I finished my coffee, showered, dressed, and made myself presentable. I had Ray's home address from the information I found on his hard drive plus I had been there once before.

I was brushing my teeth to get rid of coffee breath when the phone rang. I rinsed, spat, and rushed for the phone. I still had some toothpaste left in my mouth, but I'm one of those poor souls who can't let a phone ring without rushing to pick it up. I could probably spend a few thousand dollars on therapy to understand why, but if I found out, then I'd feel compelled to do something about it. Then I'd wonder why I felt compelled to do something about it. Thus would start a vicious cycle of self-awareness that would eventually make me insane... and broke.

I got to the phone on the third ring, just before my answering machine picked up.

"Hello?"

"Max? It's Ed. Change of plans."

"What's up?"

"The police picked up Horton last night. When they got to him, he was having some kind of attack. They--"

"Yeah, Ed. I know. Torres told me about it. They took Horton to the hospital."

"Then you know about the interview?"

"No. What interview?"

"Horton was released from the hospital and now the police have him. They used your report to get a warrant to examine his computer and his bank records. They found enough to hold him. He's at the precinct and they're going to question him. I got us access to observe the interview. Meet me there."

"Now?"

"Now." Ed hung up.

I went back to the bathroom to rid my mouth of that last glob of toothpaste, picked up my gear bag containing my Spy Shack purchase and went to meet Ed.

I crossed the South Causeway to the Mainland and drove past Bert Fish Hospital. Then I got stuck at the traffic light before I could make my turn onto US 1, the Dixie Freeway. While I waited, I admired the artwork on the pillars holding up the overpass for SR 44. The City had painted them with large colorful paintings of fish. They had even hung metal sculptures of finny ocean life from the bottom of the bridge and painted the concrete blue to look like water. This bit of whimsy used to cheer me up, but today it didn't. When the light changed, I turned right and after a few miles, I saw the police station on my left.

It was a brownish shoebox with a tall flagpole in front and taller radio tower in the back. I pulled into the lot and found Ed leaning against his car, smoking a cigarette. When he saw me pull in, he threw it down and crushed it with his black wingtip shoe. He was dressed in full attorney regalia, grey suit, white shirt and a dark striped tie. His clothing looked expensive. My cargo shorts, not so much. I parked my car and walked over to him.

"Hi, Max. Let's go." Ed turned and headed for the door. When we entered the building, there was an officer sitting behind a dark window. It looked thick and bulletproof. So did the officer. A grille in the glass facilitated conversation and a slot at the bottom provided passage for small items.

Ed shoved a business card through the slot. "Attorney Edward McCarthy to see Detective Torres."

The officer looked up from something he was doing out of sight and moved his arms, his hands out of sight. A door to our left buzzed and Ed opened it. A second uniformed officer was waiting inside. He nodded at us and walked down the hall. We followed. He stopped at a door, opened it and stepped back to allow us entry. We entered. He stayed outside and closed the door behind us.

We were in a room with Detective Torres. The room was small, dark, and smelled of stale coffee. Along one wall, there was a grey metal chair in one corner next to a grey metal wastebasket, which overflowed with paper cups. A window on the opposite wall looked in on a man in plain clothes interviewing Ben Horton. Horton looked exhausted. He sat across the table facing his interviewer and the window. Torres looked at us when we entered, tapped once on the glass and then without saying anything, went back to the watching. A speaker hung on the wall. We could hear the conversation the other man was having with Horton.

"When's the last time you saw Ray Kenwood?"

"1984"

"So you haven't seen Ray Kenwood in over 20 years?"

"No."

"But you've spoken with him since then?"

"No."

"You've had no contact with him at all in the last 20 years?"

"No."

"Look. We've seen your bank records. We've seen your emails. We know you've been in contact with Kenwood. We got subpoenas. We've got the proof." The man took some papers from a file folder and shoved them across the table to Horton.

Horton didn't look at the papers. He just shrugged and said nothing.

"OK, have it your way. We've got proof you've been in contact with Kenwood. We've got proof you lied about that. Your credibility is already shot to hell and we've got a dead Ray Kenwood literally at your doorstep. You can start cooperating with us or you can start thinking about your murder defense."

"Wait a minute here. I didn't kill Ray. I was in California when he died. I have proof. Besides, someone tried to kill me too. What are you doing about that?"

"You could have arranged Ray's death. You could have hired someone to do it. Maybe whoever you hired to kill Ray got paid and then made a run at you to keep you quiet."

"I'm telling you. I didn't kill Ray."

"But you were in touch."

Horton was silent. He looked down at the papers on the table and then up at his interviewer. In a soft voice, he said, "Yeah. We were in touch, but only by email. I haven't seen him in over 20 years. We haven't even talked on the phone. Just the emails."

"That's better. Now, you're starting to build some credibility, earn some points. Maybe even help your case. Why was Ray coming to see you?"

"I don't know. I mean, I knew he was coming, but I didn't know why. All I knew was he wanted to show me something and wouldn't say what. All he'd say was he knew I'd want to see it... and it would be profitable."

When Horton finished, the other man sat back in his chair and slowly nodded. The room filled with silence. Horton took the opportunity to ask again, "What about the guy that tried to kill me?"

"So you know it was a man?"

"No. I mean, I don't know. I never saw who it was. Never saw anybody. One minute, I'm watching TV. Next minute, I'm choking to death."

"So, who'd want to kill a sweetheart like you?"

"I don't know."

Horton watched the other man lean forward and pull two photographs from a folder. Each one was a picture of two men on a boat. Horton was in each photo.

"Ray emailed you this photo with trade secrets embedded. We recovered the product specs that were hidden inside." The man looked at Horton.

Horton stared back with a blank expression on his face.

"OK, let's start with the easy question. These pictures were taken in 1984." The man pointed at one photo. "That's Ray Kenwood." He pointed again. "That's you." He pointed at the second photo. "That's you again." He pointed at the second photo a second time. "Now, who's this third guy?"

"Skipper."

"Skipper?"

"Yeah."

"What's his name?

"Don't know. All we ever called him was 'Skipper'. He was the ship Captain. Never heard anyone call him anything else."

"Where is he now?"

"Don't know. Last time I saw him was the morning they arrested me on the boat. Skipper must have seen the police coming, slipped over the side. They searched for him like they knew he was there, but never found him. Haven't seen him since."

"Now, talk to me about how you hid the product specs in the photo."

Horton sat there silently.

"Look, you really want to tell me about this before my partner gets in. He was up all night because of you at the hospital and now he's running late because his car broke down again. He's really pissed. Not that he's a happy guy when things go smoothly."

Ed and I both looked at Torres. He didn't move. We turned back to the show in the glass window. Horton just sat there as if the man hadn't said anything. The man sat there, looked back at Horton for a minute or two, then closed his folder, got up and left the room. A moment later, the door to our room opened and the man who interviewed Horton walked in. He looked at Ed and then me.

"Hi, I'm Detective Fitzpatrick." He smiled, held out his hand and shook Ed's then mine. Fitzpatrick was tall, slim and Irish. He wore tan loafers with a basket weave on the toes, thin beige socks, tan slacks and a white short sleeve shirt with a collar. His hair was reddish blond and he looked to be in his mid forties. He wore his gun and badge on a brown leather belt. The basket weave on the belt matched the one on his shoes.

"You must be McCarthy and Fried. Thanks for the leg up. The material you provided led us to what we needed. It got us warrants, and then we found enough at Horton's place and in his bank records to make the theft charges."

Ed and I nodded in satisfaction.

"I'm afraid there's not much else we can nail him on. His alibi for the break-in checks out." He looked at Ed. "We don't have enough to tie him to bugging your office and we can't connect him to the murder. Maybe when the M. E. figures out how the killer triggered the heart attack, we'll have another go at him but for now... of course, when Torres gets his turn at Horton, who knows what he'll say. Leo's so abrasive, innocent folks confess just to get him out of the room." He grinned at Torres.

Torres looked back and slowly shook his head. "Not necessary. Spending an hour in an interview room with a grinning Fitzpatrick is enough torture to make anyone talk. Fitzie will be even worse than this when he gets over his current depression and into a good mood."

Fitzpatrick smiled again. "Look guys. You heard what Horton said. This is all we've got. Probably all we're gonna get. Anything else turns up relevant to your case, we'll give you a call. We expect you to do the same if you come across anything. Understand?"

"Sure," Ed said. I nodded assent.

"C'mon." Fitzpatrick opened the door. "I'll see you out."

When we got back to the lobby, I remembered. I was supposed to come here today and pick up my police report from the break-in.

"Ed, wait a minute."

I went back to the cop in the window. "I'd like to pick up a police report, please."

"Name?"

"Fried, F-r-i-e-d"

The cop turned to the countertop to his left. Several manila folders stood up in a holder on the desk. He counted six folders in, picked up one marked with the letter "F", opened and looked inside. "Max Fried?"

"Yes."

He took a piece of paper from the folder and passed it through the opening under the glass.

I said, "Thanks," but the cop had already picked up the phone and was writing something down. I didn't think he was listening anymore so I left the window.

Ed looked at me. "You ready?"

"Yeah."

When we got outside the Police Station, Ed walked me to my car and asked, "What do you think?"

"Too much of a coincidence that Ray's dead and someone tried to kill Horton too. There's gotta be some connection, and if Horton didn't do the murder or the break-in, then there's got to be a third person."

"OK, so who is he? Or she?"

"Well, if I'm right that the break-in is related to the trade secrets, then there has to be some connection between the third person, Ray and Horton. I think we need to look more closely at what Ray stole and how he got it. Maybe he had an accomplice?"

Ed thought for a moment, "Sounds good to me, anything useful in the police report?"

I looked down at it. Except for the name of the cop that came with Torres, there was nothing there I didn't already know. "Nah."

"Well, you need it for the insurance claim, so it's good you got it. How about now, we do that bug check at Ray's place. I'll meet you there."

"Yeah," I got into my car.

CHAPTER EIGHTEEN

I left the police station and drove south to Wayne Avenue, near Evil Twin Motorcycles where I have my bike serviced. After a couple of turns, I was in Quay Assisi. It took me all of ten minutes to get to Ray's home.

When I got there, I parked in the driveway, shut off the engine and waited for Ed. He claims he isn't a slow driver. He says he just tends to make occasional wrong turns. At the end of the wide driveway, the garage connected to what must have been over 5,000 square feet of riverfront living space. When I looked past the house from the driveway, I could see the river. Well, it wasn't actually a driveway. Pavers covered the entire front yard.

Since Ed should be arriving soon, I picked up my gear bag and got out of the car. I walked around back to look at the river, and noticed the neighbors had a beautiful, manicured, lawn. At Ray's, pavers covered his entire back yard too, except for the part occupied by a huge free form swimming pool and spa. In the river behind the pool, Ray had a covered floating dock big enough to accommodate a 50-foot boat.

I wandered back around front in time to see Ed pulling up in his silver Mercedes sedan. He got out of his car, looked over the roof at me and waved, "Hey, Max."

We started walking to the house. Ed reached inside of his shirt pocket and removed a pack of cigarettes, and then he reached in again and pulled out a piece of paper. He put the cigarettes back and unfolded the paper. By now, we were standing at the first garage door on the left. As Ed frowned and squinted at the paper, I noticed there was a keypad mounted on the garage doorframe. I had been wondering how Ed was going to get access while Kathleen was out of town. He pressed some numbers on the pad and the garage door opened providing us access to the house.

We entered the garage and headed left to a door I expected would lead us to the living area. When we got there, Ed pressed a lit button on the wall that started closing the garage. Just before we opened the door to the house, Ed stopped and looked again at the piece of paper. He quickly opened the door and rushed into the foyer where he took a moment to look around. Then he ran to a security panel and punched in some numbers.

"Well," he sighed, "We're in." We looked around us and then at each other. Somebody had tossed the place. Ed walked into a room off the foyer and reached for a wall phone.

He held the phone to his ear for a moment. "It's dead." He reached in his pants pocket. "I'll use my cell to call the Police."

I put my hand out to stop him. "Wait a minute. Was the alarm armed?"

"Yes. I think so." I followed him back to the foyer and he looked at the panel. "Yes, that's right. I remember seeing the lights change when I typed in the code and now the alarm lights show it's been disarmed. Why?"

"If the alarm was active when we walked in, I don't think anyone is here anymore. It's probably best to do our sweep before we call the police." I moved closer to the panel. "Look at this indicator light. When triggered, this alarm system dials a number and connects to a central service to report the alarm. Someone probably disabled the phone line to prevent notification to the security company."

"Yeah, but wouldn't folks still hear the alarm sound?"

"Yes."

"So, why did they kill the phone line and then let the alarm sound. I don't get that."

"Me neither. Killing the phone only prevented the dialer from calling the security company. They must have had some other way of dealing with the alarm noise. Let's look around. Do what we came to do. Maybe we'll find an explanation."

I took two pairs of latex gloves from my gear bag and gave one to Ed. Then I pulled out an AM-FM radio and tuned to an AM talk show to trigger any voice-activated transmitters we might find. I put on my headphones, switched on the bug detector and started sweeping. I started in the foyer, which was larger than Ed's office, and then moved into the kitchen. It was full of professional grade equipment like you'd see in a restaurant, but there were no bugs, no listening devices.

I stepped over things dumped on the floor and moved from the kitchen to the dining room, the living room, the office, the gym, and the bathroom. No signals detected in any of these rooms.

Ed followed me from room to room. In the office, he picked up the answering machine, turned it over and pointed to the bottom. It had a battery compartment, just like the machine in Ed's office where we found the bug. I put down my detector and took the machine from him. Pulling off the battery cover, I looked inside. The compartment was empty, no listening device, and no battery. I replaced the cover, put the machine back on the desk and picked up my detector. We found nothing but a mess on the first floor.

Ed went up the stairs. I followed him into the master suite. Photos hung in frames on the walls and sat on one of the two dressers. I looked at the ones nearest to where I stood and saw a familiar face. Ray looked bigger and fatter, but he was clearly the same man I saw in that 1984 photo he emailed to Ben Horton. In what I thought was a flash of clever insight, I looked at the rest of the photos for the third man who had been in the pictures with Ray and Horton. My cleverness went without reward.

The second floor had four other bedrooms to search. Just like the master bedroom, each had its own bathroom. I swept them all and found nothing but debris someone left from a previous visit. I turned and headed back downstairs. I wanted to talk to Ed, but just in case I missed a bug, I didn't want to do it in the house. Ed must have had the same thought as he followed me silently down the stairs and out the door.

When we got outside, there was a truck marked Coastal Caterers parked in the driveway next door. Ed and I leaned against my car. Ed lit a cigarette. I put my bag on the car roof and said, "I think it's clean in there."

Ed nodded in agreement.

"But, I don't think it was before."

"Huh?" Ed blew out smoke.

"Whoever we're looking for knew you were handling Ray's estate and bugged your office."

"Right."

"But how could they know you were handling things unless they bugged Kathleen. Where was Kathleen when she asked you to handle this?"

"Home. In Ray's office. I know because I asked her about some papers Ray kept there. She got them out of the desk to read to me."

"I think they bugged her first, and learned about you. Then

from you, they knew Kathleen left town and they could came back and search. Once they realized it wasn't here and that Kathleen didn't know where it was, they probably removed the bug."

"Sure, they also probably knew the police would come after they trashed the place and leaving the bug behind would just add to the clues leading back to them."

"Speaking of police..."

"Yeah" said Ed. He started to reach into his pocket for his cell phone when we heard a man call out "Yoo hoo." Ed and I looked up and Ed closed his phone. The man was in the driveway next door. He started waving his arm in the air to get our attention while he walked over to us.

We watched him approach. He was around five foot ten and slim with wispy, light blond hair. He wore a turquoise golf shirt, white slacks, turquoise socks, and white canvas shoes. On the left front of his shirt was a white graphic of an ocean wave over the words "Coastal Caterers." In white script, underneath the logo was the name "Bertram." He smiled, waved, and asked, "Hi, I'm Bert from the caterers. Are you men from the Alarm Company too? Are you going to test again today?"

Ed squinted at Bert, "What do you mean?"

Bert placed his hands on his hips and sighed. "Yesterday, I was next door prepping my client's place for the rehearsal dinner party and saw the alarm company truck here. The man was working on the alarm. He kept turning it on and off. On and off."

He raised both hands in the air and then returned them to his hips. "I knew my client would be concerned about the noise if it lasted so I came over to see what was going on. I was setting up the sound system for the party and they were making more noise than I was. He said he had fixed a problem and was testing it."

"No." Ed shook his head. I'm the family attorney. We're just taking care of some business here. We --"

"Good. Mr. D'Argent, my client next door, will be glad to hear that. Tonight's his Princess's wedding reception. I don't mind telling you. Even though the noise ended before the dinner party, he wasn't happy about it. Me, I like happy clients. Happy clients like my work. Unhappy ones tend to be more critical just because they're... unhappy!" Bert shook his head. "Bad for business. It –"

He spoke so fast I was having trouble finding a pause during which I could ask a question, so I just interrupted. "What did the man and the truck from the alarm company look like?"

Bertram looked at me as if surprised to hear someone else speak. "Nothing special, maybe early 50s and tall. His hardhat and wraparound sunglasses pretty much covered his face. He wore this tacky jumpsuit and drove a big white van marked Security with one of those yellow light fixtures on the roof. Why?"

"I thought we might know him. Any name on the jumpsuit or on the truck?"

Bertram thought for a moment. "No, I don't think so. No. No names."

"Thanks."

"My pleasure, if I see him again, I'll ask his name. Well, take care gentlemen. I've got a party to go to." He smiled, waved his fingers at us and headed back next door.

"Ed, I think that explains why no one reacted to the alarm. Anyone who could hear it could see what appeared to be an Alarm Company truck and probably thought the situation was under control."

"Hmmm, pretty clever."

"Let's call the police. It's getting late."

The police arrived just minutes after Ed closed his cell phone. Again, they arrived in two cars, one man in each. It seemed they got here a lot faster than they got to my place when I called them. I wondered if it just seemed that way because it was my house last time or if instead, I was learning a lesson about the quality of neighborhoods.

I was surprised to see Detective Torres exit one of the cars. He held a clipboard. The other officer, I hadn't seen before. Torres looked at me as he got out of his car. He shook his head and then he said something to the other officer. The other officer nodded, put his hand on his holstered gun and went into the house.

Torres walked over to Ed and me, pressed his lips together and stood there looking at us with his knuckles on his hips. Somehow, it looked different when Bertram did it. "Ahh, Mr. Fried, Mr. McCarthy. We meet again." He turned his gaze to only me and I showed him my best dead pan. It worked because Torres switched to staring at Ed.

Ed said, "This is the Kenwood family residence. I called it in."

Torres moved closer to him. "I know where I am. I broke the news to the widow. Where is she?"

"After Ray was killed, Kathleen went to South Carolina to be with her family. There was just the two of them, here."

"And you and Mr. Fried are here because?"

Ed opened his mouth, closed it, looked at me, and then turned back to Torres. "I'm the family attorney. I've retained Mr. Fried to assist in the location of the deceased's assets so I can handle the estate."

Torres rolled his eyes.

The other cop came out of the house and whispered something to Torres. Torres nodded and said. "It looks like someone else may be interested in the deceased's assets. Any ideas who?"

Ed and I shook, "No" like a pair of bobble head dolls.

Torres looked at me. Then as if he expected better luck with Ed, he turned to him. "And does this have anything to do with the break-in at Mr. Fried's place?"

In unison, Ed and I shrugged our shoulders.

"You guys are too much. An officer of the court and a state licensed investigator. Look, you know the drill. Just get me a list of what's missing." He walked towards the house shaking his head. I could see Bertram hustling over from next door to catch up with him. I had no doubt he was on his way to assess Torres' impact on the party next door.

Ed called after him, "Can we go now?"

Without looking back, Torres waved a hand in the air and yelled, "Please do," as he vanished into the house.

CHAPTER NINETEEN

Ed left the Kenwood home to move Sheila into his house on the river and I drove over to the EFH offices. They were on the mainland north of S.R. 44 in a corporate park between a golf course and the New Smyrna Beach Municipal Airport, Jack Bolt Field. I was feeling put out after my attempt to get through on the phone so I imagined the airport proximity a snooty convenience to suit the ipsy-pipsy family members. With Jack Bolt Field so close, they wouldn't have to travel to the Daytona Beach airport and mingle with the NASCAR fans, Bikers, Spring Breakers and me.

On the way to the airport, I saw a sign for Stevie's Sky Lounge boasting, "Just a short walk from aircraft parking." I had never been there but it was lunchtime and when I arrived, it didn't look crowded. I went inside.

A hostess seated me alone at a table for four just outside the bar with a view of the runways. The outside walls were almost entirely windows and inside walls lacked the tacky props sometimes appearing in places like this.

Although the bar crowd was small, it was noisy. Several bursts of deep male laughter accompanied a single, higher pitched feminine giggle. I ignored them and read the menu.

In case the view didn't make it clear that you were dining near an airport, the menu titles did. Appetizers were "Preparing for Takeoff", dinners "Maximum Altitude" and desserts "Landings." Despite the cutesy listings, it was a very nice upscale restaurant.

Being a vegetarian, I scanned to see what, if anything, I could eat. They had so many attractive items I was having a hard time choosing. The Pesto Bruschetta tempted me. It was thin and crispy flat bread with spinach pesto, melted mozzarella and a blend of fresh basil, diced tomatoes, garlic and olive oil.

As tasty as that sounded, I decided my interview with Corky might go better without garlic on my breath. Instead, I ordered the Caprese Salad, fresh Buffalo mozzarella and tomato fresca over baby spinach. Drizzled with a balsamic reduction and homemade spinach pesto. Served with warm Italian bread. Mmmm, it sounded good.

While waiting for my food, I heard a cell phone ring in the bar, silencing the crowd. Then I heard a female voice speaking something I couldn't make out, a click of a phone closing, the same woman speaking louder, and then an outburst of laughter from the men at the bar.

Curious to see what was going on in there, I decided this would be a good time to go wash my hands. As I passed the bar, I saw what I heard. Three men and one blonde. She wore a brown suit with a micro mini skirt and a low cut blouse. Surrounded by three men, she was brassier than the bar rail. She was Ed's ex-wife, Sheila. The ex-wife Ed had gone to move into his river view home, just about now.

I felt terrible for Ed, he'd be disappointed and hurt. It was sad to witness it, but telling him about it would serve no purpose. By now, he'd know that Sheila stood him up. She wasn't going to move in with him after all.

I washed and went back to my seat and while I sat, trying to decide how to handle this new dilemma, the waitress brought my food. I had a leisurely lunch with great service and I was still done in time to be early for my 2:00 with Corky. I paid my check and drove the short distance to my meeting.

I got there about 15 minutes early so I parked and went inside. Lunch was good but I felt bad for Ed. I was also annoyed about the way EFH treated my request for an interview with Corky. The more I thought about that, the more I began to get in a pissy mood. I figured they would keep me waiting anyway so I might as well get started. I entered the five story, red brick and smoked glass building through the double doors in the glassed in lobby. The ceiling was two stories high and contained almost as many trees inside as there were outside on the lawn. I had to admit, the place looked nice.

As I walked toward the elevator bank in the lobby one of two men at a horseshoe shaped reception desk stood and smiled at me. Both were good-looking kids in their late twenties with nice teeth. They looked like they worked out and both wore navy blue blazers with an emblem over the pocket and a two-way radio on their belts. As I neared the elevator, one of them said, "Sir?"

I wondered how far I would get if I ignored him and kept on going. I was tempted to do so, but it would have been childish and counterproductive. I had no idea where Corky's office was, so I said, "Hi, I've got a 2:00 with Corky Eastwood."

"Mr. Fried?" he asked without consulting any computer or paper.

"Yes." I was impressed they were expecting me. He also got my name right. Maybe these people weren't so bad after all.

"This way, please." He bowed his head slightly, gestured to an empty elevator and removed a key from his pocket. I entered the car. He followed me in, placed the key into a panel on the wall and turned it. He smiled at me.

I smiled at him.

He smiled at me.

I smiled at him.

The elevator stopped at "P" and the door opened. I knew "P" usually stood for "Parking" or "Penthouse." This was the first time I got off at "P" when there weren't cars all over the place.

The young man gestured towards the elevator door and I exited. There was no receptionist. I stood in a large open area. It looked like a hotel lobby or a room in a private club. It gradually dawned on me that this floor contained private living quarters instead of offices.

Several plush chairs, sofas, coffee tables and end tables sat in small groups on thick tasteful carpeting. I noticed a woman in her 40s, tall and thin with straight, blond, shoulder length, hair. She put down a glass and stood up from one of the chairs.

Her beige suit included a tailored jacket and a straight cut, tight fitting skirt that came to just below her knees. A light yellow blouse, opened at the collar, showed off a simple strand of pearls that matched her earrings.

"Mr. Fried," she showed me perfect teeth and offered her hand. I took it.

"Please sit." She said.

I gave her back her hand and we sat in a pair of matching, red, cloth, club chairs. They bordered a low redwood coffee table bordered by redwood end tables bearing green plants. A man approached wearing a black suit, thin black tie and a white shirt.

Without acknowledging his arrival, she asked, "Mr. Fried, would you like anything to drink?" It was as if she just knew he would be there in time to hear my reply to her question.

"No, thank you. I'm fine." The man in the suit nodded and left. She didn't acknowledge his departure either, so I continued. "I'd like to thank you for taking the time to meet with me."

She suppressed a grin and made a dismissive wave with her hand. "Uncle Ed tells me you have some questions for me."

"Uncle Ed?"

She laughed. "When I was about ten years old, Ed McCarthy did so much work for my father that he practically lived at our house. He spent so much time with us I began to call him Uncle Ed. That went on for about five years until the end of Daddy's real estate acquisition phase. Though he claimed otherwise, I think all of that work may have lead to the end of Uncle Ed's second marriage, or was it his third? Then when Daddy turned his investments in other directions, I didn't see Uncle Ed much after that until he started handling my own real estate a few years later. Now, he occasionally helps our corporate legal team. She placed her hands together in her lap and leaned forward towards me. "So, what do you want to know?"

"Well, I'm working with ah, Uncle Ed on a case. During the course of our investigation, we came across someone whose interests conflict with those of Ed's client. The reason I'm here is you seem to have a connection to the person with the conflict."

"You beat around the bush, very well, Mr. Fried, but I'm not that easily offended. Who are we not talking about here?"

"You appear to be a part owner of PC Gadgets. You're listed as Vice President of the corporation. Ben Horton, the President, may have interests that conflict with Ed's client. We'd like to sort this out."

"I know Ben Horton. Who's the client?"

"The estate of Ray Kenwood."

"Ray's dead? And Ben has conflicting interests?"

"Yes. You knew Ray too?"

"Yes. I was about 16. Daddy had a sailboat, a beautiful custom yacht with two masts, four cabins, and a full time crew. I used to dream about sailing away and never returning. Daddy kept it here in New Smyrna Beach, but he'd sail it back and forth to Key West. On his first trip to the Keys, Daddy captained the boat and hired Ben and Ray as crew. They were local boys who worked summers at the marina. Daddy met Skipper when we docked in the Keys. He was from around here and looking for work, so Daddy hired him. Skipper was a few years older than the boys were and he had a lot of blue water experience. That summer, I spent two weeks on that boat. I loved it. I still love the water."

When she started talking, the billionaire heiress disappeared and I saw the teenager who loved the sea. For some reason, this made me feel more comfortable with her. I sat back in my chair. "When did you last see Ray and Ben?"

She leaned forward and in a soft voice said, "Ed said this conversation would be confidential."

I leaned forward and in a soft voice, responded, "Yes, it is."

She nodded, "OK. I saw them last on the day they were arrested."

"Arrested?" I already knew Ben Horton's version of this story. Now, I wanted to see if Corky corroborated it.

"Yes. Daddy felt awful. You see, when he wasn't using the boat, Daddy let the crew go where they wanted. They worked full time crew and lived onboard. Sometimes, they went to Cuba and brought back cigars. Daddy and his friends loved those cigars and the crew was able to supplement their income. No one really cared or thought it was a big deal."

She paused. I got the impression that she was deciding whether to tell me more, so I sat there quietly, while she thought it over. She pressed her lips together and then continued.

"That is, until officers arrested Ray and Ben. I was on the boat with them on their last trip to Cuba but Ray and Ben told the officers that I wasn't. They said I was just some girl they met that day in Key West. I was wearing a bikini and the folks at the Yacht Club vouched for me so they just let me go."

"You got lucky."

"Yes. The Feds also investigated Daddy, but since he wasn't there and the boys claimed Daddy was ignorant, no one arrested him. The next day, Daddy had a crew tow the Leviathan back here to New Smyrna Beach. The day after it arrived, Daddy died on it. I loved that boat and I hated that boat."

"What became of the Leviathan?"

"I sealed it up and put it in storage the day Daddy died. I couldn't bear to use it, but I couldn't bear to part with it either."

"What about the Captain? Did he get arrested too?"

"No, he disappeared. The police were looking for him but they didn't find him. I'd guess he saw the police and went over the side. He was a great swimmer. He could probably have swum quite a distance underwater. We never saw him again. He didn't even come back for his things. He was lucky, because we later found out the police wanted him for a previous incident on another boat. They showed me his picture... said his name was Dan, no... maybe David, I don't know. It was a name I never heard him use. Anyway, they claimed he smuggled Cubans. This time, I mean people not cigars. I heard one of the police say something about wanting to talk to him about a death in Miami."

"Did the Police have the Captain's name correct?"

"Gee, Mr. Fried. I was 16. The crew seemed like old men. We really didn't socialize. All I remember is Ben, Ray, and Skipper. Everyone, even Daddy, called him nothing but "Skipper.""

"Do you remember what he looked like?"

"Vaguely. I remember he had long wavy blond hair and a Fu Manchu style moustache. Do you remember those?" She laughed.

"Yes. I remember many bad styles and I wore most of them. They all seemed like a good idea at the time. I'd really like to track down this captain. Any chance his name might be on some payroll or personnel record?"

"Possibly, I'll have Amanda check into that and call you."

"Thanks. I'd appreciate it. You've known Horton for a long time. Did you know about his food allergy?"

"You mean that peanut thing? Oh, yes. He was constantly interrogating people who prepared his food about what ingredients they used. It got to the point that when Skipper and Ray had kitchen duty, they refused to make Ben's food. He ended up making all of his own meals. Why do you want to know about that?"

"Just background information, one last question, if you don't mind."

"Sure."

"So, how did you end up as vice president on the PC Gadgets corporate papers?"

"Well, a little while ago, I got this call from Ben. I hadn't heard from him in years. He needed to borrow some money because he was having some trouble with his company. He said he had a new design he wanted to bring to market but he needed cash. I was surprised to hear from him after so long, but I wanted to help him because he helped me avoid arrest. I agreed to the loan, handed him over to our financing staff. They made him put me on the board to protect my investment."

"I guess I lied. Now, I have an additional question. Do you know what this new product is?"

"No, but it doesn't matter." She broke eye contact and looked over my shoulder. "I owed him." She was watching something while she spoke. "I would have financed anything he..."

I looked behind me and saw the elevator door closing. Detectives Torres and Fitzpatrick stood in front of it scanning the room, their gold badges and guns prominent on their belts. Torres caught my eye and the detectives started towards me with two of the EFH security men trailing behind. I turned back to Corky and saw her assistant, Amanda Finch, had materialized by her side. I wondered what was going on.

CHAPTER TWENTY

Torres stopped next to me, stared down and said, "Fried. What are you doing here?"

I didn't answer.

Detective Fitzpatrick walked over to Corky and asked, "Corky Eastwood?"

"Yes?"

"I'm Detective Fitzpatrick." He nodded his head to the side. "My partner, Detective Torres. We'd like to ask you some questions." Fitzpatrick looked at me and then at Finch as if he wanted us to leave. When we didn't, he asked Corky, "Is there someplace we can talk?"

"We can talk right here. What do you want to know?"

Fitzpatrick hesitated a moment as if considering his options, then asked, "How long have you known Ben Horton?"

Corky looked at me, then at Fitzpatrick, "Why do you want to know?"

"Corporate papers show you as Vice President of Horton's company."

"I'm an officer of many corporations."

"Yes, ma'am, but someone tried to kill Horton."

She seemed surprised. Maybe I should have told her about the attempt to kill Horton. Maybe I should have told her Ray was murdered. I held off because I didn't want to color her answers. Maybe I was wrong. She looked at me again. This time, her expression wasn't that pleasant. "And you sent Mr. Fried to see what he could learn first?"

Torres sprang to life. "What? Fried? No. He's got nothing to do with us. I'd like to know what he's doing here myself."

He didn't have to act as if working with me was so repulsive, but at least his reaction seemed to reassure Corky I was on her side. To buttress that position, I said, "I'm working for Ms. Eastwood's attorney on a private matter."

Fitzpatrick ignored the sideshow and continued to question Corky. "Are you aware that Ben Horton was buying trade secrets from a competitor?"

"No."

"How did you meet Ben Horton?"

"I'd prefer not to answer anymore questions without my attorney present."

"Is she here?"

"No."

Fitzpatrick reached out his hand towards Corky. "Then you'll have to come with us. Your lawyer can meet us at the station and we can chat."

Corky stood up and turned to her assistant Amanda. "Please arrange for appropriate counsel to meet me."

Amanda just nodded. She seemed too shocked to speak. She and I stood and watched Corky leave with the Detectives. As soon as they were gone, I ran to the elevator and pressed the button. I decided to follow them to the police station.

When I got to my car, I phoned Ed's cell but got only voice mail. When I got to the police station, I tried to get in to see Corky or Torres, but they refused me entry. I went back to my car and watched for anyone that looked like an EFH lawyer. I thought it likely that only a lawyer would drive an expensive car and wear a suit to a police station.

I watched the parking lot entrance for 10 minutes. No one came or left. Then a silver Mercedes pulled into a spot near the door. I got out of my car so I could see the driver. It was Ed. I ran over and called his name. I wanted to catch him before he went inside.

He stopped and turned to see who was calling him. When he saw me, he started in my direction so I slowed to a walk. We met halfway.

"Max, what are you doing here?"

"I was talking to Corky about Horton when Torres and Fitzpatrick came to question her. What about you?"

"I'm her lawyer."

"I thought EFH was sending someone."

"They did. Me. At this location, EFH legal only handles contracts and civil litigation. I'm on retainer to fill in the gaps. I can't talk now. I've got to go." He got about three feet and then turned back to face me, "You promised me that you'd keep Corky out of this and now she's in police custody. I should have cut you loose earlier." He showed me his back and started walking away.

I ran after him. "Wait, Ed. I had nothing to do with this. The police found the same records I did. They came to see Corky because she's listed as VP in Horton's company."

Ed stopped, "How do you know this?"

"I heard them say so when they arrived."

"For sure?"

"For sure."

Ed turned to enter the building and I walked with him. When we got to the door, he paused and gave me a puzzled look. "You following me?"

"Yeah. Corky already told me what she knows. I may be able to help you. Besides, if the police are questioning her about Horton, I may be able to learn something from their questions."

Ed shrugged and we went in to see Corky. A cop escorted us into the squad room where Corky was sitting in a side chair at Fitzpatrick's desk drinking bottled water. When he saw us, Fitzpatrick stood up. "Mr. McCarthy. Mr. Fried."

Ed said, "I'm here to represent Ms. Eastwood."

"Very good. This way please." We followed him into an interview room.

We all sat and Fitzpatrick began.

"Ms. Eastwood. How long have you known Ben Horton?"

"I'd rather not answer that."

"OK, how did you meet?"

"I'd rather not answer that either."

"How about, how did you come to be Vice President of his company?"

She shook her head.

"Ms. Eastwood. Ben Horton was your business partner. We know he was buying trade secrets stolen from a competitor. If you won't answer our questions, we can't know that you weren't involved in the theft or that you didn't have anything do with the attempt to kill him."

Ed leaned in towards Fitzpatrick. "My client is innocent until proven guilty. She has no burden of proof here. You do."

"OK," Fitzpatrick said, "How's this? I'm going prove your client and Horton were stealing from A. V. Designs. She knew that we were onto Horton and she paid someone to shut him up before he incriminated her. Plus she had to protect her investment."

Corky laughed. It seemed genuine. "Do you know how much I invested in Ben's company? Twenty thousand dollars. Do you think anyone is going to believe that I'd have someone killed over such a small amount?"

"So you don't think it's a lot of money. Working folks on a jury might not agree. Besides, even if the money wasn't a factor, you'd still want to avoid going down with him on the theft charges."

Ed stood up. "We've had enough. You've got nothing to justify holding Ms. Eastwood. We're leaving."

Fitzpatrick sat and watched us leave the room. Torres was waiting outside watching us. Just as Corky walked past him, he said, "Ma'am, you must realize that if you didn't try to kill Ben Horton, someone else did. Since you're Horton's business partner, you might be next on some killer's list."

Corky stopped and turned to glare at him. He shrugged and escorted us out of the building.

CHAPTER TWENTY-ONE

I was with Corky longer than I thought I'd be, but I still had plenty of time to get to my meeting with Clive Howard, the Security Chief at A. V. Designs.

When I drove up to the gate at A. V. Designs, a uniformed guard stepped out of his booth and smiled, "Good afternoon sir, how may I help you?"

"I've got a 4:00 with the Chief of Corporate Security. My name is Max Fried."

"Do you have some ID sir?"

This was my third chance to show off my new P. I. license, so I did. After seeing it, the guard seemed even less impressed than Detective Torres. He stepped back into the booth and made a phone call. Then he came out of the booth holding a small digital camera. He bent down next to my window and aimed the camera at me. "This is for your ID," he said and then pressed a button.

He went back into the booth and after a bit, came out with a laminated photo ID bearing my name, today's date and the word "VISITOR" in huge red letters. "This is your temporary ID sir. As indicated on the card, it is good for today only. You must wear this ID the entire time you're on the campus and you must return it when you leave." He looked at me as if to see if his instructions registered and I nodded.

"Building Two sir. Just follow this road to the left. Park in any space marked 'Visitors'." He handed me a paper tag to hang from my rear view mirror. Printed on the front was today's date, a number and the word "VISITOR." I looked at the back of the tag and saw five inches of fine, hardly readable print having something to do with the rights of A. V. Designs pertaining to my vehicle should I overstay my welcome. "Have a good day sir."

"Thanks." I drove on to the left, parked my car and walked to Building Two. I felt like I was on a college campus. It was a big place, with several buildings and nice landscaping. Little pockets of trees and plants dotted sprawling lawns. I saw some palm trees, some ferns, hibiscus and some plants with trumpet shaped flowers I couldn't name. I'd guess they probably employed more landscapers than other companies had staff. All of this green cost a lot of money.

I passed the employee parking lot for Building Two and noticed a blue four door Taurus in a space marked reserved for "Security Chief." I looked at the license plate and recognized it as the plate number Karl had seen in front of my house. I entered the building and found a semicircular reception desk just in front of a bank of elevators. As I walked in the door, a man in a dark business suit stood up behind the counter and asked, "How may I help you sir?" It sounded more like a command than a question.

I showed my new photo ID and he slapped a green sticker on my chest that read "BLDG 2" in big black letters. I guessed that instead of hiring people smart enough to know what day it was, they just changed the sticker color daily.

He made a note in a book and then directed me to the fifth floor. When I exited the elevator, it opened into a reception area. An attractive young, blonde woman sat at a desk facing the elevator door. She had shoulder length hair put up in some kind of a knot. When I exited the elevator, she stood up. She was wearing a dark blue, business suit with a skirt. Under her collarless suit jacket was a white scoop neck shell. "Mr. Fried?"

I nodded and she gestured to an alcove next to the elevator with a small sofa and two chairs grouped around a small coffee table. Someone had fanned magazines artfully across the table so that the titles were visible. A coffee maker with Styrofoam cups sat on a small table nearby.

"The Chief is on a call right now. If you'll please be seated, he should be done shortly and I'll send you right in." She smiled so sweetly I felt compelled to comply. I didn't want her to think I was a jerk. Besides, I could see the lit light on her telephone console. She sat back down and turned to a computer screen on her desk.

"Sure. Thanks." I started towards the sofa, stopped and turned back towards the young receptionist. "Hey, I noticed you have quite a fleet of company cars. Are they assigned to staff or do you have something like a motor pool where folks just sign one out when they need one?"

She looked up at me in surprise. I don't think she had expected conversation and I'm sure she thought my question was odd.

"Uh, yes. Staff can request one when needed but we assign executives their own vehicles. Are you here about vehicle leasing? The Chief doesn't handle that. Maybe you want to speak with the Director of Resource Management?"

"Perhaps another time." I don't know why, but I winked at her. "I've also got some Security business with the Chief today."

She smiled and nodded knowingly. I guess if you wink when you say "Security", it means something. I didn't know what but I decided to press on for more information. Maybe she'd take my questions as idle chatter to kill time while waiting. "Has the Chief been working here long?"

"Gee, I wouldn't know. I've only been here about six months myself. Besides, even if I knew, I probably shouldn't say." She winked at me and said, "Security."

"You know. I'm impressed. If I ever need a discreet receptionist, I'm going keep you in mind."

She laughed and looked down at her telephone console. I looked too. The previously lit light was dim. "The Chief will see you now. He has a busy schedule today but he's all ready for you. This way please."

I followed her through a double door behind her desk to the inner office where a man sat behind a large, uncluttered desk with one piece of paper in his hand. He was tall, trim and fit and sat rigidly upright in his chair, as if at attention. He carried himself with a quiet strength like someone you wouldn't want to mess with. The office was big and sparsely furnished with only a desk, a sideboard and two guest chairs in a room capable of holding much more. The result was that the room looked even bigger than it was.

He had closely cropped white hair and wore a traditional, navy blue, two-button business suit, a white shirt and a blue and white striped tie. The man put down the paper and looked up as the receptionist left. After she closed the door behind her, he said, "Ah, Mr. Fried. I'm Clive Howard. How may I be of assistance?" He had a raspy but loud and clear voice. I could hear a trace of a slight foreign accent, possibly English or South African.

Mr. Howard looked familiar. He sat there with his hands flat on his desk, palms down, making no effort to lift them to shake one of mine. He looked composed and alert, like he was accustomed to always being in control.

I looked down at my new temporary photo ID. Then I took it off and looked at it again. "You know, I don't think this photo looks all that much like me. I thought I must be better looking than this." I held it out to him. "Do you think this is an accurate likeness or do you do this simply to amuse yourselves?"

He hesitated, then smirked and took the photo ID from my hand. He held it, looked at the photo and said, "Mr. Fried, I am afraid this is a very accurate likeness. Now, how can I help you?" He returned my ID. Holding it by the edges, I clipped it back onto my collar.

"I'm a private investigator and I'm working a case that seems to have drawn the attention of A. V. Designs. Boy, you look familiar. Do I know you?"

"What do you mean, "...drawn the attention of A. V. Designs"? I don't think so. Having a familiar face has served me well in my work. Folks either don't notice me or they think I'm someone they already know."

"A man in a blue four door Taurus sedan was surveilling my home. The plates trace back to A. V. Designs." I took a small leap here. "The man looked a lot like you."

He laughed. "Well, Mr. Fried, there is no intrigue here. As one professional to another, I can tell you, yes, we have been watching you."

"Care to tell me why?"

"We're looking for something. We thought you might lead us to it."

"What is it?"

"I'm sorry. I can't tell you that."

"Why do you think I can lead you to it?"

"I'm sorry. I can't tell you that either."

"Thank you for being so forthcoming."

He laughed again. "I really am sorry, Mr. Fried. At A. V. Designs, we do a lot of leading edge design work in electronics. Knowledge and information are valuable commodities here. We must be very careful about what we tell whom and when we tell them. Please, take comfort we are following the law here. We're conducting a confidential investigation necessary to protect the interests of our shareholders. If we were up to no good, I wouldn't have been using a company car. I would not have met with you and I certainly would not have acknowledged we were watching you."

"Well then, if you believe I might be of assistance to you in finding what you seek, why not enlist my services?

"We might, Mr. Fried. While I cannot tell you what we seek, it is possible you will discover what it is on your own. Should you do so, we would appreciate it; I would appreciate it if you would contact me. If you knew on your own what it was, I would not need to reveal any confidential information and it might be fruitful for us to work together. That's why I agreed to meet with you today. If I'm correct, your investigation will eventually lead you to me again." He paused for a beat and then said. "I have a tight schedule today and I need to be elsewhere for my next meeting. Would you excuse me? It's been nice meeting you."

He rose but kept his hands palms down on his desk so that he was leaning forward over his desk.

"Sure, thank you, Mr. Howard." As I walked out, I realized he never asked me about the case I was working. I was disappointed I didn't get to throw that confidentiality speech back at him, but maybe that's why he didn't ask. On the other hand, maybe he didn't ask because he already knew.

CHAPTER TWENTY-TWO

I left Clive Howard's office and headed down to the lobby. When I got there, a guard stopped me and asked for my green "BLDG 2" sticker. I peeled it off and gave it to him. As I suspected, he didn't want my temporary photo ID so when I got into my car, I placed it in my pocket. When I approached the guard booth on my way out, there was a gate barring the exit lane. I stopped and the same guard I saw before stepped out. "Good Afternoon, sir. May I have your temporary ID please?"

I glanced down at my shirt collar, looked at my lap and then back up at the guard. "Gee, I'm sorry; it must have slipped off my collar. I didn't even notice."

The guard frowned at me. "Visitors must safeguard their IDs sir. Failure to do so may lead to you being barred from the A. V. Designs campus in the future."

"I'm very sorry. Next time, I'll be more careful."

"Please do sir," he said and then returned to the booth where he took his time writing something in a book before pressing a button to raise the gate.

When I got home, I went to my office to secure my purloined A. V. Designs photo ID. When I pulled an envelope out of my desk drawer, I noticed the blinking number two on my answering machine display. I put my photo ID in the envelope and then pressed the button to hear the first message.

"Hello, Mr. Fried. This is Amanda Finch from Ms. Eastwood's office. I've completed looking into that matter for you and I'm calling to report my results. Please call me at your convenience." She left me both her office and cell numbers.

The second message was from Ed. "Max. Call me immediately."

If it was so important, I wondered why he didn't call my cell. Then I remembered I turned it off when I met with Clive Howard and forgot about it. I turned it back on and there was a voice mail from Ed with the same urgent message. I called him back and he answered on the first ring.

"Max. Have you heard?"

"Heard what?"

"Someone tried to kill Corky."

"What? How? How is she?"

"She's fine. After I drove her home from the police station she called Amanda to retrieve her car from the EFH lot. Amanda had one of the guards follow her in his pick up so she could get a ride back to the office. After she breezed through a red light without slowing down, the guard realized something was wrong with her brakes. He pulled in front of her, went bumper to bumper and used his truck to stop her car."

"Is she all right?"

"Yeah, shook up, but all right."

"What about Corky's car?"

"Front end damage. The police looked it over and found a perforated brake fluid line and a slice in the seat belt. The guard also said that when Corky's car first made contact with his truck, they were going fast enough that he was surprised the air bag didn't deploy."

"Corky and Horton are the only people alive who have seen the Skipper."

"Yeah, and there was no reason to expect that she wouldn't be driving her own car home at the end of the day."

"...but Torres took her to the police station and saved her life."

"Luckily for Amanda, she had a smart guard with a big truck."

"About an hour before your call, I got a message to call Amanda. Think she can talk?"

"Considering what happened, it may be important. I'd call her back."

I hung up with Ed and looked at the time display on the telephone. Not only was it past business hours, it was dinnertime. Even a dedicated personal assistant like Amanda Finch probably wouldn't be at the office this late – especially after surviving attempted murder. I wondered if I should call her cell phone. Then I decided that if she didn't want to talk, she could simply turn it off. She could, but I didn't think it likely she would. I imagined Corky Eastwood's reaction should she be unable to reach her personal assistant 24 hours a day, seven days a week.

I dialed Amanda Finch's cell phone number. Ahh, perhaps now, I'll be able to put a name to Skipper. When she answered, she didn't sound like someone who almost died in a car. I offered my sympathy for her ordeal. She thanked me and got to the reason for her call. She was all business.

"Mr. Fried. I've researched our personnel and payroll records for 1984 for staff that may have worked on Mr. Eastwood's yacht. I found none, so I searched 1983 and 1985. Again, there were no records of any staff employed on Mr. Eastwood's yacht. I believe these men may have been ah, independent contractors, paid directly by Mr. Eastwood. I am sorry. I know that doesn't help you to identify Skipper."

"Thank you, Ms. Finch. I really appreciate your efforts. I was a little surprised to get your message so soon after I spoke with Corky."

"Why is that?"

"Well, right after I asked Corky for the information, the police took her and I didn't think she was too happy with me."

"The police were a bit of a shock, but that's why Corky is who she is. She says she'll do something, she does it. Besides, she's not annoyed. Since she spoke with you and the police, she's anxious to find Skipper."

"Why's that?"

"She spent part of the summer of 1984 on a sailboat with three men. One is dead. Someone tried to kill another, someone tried to kill her, and the third man, Skipper is missing. She wants to know what's going on. She thinks Skipper may be the clue. I'm sorry I couldn't find anything. We're hoping you can."

She seemed disappointed she could not find out his name. She didn't sound like she was accustomed to failure.

I hung up the phone and thought about this. I also wanted to identify this third man in the photo beyond him being "Skipper" but I really didn't know where to look next. In desperation, I went to my computer and Googled "Captain's license." In return, I found information about the types of captain's licenses, the requirements for getting one and schools where I could study for one. However, I could not find anywhere to look up who had one. Even if I had found a license directory of some sort, I had no information to feed it besides a year and a style of moustache. I doubted any existing database would respond favorably to 1984 and Fu Manchu.

Google searches sometimes provide what I want if I can guess some of the words likely to have appeared in a document that I need. Since there was a connection here involving three locations, I thought I'd see what documents contained the words New Smyrna Beach, Miami and Key West. What I got back was mainly a listing of Beach cams and tourism web sites, nothing useful.

Maybe I could find out more about the Miami incident that Corky mentioned. The first place I looked was at the online edition of the Miami Herald. I really didn't expect them to have anything back as far as 1984 but it didn't hurt to look. My pessimism was unwarranted. Their archives boasted "Miami Herald (archives from 1982 - Current)." The search page even let me specify the year.

Several articles about smuggling appeared, but one caught my eye, so I got out my debit card and paid the $2.95 to see the full article.

1437. Miami Herald - July 11, 1984 - 27A FRONT
POLICE SEEK MAN IN SMUGGLING RELATED DEATH
According to U.S. government sources, State and Federal Law Enforcement Officers have broken a profitable people-smuggling operation based in Miami that was illegally ferrying Cuban refugees to the United States. Authorities arrested seven people who are awaiting trial. Police are still seeking one man wanted in connection with the death of a smuggled Cuban national killed when smugglers and law officers exchanged gunshots during the arrest.

Government sources say the network involved local sailors, Miami Cubans and some key contacts in Cuba who accepted bribes. Rafael Domingo, a deputy director of the Immigration and Naturalization Service (INS) in Miami, confirmed a well-organized group had been operating in the area for the last year and congratulated all of those involved in the arrest. He also expressed his sorrow about the loss of life. In a statement to the press, he said, "We congratulate the brave Law Enforcement Officers who have brought this case to completion and we will continue to track the killer until we bring him to justice."

Corky told me that when the police boarded the Leviathan, they were looking for Skipper in connection with another case. This looked like it could be the other case. Reading the article made me realize I might have a way to identify Skipper but I would have to see her dad's boat first.

I printed out the article and phoned Ed. He was Zorky's lawyer, his friend and he knew boats. I told him about the article and that I wanted to see the Leviathan.

"What for?" He asked.

"A handle on Skipper. We know he's connected with Ray and Horton and Corky but we don't know who or where he is. But, he left his things behind when he ran and the ship went into storage right after he escaped. Maybe he left something we can use to identify him."

"Where's the boat?"

"Corky says it's in an EFH warehouse in New Smyrna Beach."

"Still there, huh? I know where that is. I handled the property acquisition for Zorky. When do you want to do this?"

"How soon can you get here?"

"Let me make a call first... arrange access. Say... about an hour? Oh, and I've got that Police inventory list you wanted of Ray's personal effects."

We disconnected. I took the print out of the Miami Herald article, folded it and put it in the envelope that held my photo ID from A. V. Designs. I was putting the envelope in my pocket when my cell phone rang. I looked at the display. It was Mariel.

"Ahlo", I said, using a goofy accent making the "lo" a ridiculously lower pitch than the "Ah."

She paused and then said "Ahlo," mimicking my greeting, so I guessed she might have calmed down a bit.

"How's your sister?" I figured maybe if I ignored her leaving all upset about the break-in, she might too.

"She's good. Did they catch the bad guys yet?"

Well, I thought, so much for that strategy. "No. Not yet, but I've got a plan."

I imagined her giving me that look; the one long-suffering wives give their husbands when she said. "I'm sure you do, but maybe you should leave this to the professionals. Maybe, you should come and stay here with us for a while."

"We've already discussed this. You know how I feel. Let's not go over it again. Besides, calling the Police is part of my plan."

"It's just that I love you and I worry about you."

"That's the same reason I'm glad you're there and why I'm staying here. We've got to bring this thing to an end as quickly as possible."

"You're glad I'm here?"

I was going to say, "Yes, you were right. It's not safe here." Then I realized doing so would only make her worry about me and upset her more. So, I lied and said, "I mean, I'm glad you're there because, I love you and I know you're more comfortable there."

"Oh. OK, but if you won't come here, be careful. I worry about you."

"And me you."

"Well, Goodbye. I'll tell my sister 'Hello' for you. Te amo."

"Te."

After hanging up the phone, I sat there a moment. Was Mariel right? Should I back off? I didn't see how I could. Sometimes, you just have to see things through and this time was one of them. Rummaging through my desk, I located Detective Torres' business card and gave him a call on his cell. I had lingering business and it was time to handle it.

CHAPTER TWENTY-THREE

"Detective Torres."

"Hello, Detective, this is Max Fried." I said, pausing to allow him to say how glad he was to hear from me. When he didn't, I continued, "Anything new on the break-in at my home?"

"No, Mr. Fried. I told you I'd call you if anything came up. How did you get this number?"

"It's on the card you gave me. I didn't expect you to have anything new, but I did want to tell you about something I found here."

"I've got a new batch of cards. Is my cell number really on them? I gotta pull over and look." He paused. "Damn, I have to be more careful about who I give these."

"There's a surveillance camera mounted in a tree in my yard and it's pointed at my house."

"Really? No kidding? Is it still there?"

"Yeah."

"This I'd like to see. We'll be there in about 20 minutes."

"We'll be waiting for you." I really didn't have anyone waiting with me, but I figured if he could be we, so could I.

About 30 minutes later, an unmarked police cruiser pulled up in front of the house. A city police van with an extension ladder on the roof followed it. Office Torres climbed out of the cruiser and two other men exited the van. When I saw the ladder, I was hoping one of them would be climbing it to take down the camera. I'm not that keen on heights.

"Mr. Fried," called out Detective Torres, as he came up the driveway, "these men are from our Crime Scene Unit. They're going to take a closer look at the camera while you give me some more information." He took his pad and a ballpoint from his shirt pocket.

"Sure, what do you want to know?" I spread my arms and held my hands open wide.

He clicked his ballpoint pen and looked down at his pad, "When did you first notice it?"

"Yesterday afternoon."

Torres held his pen over his pad and without moving his head, looked up at me. "And you're just calling it in now?"

"Yes."

He hung his hands at his sides and looked directly at me. "Do you have to work at annoying me or does it just come naturally to you?"

"Look, Detective Torres, I know you're a busy guy and you've got a difficult job, but like you, I've got a job to do too and yesterday, I was out doing it. I didn't have time to call it in and frankly, until I had a chance to look into something, I wasn't sure I was ready to report it."

He waved his hand around. "You mean this camera may have something to do with a case you're working; a case you can't discuss?"

"I think it may have something to do with Ray Kenwood's murder."

"Then you should have called me right away."

"Next time, I will. I've got your cell number."

He looked up at the sky. "Please, don't remind me."

"This time, I wasn't sure it was connected. If it is, it seemed that I was safer with it here. I figure that if the killer is content with watching me, maybe he won't kill me."

"Then, what changed your mind?"

"This did." I said and handed him the envelope containing my A. V. Designs ID and my print out.

He looked at me with his head tilted to the left.

"You might want to run prints on the ID card."

Torres nodded without any facial expression.

"Look, Detective Torres, it takes a long time to call you "Detective Torres." How about, I call you Leo and you call me Max."

"No."

I opened my mouth to utter a reply but was interrupted when the two guys from the van came around to the front of the house. One was carrying the ladder back to the van. The other was holding a large plastic evidence bag and walking towards Detective Torres. He held up the bag with the camera inside. "Leo, we got the camera. No prints on it. Anyone can buy one on the Internet. Transmits a radio signal to a recording device. Range isn't much, but the recorder could be anywhere. We bagged and tagged it but we're not gonna get anything more from this."

Detective Leo Torres turned to the guy, "Thanks, Bob. After you check it in, can you please leave me a copy of the report on my desk? Thanks."

Bob nodded and went to join his partner in the van.

"Gee." I said, "Bob calls you Leo."

Detective Torres turned and walked to his cruiser. With his back to me, he said "Good day, Mr. Fried," and then both vehicles pulled away.

At least the camera was gone and I didn't have to climb a tree.

CHAPTER TWENTY-FOUR

A little after Torres left, Ed arrived. I got into his car and asked him for the list of Ray's effects. Ed pulled his cigarettes from his shirt pocket and then removed a piece of paper from inside the pack. He looked at the paper and said, "Oh, crap. I left it on my desk. You want to go back and get it?"

"Nah, it'll be the same list in an hour as it is now. I want to check out this boat. Somebody got to Ray's house before we did. I don't want that to happen again. If there is something on the boat, I don't want to be beat to it."

Ed said, "Same here," and put the paper back along with his cigarettes.

We drove to an industrial park on the mainland, near the airport. Ed parked near a group of three identical buildings with the EFH logo on the side.

We got out of the car, walked towards the middle one and Ed said, "Zorky had a great gift for making money. Do you know how little this property cost twenty five years ago and how much it's worth now?"

"No." I said.

"I'm not going to tell you. It would only make you cry."

The door handle had a keypad on it, the kind with numbered pushbuttons in addition to a knob with a keyhole. I guessed you could use either one to unlock the door. Ed pulled his cigarettes out of his shirt pocket again and then fished out what looked like the same piece of paper he had before. He pressed a few numbers on the lock and then opened the door. He had to lean on the door to make it move. We went inside and I noticed a stale, musty smell.

When Ed turned on the lights, I saw the building was one huge room with a wood and metal frame in the middle. The Leviathan sat on the frame and filled the building. It reached to within a few feet of the roof and the bow and stern practically touched the front and rear walls. I had no idea how they ever got the boat inside.

Ed sighed. "Haven't seen this in about twenty years. Just after Zorky died. Guess how they got it inside?"

"No clue."

"Had to take down the back wall, push the boat in and then put the wall back up."

"Must be nice to have money."

"Oh, yeah. C'mon. Let's board."

Ed walked over to a ladder affixed to the boat. The Leviathan may have looked big on the water, but close up, inside a confined space like this, it looked colossal. As we climbed, I saw a thick layer of grime on the steps and other horizontal surfaces. My hands turned black from the dirt on the rungs. So did my pants knees as I brushed against the ladder on the way up. The stillness, the quiet and the dust made me uneasy. I felt like I invaded a tomb. As we disturbed the dust, Ed started to cough and I sneezed.

On board, Ed fumbled around for something. Then I heard a click and the boat lit up. Ed said, "They've got the boat electricity plugged into the warehouse power."

I looked around the Leviathan and realized I had no idea where to start my search. Ed said, "Looks just like it did when Zorky died," opened a door and climbed down some stairs. I followed and we entered a narrow hallway below decks. There were five doors. Yellow tape that read "POLICE LINE – DO NOT CROSS" covered the three on the left.

Ed gestured to the far end, "That door leads to the galley and the head." Then he pointed to the three doors on his left and then the one on his right. "These three are crew quarters. That one is... was Zorky's. Let's see what there is to see."

He approached the first door on his left, sliced the tape with his car key and we went inside. The room was small with a built-in bed and a tiny closet. A monogrammed, olive drab canvas duffel bag sat on the closet floor. I moved closer and read aloud the faded stenciled letters, "RK."

Ed said, "Ray Kenwood." We left the room; shut the door and Ed pulled loose the tape from the next door to the left.

I opened the door and this room looked just like the other one. Some clothes hung in the closet and I found an empty, unmarked duffel bag folded on the shelf next to a toilet kit. I took the kit down and opened it. There was a prescription bottle inside. The label said it was penicillin prescribed for Benjamin Horton. I said, "Ben Horton," shut the door and we started for the last room on the left. When I reached for the door, I saw there were already slits in the tape covering the opening. I turned the knob and we stepped inside.

This third room was identical to the other two in size, shape and style. The only difference was that this room was empty. Ed said, "This would have been Skipper's room."

I asked him, "So, where's his stuff? Corky told me that when the Police came, he escaped and never came back."

Ed shrugged, "Maybe he came back after all?"

I opened the next door and as Ed described, it led to a galley and the ship's bathroom. We looked inside and saw nothing of interest, only cooking utensils and outdated canned goods. We exited back into the hall. Ed took a deep breath and opened the fifth door. "Zorky's suite. It's been a long time since I've been here."

Zorky's quarters were as luxurious as the others were Spartan. They contained a queen size bed, a desk built into the wall and a private head with a toilet, sink and shower. He even had a tiny galley and a small table for dining with a view out a porthole.

Ed sat down at the desk and started opening drawers. When he did, I noticed an old bag style cell phone. I picked it up to look at it. "Wow, I haven't seen one of these things in ages."

Ed pulled a few folders from one drawer, looked up and said, "What? Oh, yeah. Zorky loved gadgets. He was the first person I knew that had a cell phone. It weighed ten pounds, but it still made calls." He looked back down at the files in his hand and said, "This is odd."

"What's odd?"

"Zorky had files here on Ray Kenwood and Ben Horton. Employment applications, passport photocopies, social security tax information. You know, personnel type records, but there's no file here for anybody else. No Skipper."

"That is strange. Unless... wait, Corky told me the Police showed her a photo of Skipper and asked for him by a name she never heard him use. What if he established a new identity and wanted to protect it?"

"What do you mean?"

"How about this? Skipper is on the run so he changes his name and gets some fake ID to match. Zorky hires Skipper, knows his current name, address, even his social security account number. Then Police come to arrest whatever his name was AKA Skipper for murder. Skipper escapes and the only one who knows his current identity is Zorky and the only records are on this boat. Maybe he came back to get them?"

"Well, that could explain the broken tape, the empty cabin and the missing files."

"You have any other explanation?"

"No."

I put Zorky's ancient bag phone back on the desk and when I did, I remembered something I read in Zorky's obituary.

"Ed, how did Zorky die?"

"He had a heart attack. Couldn't get to help in time."

"Did he phone for help?"

"No."

"Why not? He had this cell phone."

"Gee. I don't know."

I took a closer look at the phone and saw a break in the wire that connected the antenna. It looked like someone cut it. Maybe Zorky didn't call because his phone was broken. "Ed, what about radio? Doesn't a boat this size have a two-way marine radio?"

"Sure, up on deck."

We went up the stairs to the cabin or wheelhouse or whatever sailors called the place where the steering takes place. Ed showed me the radio and when I examined it, I found the antenna wire for the radio cut too. I showed Ed the break in the wire and said, "Zorky couldn't call for help. Somebody cut his antenna cables. Neither the cell phone nor the two-way would work. Somebody wanted him dead and they wanted it to look natural."

"Shit. Ray and Zorky both died of heart attacks. Geez, these things are so common, I never thought about it but maybe Kathleen was right. Maybe Ray didn't die of natural causes. Maybe Zorky didn't either."

"We better call Torres."

CHAPTER TWENTY-FIVE

"What? You again? I gotta learn to look at Caller ID first. What is it this time?" For some reason, Torres didn't sound glad to hear from me.

I told him, "I'm in the EFH warehouse that contains Zorky Eastwood's yacht. The boat in that picture Ray Kenwood emailed Ben Horton."

"So?"

"This is the boat Zorky was on when he died. He had a heart attack and couldn't call for help. Someone disabled his radio and cell phone."

"I don't know about this. When did he die?"

"Around 20 years ago."

"Jesus, Fried. You're too much. You call me now about a 20-year-old death that you think might not have been on the up and up? You couldn't tell me this when I saw you what? An hour ago?"

"I didn't know this then. I think it ties in with the break-in at my place and maybe with Horton and Ray Kenwood."

"You think a guy who had a heart attack 20 years ago ties in with a break-in at your home? How long you been living here? One year? Two?"

"I don't know yet how everything comes together, but I do know this. Ray Kenwood is dead and somebody stole his computer from my house. The computer ties to Ben Horton who bought stolen trade secrets from Ray. Someone killed Ray, and tried to kill Horton and Corky. Corky knew Ray, Ben, and Skipper, when they worked for Zorky Eastwood. Zorky died when he couldn't get help because his radio and phone were intentionally disabled. Lastly,

Ray and Ben's cabins and employment records are intact on Zorky's boat but the third crew cabin is empty. There are no records on board for Skipper."

There was silence on the phone. Then Torres said, "I don't know what you've got but if I don't come down there and check it out, my luck, there'll be something to it. I don't need more trouble. I've already got you."

Ed and I went outside the warehouse to wait. I was glad to get the fresh air. Ed seemed glad to have another cigarette. About 15 minutes later, Torres and Fitzpatrick pulled up followed by a van marked "Crime Scene Unit." A man and a woman got out of the van carrying equipment cases. We all went into the warehouse and climbed onto the boat. The two techs unpacked their gear and started to work.

Torres stood there watching them. Fitzpatrick said, "They're going to examine the phone and the radio, check fingerprints and see what else they can find of use."

Torres finally spoke, "Use for what? I don't even know what crime or who we're investigating anymore: Kenwood's murder, Max's burglary, the Kenwood break in, the attempt on Horton's life, Corky's life or vandalism on communications equipment?"

Torres seemed to be more upset with me than usual so I asked him, "What do you mean you don't know what you're investigating? What's really going on here?"

Torres came closer to me so that we were standing toe to toe. He was too close for comfort and I thought it was a good thing I had big feet or our faces would be touching. He leaned his head back, looked into my eyes and said, "I'll tell you what's going on. Everywhere I turn. There you are. Every call I get today, no matter what the crime, there you are."

"Yeah, well, I'm working on a job."

"Is that what you're doing? You're working on a job? I got a fingerprint report on Horton's black leather case... where he kept his epinephrine... the drugs that were out of his reach... so he almost died. You know who touched that case?"

"No, who?"

"You did. Your fingerprints were on Horton's black leather case. The one he needed and didn't have when he ingested peanuts. What do you have to say about that?"

That surprised me. I said, "I've never been to Horton's house, only his office." Then I realized what happened. "I visited him at PC Gadgets when he returned from a trip. I lifted a black leather case off a chair when he invited me to sit."

"A coincidence, huh?"

"Yeah."

"Just like you being at EFH offices an hour or two before someone put a hole in Corky's brake line?"

I didn't like where this was going but he was right. I was there. I said the best comeback I had, "Yeah."

Torres didn't seem to care. He shook his head at me. "Now, you're telling me about sabotaged communications equipment you just found and I'll probably find your fingerprints on that too."

He was right. He would find them there. "At the time I picked up the bag phone, there was no reason to think it might become evidence. Same with Horton's drug case."

"You were also the last one to see Kenwood's computer and the only one alive who saw what was on it."

It seemed that once Torres finished yelling at me, he got free of whatever was bothering him. He calmed down and Fitzpatrick watched his partner in silence for a few moments and then said quietly to Ed, and me "You guys can go now. We find anything, I'll let you know." It didn't seem like a good idea to stick around, so we left.

CHAPTER TWENTY-SIX

In the car, Ed asked me, "What was that all about?"

"Dunno, but he doesn't seem too happy with me."

"Because you keep finding more work for him without him getting a chance to make anything of what you find?"

"Maybe. I get the idea Torres likes to lead his own investigations but lately, I've been finding things that have been keeping him busy. I don't think he likes that. Do you think he really suspects me?"

"Nah, but if he does, I know a great lawyer. Me."

I didn't return Ed's grin. He stopped smiling and asked, "Now what?"

"Geez, I don't know."

"Did you eat yet?"

"No. Why?"

"I didn't get a chance to give you that personal effects list you wanted and I'm hungry. I'm thinking of going out for a late dinner and I hate eating out alone. Want to join me?"

"Sure. Where you want to go?"

"How about that place on Third Ave? The one with the outdoor seating?"

"You mean The Garlic?"

"Yeah, that's the place. I think they serve until 10."

"Sure, but I'm filthy from all of that dust and dirt on the boat. Let me change first."

"I'll drop you home, get the list, clean up myself a bit and meet you there."

Ed pulled up at my house and I said, "OK. Give me about 30

minutes. I'll be walking over."

Of all of the restaurants, which are not located on the beach, The Garlic restaurant is one of my favorites. I love their outdoor dining area and their eggplant parmigiana. In addition, they have a nice wine list and I really wanted some wine. Enough wine that I would be better off walking instead of driving.

The restaurant is a classy one, so I washed up, changed into a pair of tan cargo pants, put on a black golf shirt and black loafers. If I were going to eat Italian food with red sauce and pasta, a black shirt was the way to go. I was tired of people being able to tell what I ate just by looking at my clothes.

I locked up the house, walked north up Saxon Drive to Third Avenue and thirty minutes later, I saw Ed in the parking lot. He was leaning against his car, facing the lot entrance and smoking a cigarette. When he saw me, he waved, threw down his cigarette and then stomped it out with his shoe. He was just looking back up from the ground as I approached.

"Hey, Max. It's good we could do this. You need a break. I hate to cook and I hate to eat out alone. Especially in a nice place like this." He put his left hand on the back of my neck, and stretched out his right arm in the direction of the restaurant entrance. "After you, my friend."

We stopped at the restaurant entrance to allow folks to pass on their way out. They exited through what appeared to be an indoor hallway lined with wooden beams, benches and plants. On closer examination, the illusion breaks down revealing bushes and trees. You realize the hall is outdoors.

At the left end of the apparent hallway is Il Forno, Italian for the Oven or the Furnace. In this case, Il Forno is a wood-fired outdoor oven that reaches temperatures of over 900 degrees. It offers limited seating in front as one might find at a small bar. To the left of Il Forno is the entrance to the hostess station and the indoor portion of the restaurant. This is where the bar and the musician's bandstand are located. To the right is the landscaped and heavily treed dining courtyard. One side of the indoor restaurant was open to the air with no outside walls. This opening led to the courtyard too.

Ed walked up to the hostess station and an attractive, dark haired woman in her late fifties smiled up at him. "Are you ready now, sir?"

"Yes, please."

She picked up two menus and started walking. Due to the late hour, most of the tables were empty. When we entered the courtyard, she stopped and asked, "Any preference?"

Ed pointed to a table. "Over there is just fine, thank you."

The hostess placed the menus on the table and turned to Ed, "Enjoy your meal."

"Thank you, Darling." He placed a hand on her shoulder and smiled.

She smiled back and left us. Ed watched her walk for a moment, then pulled out a chair and sat down. While we were still standing, I took in the décor. I had only been here a few times and I still liked to admire the layout. We sat outside, next to a cypress tree, under a heater built into the eaves of the main building. A string of white lights circled its way up the tree. To our right was an outdoor fireplace tall enough for a man to stand in. A large wood fire burned brightly inside. I could hear the sound of a jazz saxophone playing from inside the restaurant.

Mariel and I came here for our wedding anniversary dinner last month. It felt strange being here with Ed instead of her. He was thumbing through the wine list and humming along with the music. I was lost in thought when I realized he stopped thumbing and humming. He looked up at me over the top of the list. "You can't let it get to you."

I nodded and picked up a menu.

"If you don't relax when you eat, you can get indigestion and all sorts of ailments. It's not worth it. Besides, things'll look up. She'll be back as soon as we clear this thing up."

He was right. I'd been through worse and getting upset wasn't going to make things better. "You're right. I'm sorry. What looks good on the wine list?"

"Red or white?"

"Red. Dry red."

He looked back down at the wine list and nodded approvingly. "They have many fine reds here."

"Unless you want something in particular, the house Montepulciano d'Abruzzo is pretty good."

"You've had it?"

"Yep."

A waiter wearing a black shirt, black pants and a long black apron came over to take our order. I didn't see a spot of red sauce anywhere on his clothing. I felt reaffirmed in my shirt choice. Ed ordered a full carafe of the house red wine and the Char-Grilled Filet Mignon with a creamy porcini mushroom sauce, caramelized onions and roasted garlic. Just in case there wasn't enough garlic in Ed's steak, it came with garlic mashed potatoes and a roasted garlic appetizer. I ordered the Eggplant Parm as planned.

After the waiter left, I asked Ed, "You got the list?"

"Yeah, they faxed it to me." He fumbled in his shirt pocket, pulled out his cigarettes and then a folded piece of paper. He handed me the paper and I unfolded it. It was a personal property inventory list from the police. It detailed each of the items Ray Kenwood was carrying when he died.

The list contained the stuff you would expect; the contents of Ray's wallet, pocket change, a wedding band, eyeglasses, Maalox tablets, cigarettes, a monogrammed lighter, a monogrammed handkerchief (both bearing the letters "RK"), a business card holder containing Ray's business cards and something odd; an eyeglass mount bicyclist's mirror.

I never met Ray, but Ed knew him pretty well, so I asked him. "Did Ray ride a bicycle?"

"No. Why?"

"Ed, where are these things now? Especially this bicyclist's mirror?"

"What's a bicyclist's mirror?"

"It's a small mirror mounted on a short, thin, stalk that clips onto a bicyclist's eyeglasses or his helmet. Because the mirror is so close to the bicyclist's eye, it can be small and still provide a view of what's behind the bike. It's odd Ray would have one in his pockets when he died."

"Yeah, I guess so. Except for the notebook computer, everything else is still with the police."

The waiter came back with two wine glasses and a colorful ceramic pitcher shaped like a chicken. He picked up the pitcher and poured wine out of the chicken's mouth. In one way, it was a cute image, but in another, it was too reminiscent of a few times I had overindulged.

After he poured the wine, the waiter produced a wood cutting board covered with a warm baguette and a huge clove of roasted garlic. This was a house specialty. He used a fork to mash the garlic and then drenched it with olive oil and balsamic vinegar. He said, "Enjoy, Gentlemen," and left the table.

Ed picked up his glass, raised it towards me and said, "May the road rise to meet you and may the wind at your back never be your own."

I laughed, raised my glass and drank.

"There, Max. That's better. I think that's the first time you've laughed since Mariel left."

"Probably."

"Mmm. I like this wine. Good choice." Ed put down his glass, broke off a piece of bread, dipped it into the mashed garlic and put it in his mouth. "Mmm."

"Thanks, Mariel and I usually order it when we come here. Ed, I'm wondering. Can you get me this bike mirror?"

"Boy, you don't stop for nothing, do you? Sure, I guess I can get it. I don't think the police are going to like me picking up things one at a time, but I guess I can pick up the rest of the stuff all at once."

"Thanks, I think this mirror may be important. If I'm right, someone may want to steal it too, so you've got to be careful. Now, it's safe with the police, but once you pick it up, someone may come after it and after you."

"You think there's a risk?"

"Not yet. We haven't discussed it anywhere we could be overheard. I think we can get our hands on it without the thieves knowing about it. Can you bring it right to me, directly from the police?"

Just after I finished speaking, the waiter returned, placed two salads on the table and said, "Gentlemen, your dinners will be out shortly." After the waiter disappeared into the restaurant, Ed shrugged. "Sure. I'll pick it up tomorrow morning. I'll call you when I've got it. Now, relax and enjoy your dinner."

"Yeah. I guess I've been a bit tense lately. I don't like the way this thing has made Mariel feel like she can't come home. I'm also not keen on the idea people have been watching me."

"You need to compartmentalize. Like when I was going through my last divorce, I was working some big cases, dealing with the break up and looking for a new place to live all at once. I had to deal with each one separately and not let my feelings about one interfere with another. On the other hand, I had experience that helped me." He paused a moment, then laughed, "My previous divorces."

I shook my head in disbelief, "How many?"

"Between the starter wife and the trophy wife? Hmm, let's just say more than one. I wouldn't want anyone to think I was hard to live with or fickle." A big smile formed on his face as he sat back in his chair.

"Ed, I don't want to pry, but if you feel like talking about it, how's it going with Sheila?"

"Did I tell you we met at my first job after law school? She had been there about a year before me, took me under her wing and under a few other body parts. We got married, had Brenda, got divorced and so on. That was before I went to work for EFH. Sheila stayed on at the firm when I left. After a couple of years with Zorky, I went out on my own, set up a practice in Manhattan. I still handled his affairs, but as outside counsel. That way I was able to leverage my accomplishments with him to obtain and service additional accounts."

Ed stopped to light another cigarette and I remembered how he tends to ramble when he's drinking.

"Outsourcing his legal work also cut down on Zorky's overhead, so it was good for everyone. Matter of fact, it was so good that after a few years, I left the New York office with one of my partners, moved down here and opened up a Florida branch. I made some friends here, bought a house where I could dock my boat and decided to stay. We spoke occasionally, but I hadn't seen Sheila in years. She's held up well though. Too bad she's not going to be moving in."

"Oh, I'm sorry to hear..." I said.

"Oh, I'll admit that for a while, it was nice to relive the time when Brenda was small and we were a family, but it's not for us. We've got a good divorce now. I wouldn't want to spoil it. You see, the reason Sheila and I hit it off in the first place was because we're so much alike. We're both aggressive in protecting our clients, clever in the law but unfortunately we both have roving eyes." Ed paused, lowered his head and without moving it, looked up at me, "and I'm not speaking ophthalmologically here. We both live for the chase."

"So she's looking for another place?"

"Yeah, it was mutual... again."

After what I heard in the bar at Stevie's Sky Lounge, I wasn't too sure about the "mutual" part, but Ed seemed to be taking the break up in stride. "What about Brenda?"

"She came down here to go to school, liked it here and stayed. That's part of the reason I decided not to go back north. Now, she's working on her graduate degree, got another year to go. Luckily, she got her mother's looks and her mother's brains. Can you imagine if she got my looks instead?"

We talked some more about Ed's family, varied legal career and his love of boating. Perhaps I should say, Ed talked while I listened and nodded. I was just as happy to sit there without the need to manufacture small talk of my own. After a while, our food arrived. My eggplant was delicious, the wine was making me feel relaxed and I was enjoying myself for the first time in a day or so. Ed seemed to be enjoying his steak. He was too busy eating to talk anymore.

We pretty much ate in silence and then stuffed and sated, sat back in our seats. The waiter brought us coffee and Ed surprised me by passing up dessert, mumbling something about keeping his figure for the ladies. When the waiter brought the check, Ed grabbed it. "Business dinner. Billable expense." It seemed either he used his allotment of words for the day or the food and wine had slowed him down.

We finished our coffee and headed out to the parking lot. I walked Ed to his car and he said, "Get in. I'll give you a lift home."

"No, thanks. I'm going to walk. Thanks for dinner."

"Thank Ray's estate. I'll call you when I've got the thing we discussed."

We shook hands and I headed home. I was still full and the walk would feel good.

CHAPTER TWENTY-SEVEN

I left the Garlic and started walking home south on Saxon Drive, a dark street bordered on the east by houses and on the west by a sidewalk and then woods. In the woods, a walking trail ran north and south and offered glimpses of the Indian River. The sidewalk was typically empty this time of night, but Mariel and I walked here many times after dark and I always felt safe, until now.

The speed limit on Saxon is only 35 miles, but the car behind me was traveling much slower than that. I became anxious when it pulled off the road and started driving behind me on the sidewalk. When I looked back at it, the headlights blinded me. I was trying to decide which way to run, when the car pulled up alongside me. The passenger side window rolled down. I knew it was fruitless to ignore the car, but I didn't want to look in that window. A man called out. "Stop." I kept walking, staring straight ahead, getting ready to run.

"Mr. Fried. Stop. Detective Torres wants to see you."

I stopped and looked into the police car that had been following me. The young cop who woke me the other night was driving.

"How did you find me?"

"I was driving to your house to pick you up when I saw you walking. Get in."

I opened the door. "Can't you people ever call first?"

The cop turned the car around and smiled. "Good idea. Why don't you suggest it to the Detective?"

"Very funny, kid. Where are we going? No, wait. You can't tell me. I have to wait for the Detective."

"You catch on quick, Mr. Fried. Maybe you should become a

detective."

We drove in silence for a few minutes. It was too dark for me to be able to read the street signs or pick out familiar landmarks, so I didn't know where we were. The cop stopped the car in front of a large riverfront home on the mainland. Parked police cars and an ambulance presented obstacles to entering. My escort led me through the maze of vehicles into the house.

Two men, wheeling a body bag on a gurney, edged past me on their way out the door. Detective Torres stood in the large foyer, watching the men. When he saw me, he nodded toward the interior rooms. The young cop left and I followed Torres into the house. He stopped in what appeared to be a high tech TV room. I think people would call this one a "Media Room." The TV screen practically covered one wall. Shelled peanuts littered the floor, clustered around a leather lounge chair.

"Who lives here?" I asked.

Torres jotted something down on his pad, "You mean, 'Who lived here?'"

"Who?"

"Horton."

"Ben Horton?"

Torres nodded, tightened his lips then said, "Yeah." He put his pad and pen away.

"I thought he was in jail."

"Out on bond."

"How did you find out he was dead?"

"His lawyer phoned it in. Horton didn't answer his calls. Guess he wanted to cover his ass about not being prepared for tomorrow's hearing."

"Any witnesses?"

"One. A neighbor noticed someone arriving. A tall, slim, older white male. What are you? Six feet? 190?"

"Six feet, three inches, 180 pounds." I didn't like the direction Torres was headed. "What happened to Horton?"

"Murder. Plain and simple. Maybe not so simple. Anaphylactic shock."

"Again? Horton just recovered from that."

"Somebody didn't appreciate his speedy recovery, so they came back and dosed him again. This time, they tied him up first in that lounger. Then they force-fed him until his throat closed. I think they also sat here watching him choke until he died." Torres pointed to another chair placed so it faced the lounger. "They wanted to make sure this time."

The image of the killer sitting and watching Ben Horton suffer until he died made me feel sick. It took a moment or so before I could speak again. When I could, I said, "This means two of the three men in those boat photos are dead. Ray Kenwood and now Ben Horton."

"What do you know about the third man?"

"Just what I told you. No one knows his name. Everybody called him, 'Skipper'. He was a boat captain. He worked for Zorky along with Ray Kenwood and Ben Horton. His belongings and personnel file are missing from the Leviathan. Law enforcement wanted him for something but he escaped. It might have something to do with that article I gave you. I haven't been able to find him."

Torres wrote something in his pad. "He may be in danger too."

"Either that or he may be the killer. Did you track down the case in the article?"

"Fitzpatrick made some calls but that article doesn't mention the kinds of things we need to identify the case. The only name mentioned is the head of INS. All the article says is that the State and Feds, including INS worked together in Miami to bust a smuggling ring. It was reported in July 1984 but we don't know when the bust took place or by whom. It's going to take a while to track it down."

"What about the fingerprints on my visitor's ID from A. V. Designs?"

"We checked them against the ones on Howard's fingerprint card from his security officer license. No matches."

"You mean Howard isn't who he claims to be?"

"No, I mean that the prints that you gave us don't match Howard's. Maybe he didn't touch it like you say he did."

"The guard at the gate made that ID while I waited. There should only be prints from three people on it, the guy at the gate, me and Clive Howard."

"Could be that somebody else handled the card laminate first. Could be Howard only touched the edges. Could be lots of things. Without proof that he actually left prints on that ID, I can't use it. Your say so isn't enough."

"Will you let me know if you find the case in the article?"

Torres ignored my question and asked me, "Do you know what these men had in common besides the boat photo?"

"No, what?"

"You."

"Me?"

Torres pulled out his pad again. "Where were you tonight?"

"You mean when I wasn't with you?"

"Yeah."

"I can't believe this. You think...Geez, Torres. I was at dinner with Ed McCarthy at the Garlic."

"Convenient. You two dine together often?"

"No. This was the first time. Why?"

"Who's idea was it? This dinner."

"Ed's. What? You think Ed and I hired someone to feed Horton peanuts until he died and we went to dinner in public for an alibi?"

Torres took a step closer to me and said, "I think, you and me." He put his pad in his pocket. "We need to talk. Come with me." He took my arm, led me out the door and into the kitchen. He sat down at the kitchen table.

"Sit."

"What's this all about?"

Torres sat there for a moment without saying anything. Then he said, "A man matching your description was seen here tonight."

"So?"

"There were no signs of forced entry. Horton knew his killer. Horton knew you."

I didn't see any point to responding so I sat there waiting for him to finish.

"The killer knew peanuts could kill Horton. You knew peanuts could kill Horton. You and Horton had a conflict. You accused him of theft. The killer took Horton's restraints with him when he left. You have a forensic background. Plus, your fingerprints are on Horton's drug case and Zorky's sabotaged phone. You were near Corky's car before the brake line was perforated. Lastly, you've been finding things that nobody else has found and you're running me in different directions all over town, like you're trying to divert my attention."

"So you do think that I killed Horton? Man, are you kidding? That's ridiculous. I can't believe that you would even think that."

He gave me his "Cop" look and said, "Stay close in case I need you."

I took it to mean, "Stay close in case I decide to pin this on you."

The kid cop appeared to drive me home. I got in the car and as we left Horton's house, I realized that he lived in the same neighborhood as Ray Kenwood. They probably used the same grocery store or marine supply shop. I was willing to bet that's how they found each other again.

CHAPTER TWENTY-EIGHT

Last night, I had no reason to set an alarm for this morning, so I got up when I felt like it. I found waking up when I wanted instead of when I had to much more agreeable. If not for two, possibly three murders if you counted Zorky, one attempt on Corky's life, Torres' accusations, the break-ins, thefts, Mariel's departure, getting knocked to the ground and the proliferation of surveillance, I'd have been in a good mood. Unfortunately, due to these things, I was not. I wanted this thing put to rest.

I sat up in bed and put on my glasses. The blank display on the cable TV box made me wonder if there had been a power outage. I looked at the clock radio in time to see 8:00 am change to 8:01 so there had to be another reason the box wasn't on. It took a moment before I remembered yesterday's bug sweep. I had forgotten to plug the box back in. Then I realized it had really been the day before yesterday that I found the camera and searched for bugs. I hadn't even had time to watch the bedroom TV for two days. Mariel had been away even longer. This thing was taking too long. It had to end soon. I got out of bed with a renewed sense of purpose, plugged in the cable box and went into the shower.

Clean and dry, I dressed and went to the kitchen for breakfast. I wasn't feeling like cooking, so I poured some cereal and skim milk in a bowl, some orange juice in a glass and some coffee in a cup. Following up the cereal with a banana, I sat in the U shaped breakfast nook that lined the walls under the kitchen windows. Finishing my coffee, I looked around the nook. It provided seating for eight but I was sitting all alone. I looked out the window. Even the street was empty.

Mariel had always wanted a restaurant style booth like this in her kitchen. When we were dating, my aunt had one. Whenever Mariel and I visited her and sat in it, Mariel loved everyone to "Squish in." In each new home we had, we planned to get one but never did until we retired and moved here. Sitting here now, by myself, just made me miss her more.

A ringing phone interrupted my thoughts. It was Ed. I recognized the incoming number as his cell phone. That was good as long as he wasn't using it while in his office. We still hadn't removed the bug.

"Hi, Ed. Where are you?"

"I'm sitting here enjoying a cup of coffee and watching the sailboats from the deck at our favorite bar."

"Sounds nice. What's up?"

"I've got the thing you wanted to see. I'll bring it by when I come over to pick you up."

It took me a minute to realize he must have been talking about the bike mirror I asked for last night. "Pick me up?"

"Yes, this morning, I got a call from an investigator at the Medical Examiner's Office. She wanted Kathleen to come in and answer some questions about Ray. I told her she was unavailable grieving with family out of state. The investigator said she was sympathetic but she didn't seem too happy, so I told her I'd be willing to come in and talk instead. She seemed even less pleased about that, but I guess there's something that she needs to know because she agreed. I want you to come with me."

"What do you want me to do?"

"Just look and listen. If I learn something useful from talking to them, I don't trust myself to be able to repeat it for you."

"Sure, when?"

"Now. I'll pick you up in ten minutes."

I rushed to clean up from breakfast so I'd have enough time to brush my teeth before Ed arrived. I hated going through the day with coffee breath. I was almost done and I was wiping my hands and face when my doorbell rang. I had timed it just right.

I opened the door and Ed stood there with his briefcase in one hand and a big, misshapen manila envelope in the other. We went inside to my office and Ed handed me the envelope. I cleared a spot on my desk and poured out the contents. The "bike mirror" tumbled out. We stared at it for a moment, and I realized for the first time how much misery it caused. I used a latex glove from my gear bag to pick it up.

This device was not what it appeared to be. In the spot where the mirror would go, there wasn't one. Instead, there was a shiny, glasslike surface. On the left side of the frame was a button. On the bottom was a small hole like the ones you see in laptop computers for built-in microphones. In addition, the back had a rectangle of grooves. They seemed to delineate a cover, like one that might hide a battery or other access compartment.

I pressed the button on the side of the frame and nothing happened. I pressed it again but this time, I held it in for a few moments. The glasslike surface flashed and I realized I was watching was some kind of miniature video display screen. I had never seen one so small. After a few letters and numbers flashed on and off the screen, so did the A.V. Design logo. Then I saw something familiar. It was a Bluetooth set up menu. I had one just like it on my cell phone. The display listed voice activated options for pairing with other Bluetooth equipment. A computerized voice said, "Ready to pair devices. Please select from the menu by saying the item number."

People could clip this thing to their eyeglasses, control their computers by speaking to them and they could see the computer display on the miniature screen. Wireless computers could be shrunk to wallet size and left in a user's coat pocket or briefcase. I think we found what Ray was dropping off. I think we found what he had stolen.

It looked like the only thing I could accomplish so far was to get Ray deeper into trouble. I looked at Ed looking at the device.

"What is it?" he asked.

"It looks like a bike mirror, but it's not. It's a miniaturized replacement for a computer screen and keyboard. Beyond state of the art, nothing like this on the market. I'm guessing this is a prototype, Ray stole it and died delivering it to PC Gadgets. I'm sorry, Ed, everything I find makes your client look worse."

Ed didn't seem as upset as I thought he would be. "I don't think it'll be a problem." He looked at his watch. "We've got to leave now for the M. E.'s office, but I'm going to talk to the D. A. again. He backed off Ray when we gave him Horton. I couldn't see him trying to convict a corpse then and I can't see him trying it now. As long as he has Horton, we should be OK. This mirror thing is just another part of that case."

"Oh, Ed?"

"Yeah?"

"Horton's dead."

"What? When? What happened?"

"Someone tied him up and force fed him peanuts. Then they sat and waited for him to die. Torres picked me up last night to talk about it."

"Torres picked you up? Is he going to charge you?"

"No, I don't think so, or I wouldn't be here now."

"If he wants to question you, call me. I've done many criminal cases in my time. You shouldn't answer any questions without an attorney."

"OK, thanks."

"Besides, maybe I can earn some of my money back." Ed was quiet for a moment and then said "I don't know how Horton's death's going to affect our deal. It might not. On the other hand, if the D. A.'s having second thoughts, maybe I can strengthen the deal if we've got something new to offer him. This mirror should do that. We'd better go now."

I handed him back the envelope minus the bike mirror and he put it in his briefcase. I got out my own briefcase and placed the bike mirror inside. "OK. I'm ready."

Ed turned to leave. I locked the house and followed him outside.

When we got to the driveway, Ed opened the door to his Mercedes and said. "Get in. I'll drive."

I got into the car and asked. "Where're we going?"

"The M.E.s office. I thought you knew that."

"No, I know that. I mean where is it?"

"Oh, I'm sorry. It's in Daytona Beach. You know the boulevard on which the International Speedway is located?"

"You mean International Speedway Boulevard?"

"Yes. That's it. Well after we get off I95, instead of driving east towards the Speedway and the beach, we drive west to the Medical Examiners' Office. It should be about a 35 minute drive."

We drove mostly in silence. I don't know what was on Ed's mind but he seemed content to stare out the window and drive. Me, I was thinking of how tired I was getting of this nonsense. I took a simple job and now my wife can't even come home. Thirty-five minutes later, Ed and I were standing at a grey metal reception desk in the building lobby. Ed looked down at the young woman sitting behind the desk. "Hi, I'm Ed McCarthy. I have an appointment with Linda Davis."

She looked at him for a moment or two as if she were trying to decide if she should believe him. Then she looked down at some papers on her desk in front of her. "You're meeting whom?"

"Linda Davis. She's a Forensic Investigator with the M.E.'s office."

She quickly looked back up him. "I know who she is, sir. Please have a seat." She glared at us and then at a single row of uncomfortable looking chairs lined up along the wall facing her. Ed and I quietly accepted our exile to the island of chairs. I felt like I was in school or more accurately, as if I were waiting in the Principal's office. While I was wondering if the receptionist's apparent displeasure with Ed was going to prolong our wait, a woman appeared.

I guessed she was about thirty-five and five feet seven. She was slim, had light brown shoulder length hair, and wore a light grey, two-piece suit. The skirt was just at knee level and fit so she would have no difficulty bending in it. The jacket was unbuttoned, revealing a white blouse. The blouse fit her loosely and covered her up to her throat. She carried a briefcase and asked the chairs, "Mr. McCarthy?"

Ed and I stood. The woman approached and reached out her hand. "Hi, I'm Linda Davis, an investigator with the M.E.'s office. Thank you for coming."

Ed shook her hand, nodded in my direction and said, "This is Max Fried. He's an investigator with me."

She raised an eyebrow, shook my hand too and said, "Oh, really. What type of investigator?"

"Private. I'm consulting with Mr. McCarthy regarding the estate." I thought about showing her my ID but I figured she probably wouldn't be impressed either.

"Do you have some type of ID?"

"Uh, yeah." I pulled out my state issued private investigator's license and handed it to her.

"Very interesting, I think if I ever got tired of working here, I might go private. How do you like it?"

"I'd rather be on the beach."

"Yes, me too" she smiled, "This way please."

We followed her past the reception desk down one short hall and then left to a longer one. We passed a different office door about every ten feet. When we got to the last door on the left, Investigator Davis held it open for Ed and me to enter. The room was windowless, small and had a capacity of no more than five or six people.

A heavy grey metal desk dominated the center of the room. Ed and I sat on one side, facing the door. Investigator Davis sat opposite us. Her back to the door and the desk between us, she put her briefcase on the floor beside her.

I admired the layout. If an interview became contentious, the interviewer had a fast and easy escape route. The desktop was clear of any staplers, telephones or other heavy objects. This positioning told me they were more concerned about threats from inside the room than from outside.

She bent down and pulled a voice recorder from her briefcase. "Our procedure requires recording interviews for the official record. Just give me a minute to verify this thing is working."

I saw Ed frown as she pressed a button and said "Testing, testing." She pressed another button and then another and then we heard "Testing, testing."

"OK, let's begin," she said pressing a button on the recorder and placing it on the table in front of Ed.

"This is Investigator Linda Davis from the Volusia County Medical Examiner's office. Today is Thursday, December 18, 2008 and it's 9:15 am. With me is Mr. Edward McCarthy, attorney for the deceased Ray Kenwood and Mr. Breed, a private investigator working for Mr. McCarthy. Mr. McCarthy. Please state your name for the record."

"I'm Edward McCarthy, attorney for the deceased, Ray Kenwood."

"Mr. McCarthy," she began, "the M. E.'s office has some questions about Mr. Kenwood's habits. We were hoping to speak with Mrs. Kenwood about them, but you tell us she's unavailable. Is that correct?"

Ed put his right hand on the table in front of him, leaned back, tilted his head, looked Linda Davis in the eye and asked, "Correct that you have some questions? Correct that you were hoping to speak with Mrs. Kenwood? Correct that she's unavailable or correct that I told you she was unavailable?"

Apparently flustered, she held up her hands, "I'm sorry. I've only had one cup of coffee today. Let's try again. Where is Mrs. Kenwood today?"

Ed relaxed his posture and leaned forward towards the recorder. "She is out of state with relatives grieving her husband's death."

"Did you personally know Ray Kenwood?"

"Yes."

While Ed was speaking, Davis was making notes on a yellow pad on the desk in front of her. "Please describe your relationship." She looked up from her pad.

"I am, I mean I was his attorney."

"Did you two have a relationship outside of the attorney client relationship?" She went back to writing on her pad.

"We were also friends. We used to get together on one of our boats and fish."

When Ed mentioned boating, Davis stopped writing and looked up. I thought I saw a glimmer of a reaction in her face.

She leaned forward on her forearms, clasping both hands and placing them on the desk in front of her. "Did you know of any medications the deceased may have used on a regular basis?"

"Rolaids. That's about it."

"How often did you go boating together?" I got the impression her questions were laying a foundation and building towards something.

Ed frowned for a second and opened his fingers. I took this as an indication he was approximating his answer. "During the warmer months, every few weeks. When it was cooler, maybe once a month if the weather was good."

"When do you last go?"

"About a month and a half. We had a good day in late October."

"Did you ever know him to take sea sickness medication?" Something, maybe it was her tone of voice, told me she had finished building.

"No, why?"

"I'm sorry, Mr. McCarthy. The purpose of this interview is for the M. E. to obtain information that may help to make a finding. I can't answer questions."

"Then this interview is over." He started to get up.

"No, wait, please. I'm pausing the record now to discuss procedural matters with Mr. McCarthy." She pressed a button on the recorder. Ed sat back down.

"What's going on here?" he asked, "What's with the question about sea sickness medicine?"

"Well, Mr. McCarthy. Please understand all we want to do here is to be accurate in determining the cause of death. That means if something stands out as odd, we need to be able to explain it."

"So, what's that got to do with sea sickness?"

"After additional test results came back this morning, we found evidence of elevated scopolamine levels in the deceased's system. One explanation could be he used a seasickness medication. Scopolamine is a common ingredient."

With his hands gripping the arms of his chair and his elbows raised in the air, Ed sat there looking as if he were deciding between standing up again or remaining seated. He sat there silently for a moment looking down at the floor. Then he released his grip on the chair arms, put his elbows down, and nodded. "OK, you can start the tape again."

She pressed a button. "Back on the record. During the break, I provided a procedural explanation to Mr. McCarthy. Mr. McCarthy, is that accurate?

"Yes"

"Did you ever know him to take sea sickness medication?"

"No."

Davis sat there for a moment, put down her pen and reached for the recorder. "OK Mr. McCarthy. Thank you for your time. The record is closed." She turned off the recorder and placed it in her briefcase. "OK, that's it." She rose from her chair, opened the door and stepped into the hall. "This way, please."

Ed remained seated. "Just a minute. I answered your question. Now, I want you to answer mine. I represent the estate of the deceased and you can tell me now what's going on or you can wait until I get a subpoena."

"What do you want to know?"

"You said Ray had high levels of scopasomething. How high?"

"Scopolamine. High enough to kill him."

"My God."

"We needed to know if he was self-medicating. If so, there was a chance he took too much by accident... or on purpose."

Ed sat there quietly as if hearing this was more than he could bear. After a while, I touched his shoulder and said, "C'mon, Ed. Let's go."

As Ms. Davis escorted us down the hall to the door, Ed asked, "Any idea when the final report will be issued?"

"As soon as we have enough information. Do we have your address in the file?"

"I believe so, but just in case..." Ed handed her one of his business cards. She gave him one of hers.

"We'll be in touch when we have something to say." She shook our hands, "Thank you for coming in."

Ed and I walked silently to his car. Once we got inside, he turned to me and asked, "Scopawhat?"

"Scopolamine. Looks like they found a lot more of it than they should have. I don't know what it is either, but I'm going to find out. Drop me at my place and how about we meet later for lunch at Bobbi and Jack's."

"OK."

"You know, Ed. I didn't realize you and Ray were that close."

"What do you mean?"

"Well, Ray was apparently into some shady dealings. He had

unknown sources of income, a criminal record and he was stealing from his employer. I mean, you went boating together on a regular basis. You knew what kind of medications he did and didn't take. Do you mean to tell me you didn't know what was really going on with him?"

"I don't like the sound of that. I thought Ray and his wife had family money. I didn't handle his taxes or his finances. I met him when he wanted a will. We both boat and fish and whatever else he was, he could tell a good joke and he knew how to sail. Look, if I knew something was wrong here, I certainly wouldn't have brought in a private investigator. Especially one as nosy and suspicious as you."

What Ed said made sense to me. "Then I'll take that comment about being nosy as a compliment."

"You do that." He stared straight ahead and drove on in silence.

CHAPTER TWENTY-NINE

Ed dropped me off at home and I went inside to research Scopolamine. I started with a Google search and found websites that detailed the drug's uses, sources and effects. I followed up on a few of the references until it was time for lunch. Then I changed into my bathing suit and walked up the beach in the surf to Bobbi and Jack's.

Mariel and I first saw Bobbi and Jack's Patio Bar when we came here on vacation in 2004. The City had closed and condemned the place due to hurricane damage. When we moved down here a few months ago, we were glad to see it rebuilt.

Their concrete and brick patio lies on the sand, separating the bar from the ocean. Heavy, unpainted, weathered and wooden Adirondack chairs surround low round, concrete tables built into the patio. The tables are just the right height for putting your feet up. Just be careful not to knock over your drink. This patio replaced the wooden one washed away by the hurricanes. Next time, Jack isn't giving up the patio without a fight.

Ed sat at one of those tables with a glass in front of him and his phone at his ear. He must have calmed down a bit because when he saw me walk up the steps from the beach, he closed his phone and waved me over.

I stood by his table. "You order food yet?" I asked. My stomach was starting to growl.

He looked up at me. "No, not yet. You want to split a pizza?"

"Sure. Mushrooms?"

"Sounds good."

"I'll get it, you want anything else?"

"No, I'm good, thanks"

I left Ed and walked over to the bar to order the pizza. Bobbi and Jack's had bar service but table service on the patio was on your own.

When I got to the bar, there was an AmberBock draft waiting for me with Jack standing behind it. "That's the trouble with this place," I told him, "the service is too damn slow." I ordered the pizza, picked up my beer and went back to Ed's table.

"Max, I spoke with my new best friend in the D. A.'s office. A. D. A. Stronberg is disappointed he missed the chance to convict Horton but he doesn't care about Ray or his estate. He's more interested in whoever killed Ray and Horton. He'd also like to find whoever fiddled with Corky's brakes. She supported the D. A. in the last election. I told him we found some stolen property that might relate to the case. I wouldn't say what. He agreed to stand by our earlier agreement not to go after Ray's estate if we continue to cooperate and produce this new evidence."

"I guess that's good news. At least, I didn't cause any problems for your client. I'm glad."

"Me too. On the other hand, Stronberg's convinced the two murders, the attempt on Corky and the stolen property, means there's more to it than he has now. He knows Ray and Horton stole trade secrets, but now that they're both dead he's confident a third party was involved in the theft. He thinks the third guy in the thefts killed Ray and Horton, and is the same person who did the break-ins, the bugging and Corky's brakes. The D. A. wants him. I said we didn't have anything yet he could use. He told me to bring him whatever I had by the end of the week or the deal on Ray's estate's off."

"Is he treating Zorky's death as a homicide?"

"They're trying to get an exhumation order."

We drank our drinks and stared out at the ocean. Two men and two women were pushing a catamaran on the sand into the water. Crashing waves impeded their progress. After a few moments, they were past the breakers and you could see the colorful sail bobbing in the distance. It had taken a concerted effort but then they all had smooth sailing.

Ed lit a cigarette. "So, what'd you find?"

"Scopolamine? Plant derivative. Small doses, they use it for truth serum and seasickness. Large doses, it's fatal. Looks like a heart attack."

"Both Ray and Zorky died from heart attacks."

"Ever notice the instructions on seasick medications? Where

they tell you to take it an hour or so before you need it?"

Ed nodded and sipped his drink.

"Well, it looks like this stuff can have a delayed reaction. You could probably slow it down further if you put it in a time delay capsule."

"Yeah, but where do you get this stuff. It doesn't just grow on trees does it?"

"Yeah. It does. There's a plant called an Angel's Trumpet. Has these pretty trumpet shaped flowers. Nice except if you eat one it's poisonous. I think I actually saw a couple on the A. V. Designs campus. Of course, you can also find it in seasickness medications."

Ed put down his glass and leaned in my direction. "So that's how they killed Ray. Poison. Do you think maybe that's what happened to Zorky too?"

"Maybe. We know somebody poisoned Horton and the three dead men spent time together on Zorky's boat. Looks like there's only one killer and he prefers staging accidents usually with poison. On the other hand, we'd be foolish to assume anything. We need to look at each murder separately starting with Ray."

"Isn't poison something female killers use?"

"I've read that they use it more than men, but not everyone fits in gender stereotypes and a clever killer may think it obscures his identity."

Ed sat back and let out a deep breath. "Geez, Max, what do we do?"

"If we're going to discover who killed Ray, we need to narrow the suspect list."

"How?"

"Start at the beginning with the simple and obvious choices. Even Ray's widow says the police usually look at the spouse first."

"No. You're not going to investigate Kathleen."

"If the police decide Ray was murdered, that's exactly what they're going to do. They're going to follow procedure."

"It's my job to keep my clients out of trouble."

"Yes it is. That's why we need to look into her."

"What are you talking about?"

"If the police question Kathleen, you're going want to know in advance what they know. You're not going to be able to protect her when they ask her about something and you're hearing about it for the first time."

Ed was silent, so I pressed on.

"If you're a good lawyer, you're not going to let a client be questioned until you've prepared her. You can't prep her if you don't know what's going on."

"You're very convincing. Ever consider a career in Law?"

"No, I like what I do better. I prefer being paid to talk to lawyers."

I don't think Ed appreciated my comment. He stared at me and then said, "I'll agree on one condition. I don't want anyone else to know we investigated her. Check her out, but don't leave any trail. Last thing I need is someone finding out that I'm investigating my own client. They might not understand."

"OK I can do that."

"If Kathleen didn't kill Ray and I'm sure she didn't, what else have we got?"

"If Kathleen didn't kill Ray... well, if Ray's killer was working with him in the prototype sale, it made no sense to kill Ray before he delivered it."

"So you think the killer wasn't working with Ray in the prototype sale."

"Yeah."

"On the other hand, an accomplice might have wanted to cut Ray out of any profits and might've wanted to kill him after he delivered it."

"Exactly, but Ray was killed before he delivered the prototype and if someone wanted Ray dead after the delivery, they would have taken a different approach. Something more certain in its timing. Maybe they would have drugged him after the delivery."

Ed sipped his drink. "So the killer wasn't an accomplice in stealing the prototype? OK"

"Well, I'm not saying the killer wasn't involved in the theft. I'm saying maybe the killer just didn't want the sale to go through."

"Oh, you mean, maybe someone helped steal it but had different ideas about how to sell it?"

"Yeah, or maybe they didn't help steal it, but knew of the theft and had their own ideas about what to do with the prototype."

"OK I can see that. Anything else?"

"Well, I think that's it. Whoever killed Ray... maybe Horton too, not only knew about the prototype, they didn't want Ray to deliver it so they killed him before he could."

"What about Zorky? Do you think the same person murdered Zorky?"

"Maybe, but we don't know for sure yet if Zorky was killed."

"You think maybe the killer is this guy, the Skipper?"

"He's a candidate, but we don't have any proof that it was him and we don't know who he is or where to find him. It's also possible that there's more than one killer. Kathleen could have killed Ray for money. Skipper could have killed Zorky to keep him quiet. Someone else could have killed Horton for some unknown reason. We should focus on Ray for now. See where it leads, first."

"Agreed, but if the Skipper or somebody else killed Ray to prevent the sale, why didn't they take the prototype from the car after the crash?"

"Don't know. Maybe they didn't want it. If Kathleen killed him, it may have had nothing to do with the prototype."

"Max, stop with Kathleen already."

"Or, if not Kathleen, maybe they tried to get the prototype and couldn't find it? Maybe the police got there too soon. Maybe they couldn't get into the car?"

"I saw the accident photos. It was horrible. When the car hit the culvert, it rolled over. Crushed the roof. Impact also pushed in the side door. They had to use the Jaws of Life to get Ray's body out. Sounds ironic, using the Jaws of Life to extricate dead bodies."

Ed shuddered and then continued. "You could be right. The interior of the car was inaccessible until the police arrived. After they arrived, everything in the car was in police custody until you and I got it. So, who are we looking at here? Ben Horton? An unknown accomplice?"

"I think we can rule out Horton. He claimed he didn't know why Ray was coming to see him. Even if he was lying, it makes no sense for him to kill Ray so that Ray dies at Horton's doorstep. Even if Horton screwed up how long it would take Ray to die, it also makes no sense for him to kill Ray with Horton being the last to see him alive. Add Horton's murder to that and there's likely a third person who knew Ray and Horton and who knows about the prototype."

Ed started counting on his fingers. "That leaves...One. Maybe a disgruntled accomplice? Two. Maybe someone else who knew of the theft and was trying to get the prototype or three, you're all wrong and it's someone out of left field. I'm not going to count Kathleen."

"Sort of."

Ed raised his hand to count again. "One, accomplices. Horton's the only possibly disgruntled accomplice we know of and you've ruled him out. Two, other people who might be trying to get the prototype for their own purposes. Uhm, we don't know who else might have known of the theft. Three, someone from out of left field and well, we obviously wouldn't know who that would be and no, I'm not going to count Kathleen here either. We're not getting too far, Max."

"Let's start with what we know and then we can speculate. We know Ray had the prototype and someone killed him. Both Ray and Zorky died from heart attacks. The Skipper is a fugitive and his things are missing from Zorky's boat. Someone made a run at Corky, planted bugs, stole the notebook, searched my place, Ray's place and killed Horton. We also know Clive Howard from A. V. Designs has been watching me, is looking for something and he thinks I might lead him to it. The only people we can name who know of the prototype are you, Ray and me. Horton claims he didn't know why Ray was coming to see him. We don't know if Howard or if anyone else at A. V. Designs even knows the prototype is missing."

"Those things are all true. So, to whom do they lead us?" Ed asked.

"Now we speculate. We can rule out you and me. You already had access to the prototype and I knew nothing until you approached me. Ray and Horton are dead. The only other person who we know is involved here is Clive Howard, the Security Chief at A. V. Designs."

"Nah," Ed shook his head as he lit another cigarette. Of course, he's involved. The prototype belongs to A. V. Designs. He's their Security Chief. He has a legitimate interest in recovering it. He also has an interest in being discreet about it. Makes perfect sense. Matter of fact, if he did know about Ray having the prototype, all he had to do was phone the Police and get it back."

"Maybe, but we're not going to get any closer to any answers without more information. Ray seems to be the focal point. He connects to Zorky, Corky, the prototype and Horton. I'm going to go back to A. V. Designs. I'll start with Personnel, see what else we can find out about Ray, and then take it from there."

Ed took a deep breath, raised his eyebrows and exhaled. I guess he had nothing else to say. A voice called out over the restaurant loudspeaker, "Ed, your order is ready."

Ed turned toward the bar. Then he looked at me and waved his cigarette. "You gave them my name for the pizza order?"

"Yeah, for some reason, people seem to screw up my name and I'm too hungry to wait. Besides, this is a business lunch, you can deduct it."

CHAPTER THIRTY

After lunch, I had a nice walk in the surf back to the house where I planned to change clothes before visiting A.V. Designs. While I walked, something occurred to me. Maybe the empty battery compartment in Ray's answering machine never had a bug. Maybe it was empty simply because it came without a battery and no one bothered to put one in. If there were no bug, then there had to be some other way someone would know that Ed was handling Ray's estate. Sure there was. That someone could be Kathleen, the woman who hired Ed.

If Kathleen wanted the prototype and couldn't find it, she could have bugged Ed's office in the hopes of locating it. All she had to do was visit the Spy Shack. When I considered this possibility, I realized that it could also have been Kathleen who tossed her house searching for Ray's hiding place. Especially since she's left the area, Kathleen is definitely a loose end I'd like to tie up

She lived with Ray. If she wanted to kill him, she would have had the opportunity to do it. Also, as his spouse, she could have a motive. Lastly, without looking into her, I'll never know if we were headed in the right direction.

When I got home, I sat at my desk and turned on my laptop computer. While I sat there waiting for it to start up, I thought about what Ed had said. He was right about protecting his client's interests, but Ray was his client too. Who was representing his interests? Surely, it was in Ray's interests to catch his killer. In addition, there was more at stake here than Ed seemed to want to acknowledge. He retained me only to locate a client's assets and I had done that.

Since then, thieves broke into my home, my wife was too scared to come back, and someone was stalking me. I had to address those personal concerns too. I was definitely going to look into Kathleen, but I promised Ed I would be discreet. I'd have to forgo the usual P. I. databases and phone calls, but I should be able to use whatever resources were available to the general public out on the Internet.

Then it occurred to me. Much of what I wanted to know about Kathleen, I could learn by investigating Ray. No one said I couldn't do more of that. I knew Kathleen and Ray lived in a house in Volusia County. I had been there to sweep for bugs. I also knew that there should be a deed on file. If the house was in only Ray's name that might be useful information. If someone else owned it, I might be able to identify another player.

Figuring the deed would be a good place to start, I went to the website of the Volusia County Clerk of Circuit Court. Under the listing "Public Records", I clicked on "Instrument Inquiry." The next page required I enter my full name. I didn't want to, but my computer IP address could identify me anyway. I typed in my name. I doubted things would get to the point where this information would come out.

Besides, I wasn't investigating Kathleen I was investigating Ray. I promised myself I wouldn't even type "Kathleen" into any of the search fields.

Instead, I typed "Kenwood Raymond" in the text box at the top of the page, clicked "Submit" and a list of Ray's county records appeared. The list included a marriage certificate, a deed, a mortgage document and a satisfaction of mortgage document.

I started with the marriage certificate. The handwritten entries told me it was the first marriage for both Ray and Kathleen and that Ray was born in Florida while Kathleen was born in South Carolina. Since the addresses on the certificate for both Ray and Kathleen were the same, I guessed they were living together when they decided to marry. She was two years older than Ray and her maiden name was Kincaid. So far, all I learned was that her premarital monogrammed clothes were still useable.

I looked at the deed next. The address on it was different from the one on the marriage certificate. It was the place where Ed and I had done the bug check. Apparently, they lived elsewhere for about ten months before buying the house as a married couple. The deed listed both Ray and Kathleen as "grantees." The mortgage document listed both Ray and Kathleen as "borrowers" and the Satisfaction of Mortgage document showed they paid the mortgage in full ten years later. I didn't see any money problems here. In addition, records I found on Ray's computer also listed Kathleen as a joint owner of all the assets listed there. If Kathleen killed Ray, it probably wasn't for money.

I didn't find any documents pertaining to any court orders or probation reports. Since they were readily available, I decided to look at the Citation records to see if anything was there. In this case, tickets issued to Ray wouldn't mention Kathleen, so I did this search on the last name alone. Nothing came up on neither Ray nor Kathleen. She didn't even have any traffic tickets.

I went back to the marriage certificate. It listed Kathleen's maiden name, birth state, and date of birth. I was thinking I could use that information to get more details from one of the P. I. databases when the phone rang. It was Ed. "We meet the D. A. tomorrow at 9:00. He wants to hear what we got in person. I'll pick you up at 8:30."

"OK. See you then." After his call I felt like I pushed as far as I could against Ed's edict without going over the line. I didn't find anything that made Kathleen look suspect but I filed her information for possible later use and sat back in my chair. It was time to go to A. V. Designs and see what else I could find.

CHAPTER THIRTY-ONE

I changed out of my bathing suit into street clothes and drove over to the A. V. Designs campus again. When I got to the gate, the same uniformed guard I saw last time greeted me. He stepped out of the guard booth, smiled and looked in my car window.

"Afternoon sir. How may I help you?"

I knew from last time he was unlikely to let me in without an appointment or at least a good reason. I also knew two groups comprised the world. One was "Us." The other was "Them." Folks bent the rules for "Us," but not for "Them." If I wanted to get past the gate, I just had to be one of "Us" and not one of "Them." "Hi, I'm Max Fried. I'm here about a job. I'm looking for the personnel office."

He paused for a moment. "You were here yesterday. You lost your ID."

I got out my wallet and showed him my P. I. license. "Yes. I'm sorry. I met with Chief Howard and now I'm here to see someone in Personnel."

I didn't feel too guilty about my story. It was true I was here about a job. I was doing a job for Ed. It was also true I had met with the Chief yesterday and I came here today to see someone in Personnel. I wanted to talk to Personnel about Ray. I figured if the guard wanted to conclude that the Chief had hired me and sent me to the Personnel office, then that was his mistake.

The guard stepped back inside and I couldn't see what he was doing. I held my breath and studied the campus map posted on the side of the security booth. After a few moments, he stepped back out of the booth. He bent down next to my window and handed me a new photo ID card. It looked like the one I had yesterday, but it had today's date and I was now a day older than my picture.

"This is your temporary ID card," he said "Please don't lose it. You'll need to turn it in when you leave and losing it could affect employment with A. V. Designs. It's only good for today." He handed me back my license and a paper tag to hang from my rear view mirror just as he did yesterday. "Personnel's in Building One, just follow this road to the right. Park in any space marked 'Visitors'. Have a good day sir."

As I drove down the road, I took a closer look at the landscaping. Sure enough, there were a few plants on the lawns with pretty trumpet shaped flowers. I parked in the Visitor's lot and walked up to Building One. From the outside, it looked exactly like Building Two. I was willing to bet that inside, it was also the same layout. Why pay someone to design two buildings when it's cheaper to design once and build twice?

I entered the building and went up to the semicircular reception desk. I half expected to see the same receptionist I saw in Building Two. This receptionist wasn't the same man but he wore the same dark business suit and could have been his brother. "How may I help you sir?"

"Hi," I smiled, I'm Max Fried. I'm here to see the Human Resources Director.

He looked down at something hidden behind the reception desk. "Is she expecting you sir?"

"No. We don't make appointments. We're investigating the death of one of your employees."

"Oh, well, I'll call ahead and let her know you're coming up." He stammered. He must have been new there. A pro would have asked to see a badge first.

He made a call and then put down the phone. "Take the elevator to three. The receptionist there will direct you."

"Thanks." I rode the elevator to the third floor, enduring an orchestral rendition of the Beatles "Come Together" that featured violins. Grateful I didn't have to ride to the top floor, I stepped out of the elevator into the third floor reception area.

A woman in her early twenties looked up at me from her elevator-facing desk. She had her phone to her ear. She put her hand over the mouthpiece and looked at me. "Sir?"

"Hi, I'm here to see the Human Resources Director."

"Just a moment, please, sir."

She uncovered the mouthpiece, said, "He's here now. I'll send him in as soon as she's free," then she reached for her telephone cradle and pressed a button. I guessed the folks in the lobby wanted to make sure I went where I said I was going.

After a moment, she spoke softly into the phone. I couldn't hear what she said. Then she hung it up and stood. "This way please."

As I followed her down the hall, I wondered what would happen if someone else got off the elevator. Was someone else staffing her desk while she escorted me? Did they have a closet full of folks standing by; making certain all visitors always had an escort? Security seemed tight here. My experiences at A. V. Designs so far, indicated they didn't tolerate folks strolling around without authorization. I wondered how Ray, a sales rep, could get his hands on a prototype. From what I had seen of the campus map at the entrance gate, Sales was in a different building from Research and Development.

My escort led me into a large office. A woman in her late 40s with short blond hair rose from behind a desk and offered her hand. She looked slim, but it wouldn't take much weight for her to lose that distinction.

"Hi, I'm Bev Ryan, Director of Human Resources for A. V. Designs."

I shook her hand. "Max Fried."

"Please sit. I understand you're here about Ray Kenwood's death."

I followed her to the sofa across from her desk and we sat. "Yes, how did you know that? I didn't mention his name."

"Yes, but you did say 'employee death'. Fortunately, there've been no other recent company deaths. Why are the police investigating?"

"I don't know that they are. I'm working for Ray Kenwood's family. We need to settle his insurance claims and his estate and there are a few loose ends. Ray's family lawyer asked me to see if I could tie them up. You see, he bills at a higher hourly rate than I do."

She smiled. "Yes, I can imagine. I'm familiar with the payroll over in legal. How can I help?"

"Can we start with some background? Like how long did Ray work here. What was his job title...?"

She hesitated. "I guess so... Ray was one of our sales reps. Worked here about a year." She typed something on her computer, and then read the screen. "Thirteen months, started November 15th last year."

"Was that long enough to qualify for company life insurance?"

A smile formed on her face. "Oh, I see. When we learn of an employee's death, we have an informational package we send out to the beneficiaries. It contains all of the information about pensions, 401K, survivor's benefits, final pay, life insurance... The package details all of the benefits the deceased may have had. I don't believe we sent anything out yet in Ray's case. We just learned of his death yesterday. It should go out tomorrow."

"By the way, did you know Ray?"

"Oh yes. Boy, did he love to tell bad jokes. Her smile disappeared. It's hard to imagine him gone. He certainly seemed to enjoy life. I met him when the Chief brought him in."

"Chief Howard, from Security?"

"Yes," she nodded. "You know the Chief?"

"We've met."

She shook her head. "It was very unusual for the head of Security to bring a salesman onboard." She raised an eyebrow. "There were a few noses out of joint. Corporate turf wars." She shrugged. "The Sales VP thought the Chief was overstepping. The Chief placated him by hiring the Sales VPs brother in law... security guard. Quid pro quo and all was fine." She held her hands in front of her, turned her palms up and shrugged again.

"That does seem odd. I guess Ray and the Chief must have been old friends from somewhere else."

Her eyebrow went up again. "I thought so, but if you saw them together, they really didn't seem to even like each other." She let out a breath. "Well, Ray seemed to like the Chief, but the Chief didn't seem to like Ray. I remember one incident when Ray first started. Saw them both in the cafeteria." She lowered her voice as if divulging a secret. "Despite their apparent friction, they ate together once a week on Fridays. At first, I thought they liked sushi. Friday's sushi day, but I never saw them at the sushi station." Her expression brightened for a moment. "I love the Negihama, don't you? You know the yellow tail and onion roll? Yum." Then she went back to her soft voice. "Anyway, Ray had called the Chief, "Skipper" and the Chief became upset with him."

She leaned forward in a conspiratorial fashion, "I thought the Chief's reaction was extreme." She leaned back. She paused, then leaned forward again and in a stage whisper said, "I thought it was harsh. He should have understood how a new employee could confuse the titles." She sat back with a smile as if she were pleased to have made her feelings known.

I felt like I had been watching a bad actress audition for a part. Her exaggerated mannerisms were wearing me out. I cringed when I realized I was in the presence of an effusive "people person" who apparently took great pleasure in personal interaction, but all I said was, "Sure, it takes time to get used to new surroundings."

She waved a hand in the air as she shook her head. "I never got it. They just didn't seem to be all that buddy-buddy. Ray was always jovial, but there seemed to be tension between them. It didn't seem the Chief really cared for Ray, but yet they ate together on a regular schedule." She shrugged.

I added, "Plus the Chief ruffled feathers to get Ray hired. Strange..."

"Yes, but I'm talking too much, as usual, and I've got work to do." She slapped her hands into her lap palms down.

Knowing she was finished brought me a sense of relief but I had to press on. I had only one last question and then I could go. "I'm sorry. One last question, please. The family is going to go through Ray's things, probably sometime next week. Did he have anything we have to return to the company? A laptop, sales materials, samples, stuff like that?"

"I don't think so. He used his own computer. All we gave him were flyers, handouts, things like that for public use. You need not return those. Though ever since 'the incident', we started keeping the Sales Reps informed about R and D specs. For security reasons, we don't allow Sales staff in the R and D building, but we do provide them the ability to view that information here by computer. However, Sales is limited to viewing that information here. Taking it off campus is not allowed and we don't provide samples of R and D products to the sales reps until they're released to market."

I didn't want to witness her performing another story for my benefit. I didn't think I could take it, but I knew I had to ask. "The incident?"

"Yes," she grinned. "I probably shouldn't tell you this but it's such a typical corporate screw up. It's like a Dilbert cartoon." She smiled widely, too widely as she shook her head from side to side. "We had an embarrassing situation when our Sales Reps were out in the field, selling our product, knocking the competition for using an alternative technology."

Uh oh. She raised her eyebrow again. "Unfortunately, our R and D staff was switching to the same alternative technology for the next year's model. Ever since then, we make sure to keep the sales staff informed." She laughed and clapped her hands.

I smiled politely and stood. "Thank you for your time."

She got up and escorted me to the elevator lobby, shook my hand and smiled. "Good bye, Mr. Leeds. If you need any more information, just let me know." Her demeanor became somber, her lower lip protruded slightly. "Oh, and please, tell the family I'm sorry for their loss." She smiled at me -- again, turned back towards her office and left me under the watchful eye of the third floor lobby receptionist.

I went downstairs to my car and drove to the Security Gate. When I got there, the barricade was down blocking my exit. The guard stepped out and I handed him my ID card. He smiled at me and nodded, apparently taking the fact I didn't lose this one as a personal triumph.

"How'd it go?" He asked.

It took me a minute before I realized he was asking me about what he thought was a job interview. "Gee, I don't know. Who can tell with these things?"

"Yeah. I hear you. Good luck." He vanished into his booth. The gate opened and I drove off. In my rear view mirror, I saw him waving goodbye. Like I always say, "The world is made up of Us and Them."

I drove back home, anxious to look again at Ray's computer disk. It's a lot easier to find something when you know what you're looking for and now I had something.

When I pulled into the driveway and Mariel's car wasn't there, I wasn't too surprised. I didn't expect her back until this whole thing came to an end. I pressed the button on my garage door opener and crept forward to navigate the tight fit between the lawn mower and my motorcycle. I liked to keep my car in my garage. It lessened the need to clean off bird shit and made the car tougher to steal. I locked the car and entered the house from the garage. I was thankful there were no signs of unwelcome visitors. I went to my office and turned on my laptop computer. My replacement desktop computer wasn't due to arrive until tomorrow.

Now, I knew how Ray had gotten the product information he sold to Horton and he didn't need any help to accomplish that. He just copied it off his computer. On the other hand, I also knew he couldn't have gotten the prototype on his own. The campus map showed Research and Development was in a separate building from sales and Bev Ryan told me R & D shared nothing beyond specs with the sales staff.

Ray would have needed the help of someone with the appropriate security clearance to get the prototype. That meant Ray had an accomplice at A. V. Designs for at least that part of the theft. My problem was that I found had no reason for anyone with access to help him. Unless I could find a reason, I'd have a hard time making a case for an arrest.

I loaded the image from Ray's notebook into my forensic software and narrowed my search to cash deposits in Ray's money market accounts. I saw them earlier, but couldn't make any sense of them. Each of a series of deposits was the same amount. The records showed one deposit each Friday evening starting in November of last year. November was when Ray started at A. V. Designs and the deposit pattern matched the sushi schedule in the A. V. Designs cafeteria. These were the days Ray had lunch with the Chief. The Chief who got upset when Ray called him "Skipper." I could probably come up with a theory why Ray would pay the Chief, but I had no idea why the Chief would pay Ray. All this effort did nothing but confuse my case theory and raise yet another question, "Who was paying Ray and why?"

I wanted to investigate further but after Horton's death and my M. E. visit, I knew I was getting too close to a murder investigation. It was time to call in the pros so I looked forward to tomorrow's meeting at the D. A.'s office. I didn't want to surprise Ed at the meeting so I called and told him what I had learned.

I was facing yet another dinner alone. I missed Mariel, but now that Horton was dead and I suspected that Ray was possibly murdered, I was glad she wasn't here. It seemed likely whoever killed Horton and Ray planted the bugs and broke into our home. It was good that she was somewhere else. I didn't even want to call her. It made no sense, but I believed that if I ignored her, maybe the killer would too.

I tried to get excited about dinner. I love to cook and here was another opportunity to make whatever I wanted. I had no appetite, so I nuked a veggie burger, poured some wine and called it a night.

CHAPTER THIRTY-TWO

Once again, I slept poorly. I must have been in constant motion all night. Investigating misdeeds is one thing. Dealing with a killer is another. I was out of my league. I didn't even belong to a league. Hell, I didn't even own a gun. I probably had fifty dreams about this case that night. They were vague scenarios where bizarre things happened. In one snippet, I was looking at a case file on line and when I clicked a link with my mouse, a gun went off. Someone shot me, but clicking again somehow saved me. When my alarm finally went off at 7:00 am and I woke with minimal sleep, I was glad to get out of bed.

I dragged myself into the bathroom, showered, shaved, and got dressed. I went to the kitchen, made coffee and a cheese omelet with sharp shredded cheddar and waited for Ed.

The doorbell rang at 8:25. I put my dishes in the sink, went to the door and looked through the peephole. How the hell can anyone see anything through these things? All I could make out was a blurry, round shape smoking a cigarette. I knew it had to be Ed so I opened the door, "How're you doing?"

He exhaled some smoke out of the side of his mouth and said, "A lot better than you. What'd you do? Stay up all night?"

I shook my head. "Gimme a minute to brush my teeth."

Five minutes later, I grabbed my briefcase, stepped outside, shut and locked my door. Ed was still standing there smoking. He put out his cigarette and said, "Let's go."

We got into his Mercedes and drove to the D. A.'s office in Deland. As we crossed the bridge over the Indian River to the mainland, Ed said, "I spoke with Torres."

"Detective Torres? When?"

"Early this morning. Supposedly he called me in regard to his report on the break-in at the Kenwood house."

"What did he want?"

"He's not buying it. Ever since he learned a client's computer was the target of the break-in at your place, he's known you weren't telling him everything." Ed took his eyes off the road a moment to look at me. "Torres likes to know everything, especially when it involves a murder victim."

"Yeah", I sighed.

"Then the very next day, you mysteriously develop this case against Horton. He sends guys to pick up Horton and they find him poisoned. Right after that, Torres sees you again when they send him to yet another break-in. Then Horton gets killed. Add to that, the camera you had Torres remove from your tree, the business on the boat, Corky's car and well... you get the picture. He knows you know things he wants to know."

"Ed, It's too early for complicated sentences. I just got up and I didn't sleep much."

"Well, he knows you're holding back. He thought I might give you up."

"So now that you've talked, what does he think?"

"He didn't say, but now I think he thinks I'm involved, too."

I shook my head. I was still trying to absorb 'He knows you know things he wants to know' and now Ed was throwing 'I think he thinks I'm involved, too.' at me. If Ed's going to continue like this, I'm going to need more sleep... or more coffee. Maybe both. I was fantasizing about the idea of somehow having coffee while sleeping, when Ed asked, "Were you discreet when you checked out Kathleen?"

"Yeah, all I did was look at Ray's marriage certificate, deed and mortgage."

"...and Kathleen's name just happened to be on them."

"Yup," I said. "Actually, they support a case for her innocence. The marriage appears legit. It was the first one for each. They lived together before they were married. She owns half the house and it's all paid off. Plus the documents on Ray's computer show joint ownership of all of his assets."

"I hope you're happy now, Fried." Ed shook his head and drove on in silence.

The drive took about 30 minutes and we had about 20 to go so I tried to use the time to try to figure a few things out. I needed a plan.

When we got to the office building where the D. A. was located, Ed parked the car and we went in. In the lobby, there was a uniformed officer leaning against a desk in front of a metal detector. Next to the metal detector was a table with a scanner. A second officer sat at the scanner controls. A third officer was on the other side of the detector with a wand in his hand. They were apparently discussing some ball game and waiting for the next visitors to arrive. Ed and I approached the metal detector and the leaning officer stood up in front of the detector entrance. He looked at Ed and lifted his head inquisitively.

"I'm Ed McCarthy. I'm an attorney. I've a 9:00 with A. D. A. Stronberg."

The officer moved his head to look past Ed at me.

"Max Fried. I'm with Ed."

"ID and sign in, please." The officer held out his left hand for our ID and pointed with his right to a book on the desk.

Ed pulled his driver's license out of his wallet and showed it to the officer who nodded and gave it back. As Ed was signing the book, I showed the officer my P. I. license. He looked at me, tilted his head back, looked at the license and then handed it back. I probably shouldn't have shaved my beard until my new license photo was due. I signed the book after Ed. We put our metal objects in Rubbermaid dishes. I put my briefcase on the scanner conveyor belt and we walked through the metal detector.

After we passed through without incident and reclaimed our belongings, Ed turned to the officer with the scanning wand. "A. D. A. Stronberg?"

The officer pointed with the wand. "This hall, on the left, 109."

Ed nodded his thanks and we went down the hall. The door to Room 109 had a frosted glass panel so you could see if you were opening the door into someone on the other side, but you couldn't see who. All the gold lettering on the door glass said was "109." Ed opened the door and we walked into a reception area. Behind the reception area were a number of cubicles and a few offices with doors. Ed turned to the receptionist. "Ed McCarthy. I've got a niner with Stronberg."

She nodded and picked up the phone on her desk. "Dave, your nine is here." and hung up. Just as she finished telling us to have a seat, a man appeared at the reception desk and said, "Thanks Sara." He turned to us. "Ed McCarthy?"

Ed nodded. The man reached out his hand. "I'm Dave Stronberg. Nice to finally meet you. This Mr. Meade?"

"I'm Max Fried." I shook his hand.

He nodded and pointed with an open hand. "This way, please."

He showed us into a conference room and closed the door behind us. When we got inside, I recognized Linda Davis from the M. E.'s office sitting at the conference table reviewing a file. "I think you both know Linda Davis from the M. E.'s office?"

We assured him we did and said how good it was to see her again. She smiled at Ed, but just nodded at me. Ed sat down across from her. I took the chair next to him. She and Ed looked happy to see each other.

Stronberg sat at the head of the table with Davis on his right and looked at his watch. "We're waiting on just one more person, so please, just relax for a few minutes."

I looked around the table. Everyone seemed to be interested in whatever papers they had in front of them. I had no papers so I just stared off into space and wondered if the D. A.'s office had good coffee. After just a few moments, the door opened.

"What are these two doing here?" Detective Torres glared at Ed and me as he entered the room.

"And here he is," said Stronberg. Torres sat down next to Davis and scowled across the table at me.

"We are here," Stronberg began, "because Attorney McCarthy has information regarding criminal activity. He's doing his duty as an officer of the court in bringing this to our attention. Mr. Meade, a private investigator, is here because he has possession of evidence supporting Mr. McCarthy's information. Mr. McCarthy?" Stronberg held out his hand palm up in Ed's direction.

"We are here today because the D.A., the M. E.'s office, the police and I each have some information which is inconclusive when viewed separately but when viewed together presents a clearer picture of recent criminal acts." Torres and Davis looked at each other. Ed and Linda Davis smiled at each other... again. I was beginning to suspect some extracurricular activity between them.

Ed continued. "I represent the estate of Ray Kenwood. We all know Ray was murdered but here's what else we know." He paused and looked around the room. "Someone bugged my office."

Torres reached into his pocket and pulled out a cell phone. I could hear the buzz as the phone vibrated. He looked at the display, and then left the room opening his phone as he walked.

Ed watched him leave and then said. "The bug is still there. Whoever planted it doesn't know we know about it. We believe the bug was an attempt to locate and take Ray Kenwood's property. We think so because someone broke into Max's office and stole Mr. Kenwood's notebook computer. That notebook contained proof Ray Kenwood was selling trade secrets from his employer, A. V. Designs to a competitor, Ben Horton, owner of PC Gadgets. We don't know for certain if there is any connection here, but somebody also tried to poison Horton and somebody eventually succeeded in killing him."

Linda Davis interrupted, "Excuse me Ed, I'm not familiar with the Horton case, what kind of poison?"

"Horton had a peanut allergy. Someone put peanuts in his food."

Davis nodded and wrote something on her pad.

Ed continued, "We don't think the computer thief found everything he wanted. I say that because at some point, someone broke into Ray Kenwood's home and tossed the place. Also, because A. V. Designs Corporate Security was surveilling Max and lastly because Max found a hidden camera at his home."

Stronberg spoke up, "Anything new that proves the sale of secrets?"

"Just the stuff I emailed you the other day," said Ed.

Stronberg nodded and then turned at the sound of the door opening. Torres came back into the room and sat down.

Davis leaned forward and asked, "What stuff is that?"

I answered, "Emails from Ray Kenwood to Ben Horton contained hidden specs from A. V. Designs products. Spreadsheets detailing Ray's sales to Horton and Ray's bank records showed matching deposits. Plus, they knew each other from prior criminal activity."

Torres added, "Fried's information enabled us to get warrants which led to documents on Horton's computer and bank records confirming what Fried said. We interviewed Horton but didn't get anything useful from him except he was out of town when the Fried break-in took place. His alibi for that checks out. He was killed before we could get more."

Stronberg paused for a moment as if he were considering the information. "So, what have we got? A theft where both thieves are dead, two murders and one attempted murder all possibly connected with the theft. Let's work the theft connection on the first homicide and see what comes up." He looked around the room for a consensus.

Ed lifted his hand off the table, "Wait. There's something else. Mr. Kenwood had his induced heart attack on the road leading to PC Gadgets. However, all of his transactions with Horton were electronic. We don't see why he would go there unless he had something to drop off. We think that when he was killed, he had not only the notebook but also something else in his possession."

This time Torres interrupted, "Why are you so sure he was dropping off and not picking up?"

Ed responded, "Because we found the missing object. It was still in Ray's possession when he died."

Torres and Stronberg looked at each other and then Ed.

Stronberg asked, "What is it?"

"This." I said and pulled the prototype out of my briefcase. "This is a working prototype of an A. V. Designs product yet to hit the market. It was among Ray's personal effects."

Davis looked confused. She asked, "What is that thing?"

"A computer interface."

Davis shook her head so I said, "A new product. Nothing like it on the market."

She still looked confused.

Stronberg turned to Ed. "So, you think maybe Horton killed your client?"

"No." Ed looked at me. "Max?"

"Horton was out of town when Ray died. It's possible he hired someone to kill Ray. It's even possible a hired killer killed Horton to cover his own tracks. However, I don't think Horton killed Ray."

I looked around the room. They were still looking at me so I continued. "You see, Ray Kenwood had access to the documents he sold Horton, but he didn't have access to the prototype. He needed assistance from someone else at A. V. Designs. Also, it didn't make sense for Horton to kill Kenwood until he had the prototype. Ed and I think Horton is only a thief. We think someone else is involved. Someone who planted the bugs, stole the notebook, stole the prototype and then killed Ray to get the prototype back."

"Why would someone do that?" Torres asked.

I answered. "We don't know, but we do know Ray couldn't have gotten the prototype by himself. I think when we find out who helped him, we'll find out why."

Stronberg spoke up. "We need to notify A. V. Designs. We need to alert them to beef up their security and we need them to file a complaint."

Torres opened his mouth and sat forward as if he were going to say something. Then he closed his mouth, sat back, and looked up at the ceiling.

When it became apparent he wasn't going to say anything, I suggested, "If we notify the wrong person we're in trouble. Ray's killer could be working there and notifying them could alert him or her we're onto them. On the other hand, their Security Chief, Clive

Howard, already told me he was looking for something he thought I might lead him to. I think I've found it. How about I bring him in on this?" I asked. I was thinking about my last visit with Howard and an idea was starting to form.

When I mentioned Clive Howard, Torres stuck his tongue in his cheek and started nodding his head.

Stronberg grunted his approval, but his expression made me think he wasn't completely sold on the idea.

"How about this?" I said. "We use the prototype to flush out the thief and possibly a killer."

Torres looked interested. "How?"

"Well, we can use the bug in Ed's office, if we want to get them to go someplace or go after something, we can use that to tip them off." I suggested.

"Where are you planning to send them?"

"They already stole the computers from my place, so we know that's one place they would go. I'm thinking that if I'm right about the prototype, it might be enough on its own to flush them out. Just in case it's not, let's also mention I have a forensic image of Ray's notebook computer on my IPod. We just need a way to make their need for action immediate. I mean, we can't just wait around for them to act at their convenience. We need to set it up so they have to act within a time frame we control."

Stronberg looked at his watch. "It's about nine thirty. How about this? At 1:00 p.m., Ed calls me at the D.A.'s office, from his office phone. He tells me you've recovered a stolen prototype. You're keeping it safe along with your iPod and that the iPod contains a copy of Kenwood's notebook. I'll tell Ed I'm coming over to your place at say, three o'clock to get them."

"Sounds good, I'll call, Clive Howard, the Security Chief, from A. V. Designs and I'll tell them I found what they're looking for and invite him to come over too."

Everybody nodded their heads in approval, gathered up their things, and started filing out the door. Only Torres and I were still in the room and he said to me, "Before you go..."

I was with him for about five minutes. When I came out of the room, Ed was waiting for me. "What did Torres want?"

"He checked something out for me. If you tell me about you and Linda Davis, I'll tell you about it in the car."

Ed grinned. We left the D. A.'s office and got into Ed's car. As soon as we closed the doors, he asked. "OK. What's going on? What did Torres say?"

I told Ed about the Miami Herald article about the missing

murder suspect.

He started the car and said, "So?"

"It took a while to track down the case in the paper but when the Miami Police found it their records included their suspect's fingerprints. The prints matched some found on the Leviathan. They sent a copy to Torres and he matched them to prints from my ID badge. Clive Howard is not Clive Howard."

Ed's mouth opened as if to say something. Then it closed. Then it opened. Then it closed. Finally, he said, "What? You're inviting a killer to your home. You're going to tell him that you have the thing he wants, the thing that's keeping you alive. Are you nuts?"

"Maybe, but I've had enough of this."

"What about Zorky? Did the bastard kill Zorky too?"

"They don't know. We won't find out until they exhume the body. Even then, we might not learn anything new. Besides, there isn't enough time for that now."

"Why don't they just arrest him for the Miami murder and be done with it?"

"Too long ago to make conviction a sure thing. A key witness is dead now. Case could go either way."

"Howard's not going to wait until three o'clock. He's going to come as soon as you call."

"Yeah, that's why Torres just passed us. He's going to be waiting at my house when I call."

Ed shook his head, "Max, this is dangerous. Things could go wrong."

I didn't want to discuss it anymore for fear that I'd agree and change my mind so I asked, "So, Ed, what about you and Linda Davis?"

He said, "Gentlemen tell no tales," gave me a sideways look, shook his head and then drove on in silence.

CHAPTER THIRTY-THREE

When I got in the house, I went to my office, turned on my laptop computer, hooked up my iPod and emptied my briefcase. After my computer started up, I moved some files around and went to the A. V. Designs web site. I looked up their number, picked up the phone and dialed it.

"Good afternoon, A. V. Designs. How may I direct your call?"

"Clive Howard in Security, please."

"Yes, sir. Please hold while I connect you."

"A. V. Designs, Corporate Security Office. How may I direct your call?"

"Max Fried for Chief Howard, please."

"One moment, sir."

The line went quiet for a short time. Thankfully, there was no canned music.

"Mr. Fried. Chief Howard. What can I do for you today?"

"You told me you were looking for something and you thought I may be able to lead you to it."

"Yes, I did."

"Well, I think I've found it and I think whoever stole it bugged a lawyer's office in an attempt to locate it. We're planning to use that bug to set a trap for the thief. At one o'clock, the lawyer, Ed McCarthy, will be calling the D. A.'s office to tell them I have the device. The D. A. is going to tell Ed he'll be at my place in two hours to take custody of it. We expect whoever planted the bug will attempt to recover the device during that two hour window."

"And you're certain I'm interested in this device?"

"Yes."

"Why?"

"It's an unreleased A. V. Designs product."

Silence. "Where is it now?"

"I have it here. At my place."

Another pause on the line, then, "Mr. Fried, why are you telling me this?"

"It's 11:00 now. You're invited to join us at 1:00, when the police arrive."

"How come I'm invited?"

"It's an A. V. Designs product. You're their Security Chief. If you're a part of the recovery, you look good. If you're out of the loop, you don't look as good. Consider it a professional courtesy."

"I like that. Good. I have a couple of guards licensed to carry. I'll bring them. We can station them around the house to make sure no one gets away. See you at one."

About 11:05, my doorbell rang. I wasn't expecting anyone yet. Clive Howard couldn't have gotten here that fast. I took a deep breath and went to the door. I opened it just in time to see the back of a UPS deliveryman as he headed back to his truck. I looked down and saw my new desktop computer had arrived. I picked up the boxes and lugged them into my office. I started unpacking the boxes, and ten minutes later, the doorbell rang again.

When I got to the door, I looked in the peephole. I couldn't make out who it was, but he was alone. I thought he looked like Clive Howard. I opened the door and I was correct. I invited him in.

"Good afternoon, Mr. Fried. I hope you don't mind I'm early? I thought it would be prudent. I've also stationed my security staff outside. May I see this device you spoke of?"

"Sure." He followed me into my office. I pointed to the devices lying on my desk. "Why don't you have your security team come inside? You're way too early. Ed hasn't even made the phone call yet."

The Chief reached for the iPod. "I'm sorry I missed this when I took the computers but then, I would have had to come back anyway for the prototype." He put the iPod in his pocket and held out his hand for the "bicycle mirror." "Funny, this is the second time I had to steal this. Oh, and since I'm the one you are trying to catch, there wasn't any point in bringing a security force. So I didn't. Well, except for this." He smiled and pulled out a handgun.

It was a Smith and Wesson .38 snub nose revolver. It had a concealed hammer so it wouldn't catch on your clothes when you took it out of a pocket. I think it was the model 642. I was familiar

181

with the gun as I was thinking of buying one. It was small, lightweight and easy to carry concealed. However, all I could think of now was it looked a lot bigger from this end and I wished I had already bought one. Involuntarily, I took a step back. If he fired, being a foot further wouldn't help me, but my movement was instinctive. I tried to recover from the shock of the gun in my face and speak normally. I'm not so sure I succeeded.

"I don't think you want to shoot me."

Howard smiled. I think my comment actually amused him. "Why would you say that?"

"Well, you may want me dead, but shooting me wouldn't be your style."

"It wouldn't?"

"No. I know Ray was blackmailing you for money and he coerced you into stealing the prototype. However, when you killed him, you tried to make it look like an accident. You did the same thing when you murdered Zorky Eastwood."

"Mr. Eastwood's demise was unfortunate. He had information that could hurt me, but Ray, he deserved it. Did you know that even after I gave him that device, he was still demanding cash? At that point, I realized the only way to extricate myself would be to eliminate him and retrieve the prototype. No one would even know it had been missing."

I didn't like standing in front of a loaded revolver, but I felt an odd calm. When a suspect actually shot me on the job, I never even saw the gun. The guy sitting across the table from me just opened his attaché case and started firing. No one expected that kind of thing at an employment termination hearing. No one figured a guy who was fired for running his own business on State time and equipment would find shooting the investigator a viable solution. At least this time, I could see the gun and hope that if Howard hadn't shot me yet, maybe he wouldn't.

There was one more thing I had to know. I needed complete understanding. "You also tried to make it look like Horton died from an accident too. I just don't get why you killed him."

"Then you're not as bright as you think. If the police prosecuted Horton for thefts from my company, Horton would likely see me. If he recognized me like Ray did, all of my efforts to hide would be for naught."

"All of this time, everything you've done, you've done so you could remain hidden. If you shoot me, there will be an inquiry. You'll be fingerprinted and then your fingerprints will connect you to the very thing you've been trying to hide."

"Once again, Mr. Fried, you've missed the point. I'm no longer trying to hide. That option died with Ben Horton's obvious murder. It's too late now. If the authorities are close enough to attempt a trap, then there's no longer any point in hiding who I am. I've changed my plans. After I shoot you, I take the prototype, leave for Asia and sell it to one of my employer's competitors. They have all been racing to get to this point. Any one of them could reach success without being suspect."

"Well, Mr. Howard, in that case I should tell you there is nothing but music on the iPod and this 'bicycle mirror' is well, a bicycle mirror." I tossed it to him and for a moment, he flinched to catch it. That was enough to minimize my risk and give the police a chance.

"And this" said Detective Torres from behind Clive Howard, "is an arrest." Two additional police officers came in. One placed his gun against Clive Howard's back while the other took Howard's gun from him. Howard dropped the mirror and raised his hands into the air. The two officers led him out of my now crowded office into my living room where there was room to cuff him.

"Good job, just like we planned," Torres said to me. "For once, you followed directions." We followed the officers out to the living room and encountered Ed and A. D. A. Stronberg.

Clive Howard turned to me and asked, "How did you know it was me?"

"I didn't know for sure until now. We knew that besides Ray and Horton, a third person was involved. We didn't know whom, but each email containing trade secrets, that Ray sent, included a picture of three men on a boat. One was Ray. One was Horton and we didn't know who the third man was. After I met you, I thought I recognized you from the boat pictures and possibly as the man who knocked me down, but I was only suspicious. I had no proof, so I got your fingerprints on my ID badge. Then when I heard you got upset with Ray for calling you "Skipper" at work, I was sure you were the man in the photos. Ray had an odd sense of humor. He was using you to sell technology to Horton and was hiding secrets in pictures of the three of you. When we finally matched your fingerprints with the death in Miami, we knew what you were trying to hide."

I had an almost captive audience and I felt pumped up due to surviving my close encounter with a .38 so I went on. "But, even if it was you in the photo, you could have been an innocent sailing buddy. We didn't even know whom you were until your prints IDed you. Even then, while we knew Miami Police wanted you, I had no proof you were involved in killing Zorky, Ray and Horton or the attempt to kill Corky. Not until you pulled that gun on me. Then I knew for sure. Luckily, the Police shared my suspicions. We knew a sales rep like Ray would not have access to developmental prototypes. We knew Ray would have needed help to get it and that a Security Chief would have the needed access. We also guessed you killed Ray to get it back."

The officer who had taken Howard's gun had placed it in his belt and was taking out his handcuffs.

"That blackmailing scum deserved what he got. Besides, you have nothing on me besides a menacing charge and I'll swear I was simply recovering company property you stole. That I pulled my gun in self-defense."

"You do that, Skipper, but you might be busy planning your defense on the charges related to that dead Cuban you tried to smuggle into the country."

The officer had one of Howard's hand's cuffed and was about to cuff his other one. A loud noise came from the foyer. Everyone's head turned as the front door slammed shut. Mariel had just walked in. She didn't know anything about the plan to capture the Chief. I hadn't told her. I was afraid she would have gotten upset. I never expected her to come back home until everything had been resolved.

The distraction of her entrance enabled Howard to step away from the two officers. He ran for the front door and for Mariel.

"Stop!" yelled Torres. The officer that had been pointing his gun at Howard turned to point at him again. Seeing how close Howard was to Mariel, he pointed his gun towards the ceiling. He kept both hands on it and poised himself to aim quickly and fire if needed. Ed and Stronberg moved out of the way, to the back of the room. The third officer pulled his gun and moved to the side to flank Howard. As he did so, Howard grabbed Mariel by the neck, stepped behind her with his right arm around her neck and said in a calm, quiet voice, "No. You stop." He then grabbed his left elbow with his right hand and placed his left hand behind her head. "I can snap her neck faster than you can aim and shoot."

No one said anything. I looked at Mariel. She looked strangely calm. I was never so scared in my life. I didn't want to lose her.

Mariel is a small woman but Howard crouched down behind her so shooting him without hitting her would be a tough shot to make. I didn't think the police had any plan other than to try to talk Howard down.

Torres told him. "Even if we let you go, we know who you are.

You won't get far. In addition, as an armed and dangerous fugitive who has held a defenseless woman hostage, there's a very good chance you may not survive capture."

As Torres talked, he and the other officers moved slightly and slowly to their sides, flanking Howard and forcing him to keep shifting his eyes between them.

"Stop, stay still." Howard shouted. "Stop moving."

His command came too late for as he was speaking, Mariel lifted her right leg and bent her knee all the way up to her chest. With a fast downward motion, she put her entire body weight into the effort. She only weighed one hundred pounds, but it was enough. One hundred pounds of fury drove the slim metal spike that was the high heel on her shoe into Howard's instep. The spike heel broke off her shoe, embedding itself in his foot. I could hear bones crunch. Screaming, he bent over in pain to remove the broken heel. He weakened his hold on Mariel. She pushed him away. On her toes, she ran to me. I grabbed her and held her tight. Torres and the two police officers converged on Howard. They threw him down hard, face first on our tile floor. I was glad to see his nose bloody when they picked him up with his hands cuffed behind his back.

The two police officers led Howard out the door. Mariel, Ed and I grinned like idiots. Mariel and I hugged as if we were never going to let go. Ed kept on grinning, nodding his head, and clapping us on our backs.

Detective Torres laughed at us on his way out, then looked back over his shoulder and said "Thanks, Max and thank you, Mrs. Fried."

"Thank you, Leo." I kept a tight grip on Mariel and turned to him. "You guys were great."

Leo smiled and left.

CHAPTER THIRTY-FOUR

Mariel and I sat on the patio of Bobbi and Jack's and congratulated ourselves on how well things turned out.

She reached over and took my hand as I told her how Clive Howard came to be in our house.

"So, this Howard man, he's Skipper?"

"Yes, and it looks like the only one who knew he was using the name Clive Howard was Zorky Eastwood. Howard killed him to keep his secret. Then years later, Ray Kenwood goes to A. V. Designs for a job interview and recognizes him. Kenwood used the information for advantage and did pretty well until he got greedy. Then Howard decided the cost was too high and killed him and Horton too."

Mariel shook her head. "Those poor men, that Zorky was innocent and he died because he gave someone a job. How horrible... and those other two may have been thieves, but they didn't deserve to be murdered."

"Ray was more than a thief. After the police got Howard in custody, they were able to get warrants for his financials. They found proof Ray was blackmailing him, probably about the death in Miami. Apparently, Ray stumbled across the Skipper by chance when Ray was job hunting at A. V. Designs. He coerced Howard, AKA Skipper into making sure he got the job at A. V. Designs and into paying him weekly to keep his mouth shut. Once Ray got into A. V. Designs, he hooked up with his old buddy Ben Horton. Ray was scheming to help Ben's company and himself by selling Ben A. V. Design secrets. When Ray decided he needed the prototype to go with the plans, he pressured the Chief who got nothing out of the deal to help him. Once that happened, the Chief saw Ray wasn't going to just leave him alone. The only way Chief Howard could extricate himself would be to kill Ray, recover the prototype, and put it back before anyone noticed. Then as we got closer to catching him, his plan changed. He wanted the prototype for himself."

"So you used a trap to set a trap. I married such a clever man. I know you didn't mean for this to go this far and you couldn't just walk away from this. But we didn't retire here for you to put us or yourself at risk. This is supposed to be our time together... to make up for all of the time we were too busy doing the daily things we needed to do to get by."

"Yup, you're right. I never wanted you to be at risk. I pursued this because I thought it would make it safe for you to come home. I also tried to protect you by not telling you we had set a trap to catch Howard. Instead, I put you at greater risk. In addition to the danger, this whole thing was way too much work. I missed a couple of days of running and a couple of naps. I couldn't always wear a bathing suit. I actually had to wear underwear a couple times. Matter of fact, I missed a couple days of something else too. You know, I'm really not too big on sleeping alone."

"Hmmm, I would think being big and sleeping alone might go together, but we can take care of that later. For now, I have only one question. Were the bad people wearing business suits or bathing suits?"

"Business suits."

"It's like I always say," smiled Mariel looking over at me lying on a deck chair in my bathing suit. "Never trust a man who is wearing underwear."

"Yeah, but I'm really proud of you. I can't believe how brave you were to stomp on Howard's foot like that."

"I had no choice. When I walked in, I could see he was dangerous and I could see the police had no realistic way of rescuing me. Howard had no reason to keep me alive after he got away. I did the only thing that could be done."

"But still, it was incredibly brave."

"Sometimes to be safe, you have to do the thing that scares you the most."

ALSO FROM AUTHOR FALAFEL JONES

PAYBACK'S A BEACH

MAX FRIED MYSTERY #2

When Brenda McCarthy wakes to the sound of police pounding on her door, her clothes are bloody and she doesn't know why. After detectives say her date's dead body washed up on the beach, she turns to private investigator Max Fried. Max wants to help her but neither he nor Brenda are so sure she's innocent.

THE KEWPIE KILLER

It's hard to be a tough investigative reporter when Mommy owns the paper, you lose your apartment and you have to move back home. There's also no solace in your social life when you own at least one bridesmaid dress for every friend you have. Just ask rookie reporter, Raquel Flanagan.

The night Raquel covers a carnival opening, a Bearded Lady of questionable gender finds a dead farmer planted next to a Kewpie doll. Both the farmer and the doll sport straw hats and overalls. Anxious to prove herself to Mom, who is a pathological perfectionist, Raquel locates reports of additional victims dead next to dolls that match their occupations.

At first, no one believes Raquel's theory that a serial Kewpie Killer exists. Then Raquel meets and falls for Eddie Franklin, a cop working Kewpie Killings in Florida. Eddie can't leave his job and Raquel's mom wants her to run the paper in New York. Raquel doesn't know what to do. She still hasn't found a place to live and now someone's sending her Kewpie reporters with tape over the eyes and mouths.